AF614890

LAST KID BOOKS
by David Benjamin

Three's a Crowd

A Sunday Kind of Love

Almost Killed by a Train of Thought: Collected Essays

Skulduggery in the Latin Quarter

Summer of '68

Black Dragon

Jailbait

They Shot Kennedy

The Life and Times of the Last Kid Picked

Bastard's Bluff

Fat Vinny's Forbidden Love

Woman Trouble

Witness to the Crucifixion

Also by David Benjamin

SUMO: A Thinking Fan's Guide to
Japan's National Sport (Tuttle)

CHOOSE MOOSE

BY DAVID BENJAMIN

LAST KID BOOKS

Madison, Wisconsin USA

Last Kid Books
309 W. Washington Avenue
Madison, WI 53703

First Edition
August 2022

Printed in Wisconsin, United States of America

For more information or to order books:
visit www.lastkidbooks.com

Library of Congress Control Number: 2022913023

ISBN-13: 979-8-9863129-8-9

A NOTE ON THE TYPE

This book was set in Athelas, a serif typeface designed by Veronika Burian and Jose Scaglione and intended for use in body text.[1] Released by the company TypeTogether in 2008, Burian and Scaglione described Athelas as inspired by British fine book printing.

Printed and bound by Park Printing Solutions
Verona, Wisconsin

Designed by Kristin Mitchell, Little Creek Press and Book Design
Mineral Point, Wisconsin

For Junko,
again

“

In the first place,
God made idiots.
That was for practice.
Then he made
school boards.

”

—Mark Twain

ROUND 1:

HENRY HITS THE WALL

CHAPTER 1

16 AUGUST

Henry Haddock was incensed—and he said so.

Amy, the elder of Henry's two sisters, sniffed the air histrionically and said, "I can't smell a thing."

Penelope, younger than Amy but nonetheless senior to Henry by three full grades in school, was more direct. She replied, "What do you mean, incensed?"

"I see no smoke," said Amy. "I smell nothing burning."

Henry Haddock made a growly sound deep in his throat and began: "I didn't mean—"

Penelope broke in. "What *did* you mean?"

"I meant that I was burned up, ticked off. Mad!"

"Insane then," offered Amy. "Not incensed."

"I'm not insane," snapped Henry Haddock, increasingly incensed. "I'm ticked off."

"Well, if you're ticked off," said Penelope, "why didn't you just *say* you're ticked—"

"Henry." Henry's mother had listened long enough to her daughters teasing her son. She said, "What's bothering you?"

"What's bothering me," said Henry, "is somethin' that

should bother Amy and Penny, too."

"I'm Penelope," replied his sister, who refused to be nicknamed, especially in honor of an insignificant unit of currency.

Henry, pausing to curl a lip at Penelope, said to his mother. "They took away Ms. Webster, who was gonna be my art teacher."

"Who took her away?" demanded Penelope.

But Henry's mother, Helen Haddock—who understood—nodded sadly.

"I know," said Helen Haddock, in a tone of genuine sympathy. Henry's mother was a teacher. Alice Webster had been one of her colleagues in the public schools of the town of Blackhawk.

For the first time in that morning's breakfast conversation at the Haddock household, Penelope betrayed genuine concern. "Took her away? Who took her away?" she repeated. "I love Ms. Webster."

"The stupid School Board took her away," said Henry. "Dumped her. Cast her adrift!"

Helen Haddock chose not to correct her son's harsh characterization of the School Board. She simply moved a morsel of egg from her plate to her mouth.

Henry glared across the breakfast bar at Penelope. "Haven't you looked at your class schedule, baconface?"

"Henry," said his mother warningly.

"No, I haven't! Why should I?" replied Penelope. "School doesn't start for two weeks. I don't wanna *think* about school 'til then."

"Yeah, well, you better check it out before then, Penny."

"Penelope!"

"'Cause you're not gonna have clarinet lessons with Mr. Hurst."

"Yes, I am! I'm his favorite."

"Well, he's gone, clarinetface!"

"Who's gone?" Penelope looked stricken.

"Mr. Hurst. They fired him, too," said Henry. He was both triumphant in his knowledge and incensed at its unfairness. "They nuked the whole music department, lock, stock and tuba—except for the stupid marching band."

"Wha-at?" wailed Penelope.

"Wait a minute," said Amy.

"I'm afraid it's true, girls," said Helen Haddock with a sigh. She began to explain to her daughters about the school budget. She said the School Board had begun to operate—just this year—under a very strict spending formula that had been mandated statewide by popular vote.

"There was a referendum," said Helen Haddock.

"What's a referendum?" asked Penelope.

"Aw jeez," said Henry, "you don't even know what a referendum is?"

"Well," said Penelope, "it sounds like a bird with a deep voice."

"Well, it's not, parrotface," snapped Henry. "It's a vote, on a law. A referendum, for your information, pelicanface, is a direct vote, by the people, on some issue or another. The senate and the state assembly can't stop a referendum, even if it's a rotten, dumb idea dreamed up by a lot of people who hate art and music, and French!"

"French?" bleated Amy, wrinkling her brow.

"Yeah," said Henry. He pointed his fork at his sister. "No French for you."

"No!"

"I'm afraid that's true, Amy," said Helen Haddock. "The Board reduced foreign languages at the high school to just Spanish and German."

"You mean?"

"Yes," said Amy's mother. "Madame Celestine was let go, too. And Jeanne Brady, who also taught French. And Mr. Vricella, the Italian teacher."

"And that ain't all!" Henry interrupted.

"True," said Helen Haddock. "Instead of two teachers in Spanish and German, there will only be one each."

"Oh no. What about Herr Haushalter?" asked Penelope meekly. "He's so cute!"

"Gone! Cute no more," snarled Henry. "Kaput!"

"Oh my God! No *French!*" wailed Amy, reaching for her phone. "I've gotta tell Tiff about this!"

"Amy." There was a note of warning in Helen Haddock's voice. Phones were strictly forbidden at mealtime.

Amy threw up her hands, "But, mom!" she cried. "This is a crisis!"

"Hm," said Henry. "Amy, dear sister, you look ... incensed."

"Oh. Shut. Up!" said his sister, bolting her breakfast and fleeing the table.

For a moment, Helen Haddock sat silently regarding Henry and Penelope, still seated at the breakfast bar.

Penelope, almost fourteen and a freshman at Blackhawk High, was in the gangly stage of adolescence, consisting mostly of bones and angles, but with long auburn hair shiny with natural highlights that her big sister secretly envied. There were signs around Penelope's eyes and lips that suggested she would grow up to be almost as pretty as her mother.

Henry, who would be entering sixth grade at the Blackhawk Middle School, was eleven, average in height for his age, with a wiry build, quick feet, subpar vision (and glasses that rarely went more than three weeks without a cracked lens or a mangled frame), freckles across his nose, a conspicuous gap between his two front teeth and brown hair kept right around hedgehog length because, when it grew out, Henry's head became—according to his father, Ralph Haddock—"the world capital of cowlicks."

Henry earned pretty good grades in school. He didn't do quite as well as his two sisters because he had an independent streak that clashed occasionally with authority. His all-time worst antagonist had been his fourth-grade teacher, Mrs. Reed. She had once summoned Henry's parents to school to discuss his difficulties with "self-restraint." Henry was, Mrs. Reed inferred, "insufficiently socialized."

During that meeting, Mrs. Reed had done almost all the talking. Afterward, Henry and his parents were silent for a while. Henry wondered how much trouble he was in. His father, as he drove the family car out of the school parking lot, said, "Hoo boy. Gene Debs, Clarence Darrow, Henry Wallace, Bernie Sanders and now, Grace Reed!"

Ralph Haddock had a habit of dropping obscure historical references. He had grown up hoping to become a famous popular historian like Simon Winchester or Daniel Boorstin. But in college, his aptitude for chemistry proved so exceptional that he changed his career path and ended up a chemical engineer. Still, history was his intellectual passion. Henry was his protégé.

"Ralph, what on earth are you talking about?" asked Helen Haddock.

"Socialism," said Henry.

"Oh, for heaven's sake," said Helen Haddock.

"Well, you heard what Mrs. Reed said, Helen. The woman's a socialist all the way down to her red underwear. She wants Henry to be *socialized*, like health care in Canada and oil in Venezuela!" said Henry's dad. "And more power to her. If the big political parties in America can't manage things any better than they've been doing lately, maybe the Socialists—"

"Oh, Ralph, enough!" said his wife. "That's not what the woman meant by 'socialized'."

But Henry's father was laughing so hard that Henry started laughing, and pretty soon, his mom, too. And they all decided to take a detour to the Dairy Barn in downtown Blackhawk for a little "ice cream socialism."

Three weeks after that parent-teacher conference, Henry turned in a theme about "famous American socialists," for which Mrs. Reed gave him an "A." By turning in his theme, Henry was making a roundabout play on words about "socialization" and "socialism." Luckily, Mrs. Reed, who lacked a sense of humor, never got the joke. If she had, Henry might have ended up on the hot seat for another conference.

Henry's dad was kidding around that day about socialism, but that conversation piqued Henry Haddock's curiosity and marked the beginning of his interest in politics. Henry didn't think he was personally a socialist (or any kind of an "-ist"), but he loved reading about grand old American rabble-rousers like Eugene V. Debs and Mother Jones. Next thing he knew, Henry had started reading, cover-to-cover, both a daily newspaper and the local weekly, the Blackhawk *Weekly Argument*. Every day after school, he also logged online to other, bigger newspapers.

It was a story in the *Argument* that alerted Henry to the school budget bombshell. According to *Argument* editor Darren Flack, a recently passed statewide law had forced Blackhawk to reduce its property taxes, which provided most of the money to pay for public schools. The five elected members of the School Board had to make a cruel choice. They could either find new sources of income for the schools—which would be unpopular with voters if a tax hike was involved—or they could make drastic cuts in the budget.

As Darren Flack explained in his budget story, the second choice would also be unpopular. Politically, however, budget cutting was the lesser of two evils. To raise money meant raising taxes. Or, the School Board could try to pass a "bond issue," which would require townspeople to vote on raising a large sum of money by borrowing it from investors and repaying it later (with another tax).

Flack wrote that the best thing, politically, about cutting expenses was that the Board could do it in the middle of the summer—at "budget time"—when no one in town was paying attention to the school system's affairs.

But Henry Haddock was paying attention. He read the whole article in the *Argument.* Then he read it again, and he was incensed—not just because of the big spending reductions, but because the School Board had been so sneaky. Behind everyone's back, the Board had dumped dozens of teachers and wiped out whole subjects, including art and music.

Henry was just beginning to reveal the horrific details of this catastrophe to Penelope when a cocoa-colored tornado roared into the Haddock kitchen, followed by a large dog.

"What the HELL do they think they're doing?" shouted Fantasia Fulton, who was clutching a crumpled copy of her sixth-grade class schedule. "Where the HELL is my gym class?"

Helen Haddock would have disciplined her own children immediately had they spoken so profanely in her presence. But she had a soft spot in her heart for Fantasia.

"Fantasia, my goodness!" said Helen Haddock. "Such language."

"Aw, to HELL with language!" cried Fantasia. Do you know what those pigface dog-doodies did?"

Helen Haddock simply gazed in amazement. Henry reached down to pet the dog, who belonged to the Fulton family. His name was Sarge. He was a gangly, tongue-floppy, caramel-colored Labrador with a wry smile and an easygoing disposition. Sarge looked up at Henry, hoping for food. Henry shared a crust of toast.

Fantasia continued to rage.

"They fired Ms. Hayes, DAMN it!" Fantasia replied. "That's what they did, those dogface pig—"

"Fantasia! I know," said Helen Haddock. Sadly but firmly.

"I was just sayin'," added Henry.

"Ms. Hayes?" said Penelope. "Ms. Hayes is gone?"

"Gone, DAMMIT!" raged Fantasia.

"So, no gym class?" said Penelope. "Good."

Penelope Haddock hated gym. Fantasia Fulton, on the other hand, loved it, and all the games kids got to play in gym class. She was a charter member of the Blackhawk Independent Baseball Organization (BIBO), which Henry had founded that very summer.

Fantasia's explosive arrival in the Haddock kitchen was hardly unusual. She and Henry had been best friends since meeting—at age two—in Fantasia's playpen. Henry, at the time, required the occasional babysitter. Fantasia's mother, Delia Fulton, one day offered to watch Henry so that Helen Haddock could run a series of Saturday morning errands. Delia Fulton sat Henry next to Fantasia in her playpen.

"Now, you two," she said, turning away, "play nice."

But Fantasia saw Henry's arrival as an invasion of her turf. She wrapped her hand around a Weeble policeman and gave Henry his first black eye.

They had been inseparable ever since.

"I LOVE gym, DAMN it ALL!" cried Fantasia, who had a tendency to speak in capital letters.

"Hi, Fancy," said Henry, using the nickname he had invented at age two when he found himself unable to pronounce "Fantasia."

"Yo, Hank," said Fantasia, hauling herself up onto a stool beside Helen Haddock and shoving two slices of bread into the Haddock toaster. She turned grimly to gaze upward at Henry's mother.

"Mrs. H," she said. "We gotta do somethin' about this. They're KILLin' us here."

Helen Haddock smiled at Fantasia's earnestness, but quickly grew serious again.

"Oh, Fantasia, I wish we could. But I don't know how ... "

Helen Haddock's voice trailed off. She was clearly upset at the School Board's budget cuts. She knew the harm they would cause for all the children in Blackhawk. She felt both relieved and guilty that she still had her own job, teaching second grade at Blackhawk Elementary. Mrs. Haddock was reluctant to make any trouble that might put her position at risk. Several School Board members, after all, had a reputation for vindictiveness. They especially did not like outspoken teachers.

"Organize!" said Henry, articulating the lessons he had learned from studying the careers of Sam Gompers and John L. Lewis. "Collective action, public protest. We gotta do stuff like that."

"Well," said Helen Haddock, "collective action can be effective, Henry. But so far, you haven't collected anybody. Have you?"

Henry Haddock got the message. Being "incensed" all by yourself was pretty lonely. Plus, it was useless. He needed to either find other incensed people or he had to start incensing the un-incensed. He certainly needed more troops than just Fantasia and certainly not Penelope, whose commitment couldn't be trusted. After all, Penelope was happy about the abolition of gym class. Moreover, she was in the high-school band, which took up a lot of her time.

"I'll help," said Fantasia.

"Great," said Henry. "Two sixth-graders. Big deal."

"Even sixth-graders," said Helen Haddock very gently, "are allowed to attend School Board meetings."

"School Board meetings?" asked Fantasia.

"Yes," said Henry's mother. "Anybody can go. It's public."

"Public?" asked Henry.

"Yes, indeed."

Henry Haddock bounded from his stool. "Yes!" he roared. "I'll beard the lion in his den!"

"Huh?" said Fantasia.

"Lion?" asked Penelope. "What lion?"

Helen Haddock just laughed.

Fantasia Fulton crossed her arms and gave Henry her severest glare. "Boy, you read too DAMN much," she said. "You better not be talkin' like that to those School Board people."

"You should talk," replied Henry ironically, "about how to talk."

CHAPTER 2

17 AUGUST

For his first-ever appearance at the School Board, Henry Haddock was wearing clean blue jeans, hard shoes, his only white shirt, a Navy-blue crested blazer and a matching dark-blue tie whose only embellishment was a small, tasteful portrait of Bart Simpson.

When forced by his mother—one day at J.C. Penney's—to choose a tie, Henry had been sorely tempted by the one on which Bart Simpson was pulling down his pants and "mooning." Now he was glad he had selected the more understated image.

Henry was alone. Fantasia had promised to stand by his side. However, that afternoon, Fantasia had been apprehended by her father, Lt. Col. Lafayette Fulton, videogaming on her laptop during what he called "restricted hours." This infraction had rendered Fantasia "confined to quarters" 'til the weekend.

Helen Haddock had volunteered to accompany her son. But Henry knew that opposing the School Board was risky for his mother. He had told her, no, he'd rather do this himself.

Henry had sacrificed a whole day of summertime baseball

for the sake of this encounter. He'd gotten to the Blackhawk Public Library at opening time, and told Peg Bradner, the head librarian, that he needed to read up on the School Board. Ms. Bradner took Henry to the newspaper "morgue," where he read back issues of the *Weekly Argument* both on paper and on disks.

Henry got to know, pretty well, who the School Board members were and how they thought about a lot of topics.

The Blackhawk School Board held its weekly meetings at 7:30 p.m. in the Blackhawk High School library, where six rows of folding chairs were regularly arranged, facing a broad table. Behind the big table, the five School Board members conducted their business and occasionally looked out at rows of mostly empty chairs. On that night, besides Henry, there were only a few spectators, including Buzz Skelton, one of the middle-school teachers. Henry knew from reading the Blackhawk *Weekly Argument* that Mr. Skelton "monitored" the meetings for the teachers association.

Henry, who was prepared to speak when called upon, sat right up in the first row, in the middle, facing the spot where the Chairman, Farrell McDuff—whose lifelong nickname was "Scooter"—would be sitting if he were there. Scooter McDuff had not yet arrived when Henry entered the room. In fact, only one member, Mrs. Annabella Moss, had gotten to the meeting ahead of Henry.

Mrs. Moss peered curiously at the boy in the front row. After a moment, a light shone in her eye and a smile creased her already creased (but amiable) face.

"Henry?"

Henry, squirming a little, met Mrs. Moss' gaze.

"Henry Haddock?"

"Um. Yeah. I mean, yes."

"Oh, Henry, you rascal. You've gotten so tall!"

Tall? Thought Henry. Boy, didn't he wish he was tall.

"Henry, come up here."

Henry approached Mrs. Moss, who had been his third-grade teacher many years before—as well as Amy's and Penelope's third-grade teacher, and third-grade teacher to kids in Blackhawk going back roughly to Paleolithic times.

Several years ago, Mrs. Moss had retired, and—loath to just "sit around feeling my arteries harden"—she had run for School Board. And won. And then, just this past April, she'd been elected to a second term.

Mrs. Moss, as Henry knew from reading the *Argument*, was the only member of the Board who had voted against the huge budget cuts.

Tonight, Annie Moss didn't talk about the budget to Henry. She asked about Amy and Penelope and insisted that Henry say "hello" to his parents. And she enthused about how big and handsome Henry had become.

Henry answered all Mrs. Moss' questions politely but he felt self-conscious, especially as the other School Board members began filtering into the library, taking seats at the big table and looking curiously—and not in a very friendly way—at the kid schmoozing with Annie Moss.

Henry was eager to return to his seat, but Mrs. Moss was still asking questions. Finally, she said, "Henry, I must say I'm surprised to see you here, of all places. What on earth—"

A loud and forceful throat-clearing sound, rumbling from the depths of Chairman McDuff, interrupted Mrs. Moss. She winked at Henry and whispered, "We'll talk afterward, all right, Henry?"

Henry returned to his seat, with alacrity.

Scooter McDuff, whose moniker went back to his school days as a tight end for the Blackhawk High School football "Blackhawks," seated himself widely and ponderously. He reached for his gavel.

"This meeting of the Blackhawk School Board will come to order."

For the first half hour of the meeting, Henry barely heard a word exchanged among the Board members. He had read about them. He had seen each of them around town from time to time. But, in places like the Blackhawk Cash Store or the All-State Truck Stop Diner, they seemed like ordinary people. As members of the town's second most important deliberative body (some said the School Board was number one, more important than the Board of Aldermen), they looked different to Henry. Even Mrs. Moss seemed somehow larger and weightier than normal, even a little scary.

Viewed from Henry's left, the Board members were Randy Zink, who'd been selling insurance for State Farm since his graduation from Blackhawk High eighteen years before, Lyle Lehnherr, who worked at the Farmers & Merchants Bank, Chairman McDuff, proprietor of McDuff's Monster Tire Depot, Mrs. Moss and—farthest to Henry's right—Darlene Gazelick, who didn't work outside the home because it was against her religion.

From his library research, Henry knew that Chairman McDuff was the talkingest—and shoutingest—member. He bullied everyone, especially Randy Zink, but was careful not to antagonize Mrs. Moss. Mrs. Gazelick, whose opinions were very strong, offered frequent proposals to "reform" the schools, mostly by having students pray in class, study the Bible and "practice abstinence." She also wanted to remove a lot of books she thought were "indecent."

Henry knew also that Mr. Lehnherr called himself a "financial expert," probably because he worked at the bank. He always favored spending less money on schools, never more. He was the main author of the list of teachers who had been fired. Henry stared hard at Mr. Lehnherr, searching his face for signs of malice and heartlessness. But all he saw was a squinch-faced man in his thirties, with wavy brown hair, walrus whiskers and watery eyes behind wire-rimmed glasses. He had a shaving cut on his chin.

Henry actually liked Lyle Lehnherr's face—for "artistic" reasons. It occurred to Henry that if he ever came to another School Board meeting, he should bring along his sketchbook.

It took Henry an hour or so, but he figured out what was going on. This was the Board's first meeting after many weeks of budget talks. So, Chairman McDuff put the Board to work catching up on "old business," none of it very interesting. As 10 pm approached, the audience consisted entirely of Mr. Skelton—who was obligated to be there—and Henry. A news "stringer" for the *Argument*, a student from Coulee Junior College just up the road from Blackhawk, had spent a fidgety hour in the audience and then departed.

Henry was getting a little drowsy.

But he sprang back to attention after the Board voted unanimously on something and Chairman McDuff said, "Okay then. Let's get on to new business."

Instantly, Henry raised his hand.

Chairman McDuff ignored Henry.

Henry waved his hand.

Chairman McDuff kept his eyes lowered and read from his agenda, proposing that the Board pass a resolution commending the drum-and-bugle unit of the Blackhawk High School Band, also known as "The Thundering Three Hundred," for their gold-medal performance in the tristate summer "marching music showdown." Scooter McDuff spoke enthusiastically about the drum-and-bugle corps' excellent performance, under the leadership of Band Director W.C. Wilcox, in "an intensely competitive atmosphere." McDuff added that he had been present in person to witness the victory.

The vote was unanimous.

Through seven other "new business" items, Chairman McDuff did almost all the talking. Each time, Henry raised his hand. Each time, Scooter paid no attention.

It was a few minutes before 11 pm when Chairman McDuff

said, "Well, I guess that about does it," and raised his gavel.

Henry sprang to his feet, waving a hand wildly, almost in the Chairman's face.

"Move to adjourn," said Randy Zink, his first utterance of the meeting.

"Second," snapped Mrs. Gazelick.

The gavel rapped.

"Okay then," said Chairman McDuff.

Henry was unable to contain himself.

"Hey! Wait a minute!"

The entire School Board (except Mrs. Moss) looked suddenly in Henry's direction, glaring at him in surprise, as though he had just run into the room with his hedgehog hair on fire.

"Wait!" said Henry a little more softly.

Chairman McDuff drew in a vast lungful of air, swelling to something like twice his normal size. He lowered his chins and adjusted his glasses, peering over them at Henry. He leaned forward slightly, knitting his eyebrows so grimly that they met above his nose, and he spoke in majestiferous tones.

"Young man?"

"Um." Henry backed up a step. He found himself fighting the urge to run away, like a little kid.

He might have run, if he hadn't noticed Mrs. Moss, nodding at him with a motherly smile.

"Um," said Henry.

"Yes?" said Chairman McDuff impatiently.

"Well, um," Henry finally managed, "I wanted to say something ... to the, um, Board."

Chairman McDuff shook his head, scowling. Dismissively, he said, "Meeting's over, son."

McDuff turned away. "But I raised my hand," Henry protested.

Chairman McDuff turned back, once more inflating himself to maximum size.

"Raised your hand?"

"Yes," replied Henry, "er ... sir."

Splaying his own hands on the table, Chairman McDuff leaned toward Henry. "Well, son, I saw you raise your hand."

"Oh," said Henry. "Then why didn't you—"

"Call on you?" McDuff broke in, his voice louder. Henry noticed Board members Zink, Lehnherr and Gazelick arrayed behind the Chairman, like one of those phalanxes of Roman times that he had read about.

"Yeah. I mean, yes sir."

"I didn't call on you, son, because this is not fourth grade. Nor is this a forum for random commentary from the general public. This is a School Board meeting, young man. We have important public affairs to conduct. We have an agenda, and we have rules."

Chairman McDuff seemed to be finished. He stood up straight again, apparently poised to leave the library.

"Um," said Henry.

The Board scowled at him.

Annabella Moss intervened. "Henry," she said, "during our regular meetings, it isn't customary for the School Board to solicit comments or questions."

"Oh," said Henry, surprised.

"If we did, we'd be here the whole damn night," said Chairman McDuff.

"Oh," said Henry. "Can't I ever—"

"You have to get on the agenda, son," said McDuff.

"Oh. Well, how—"

"It's late, son!"

With that, the Chairman, quickly followed by members Zink, Lehnherr and Gazelick, departed the high-school library.

Henry found himself alone with Mrs. Moss, who was tucking a handkerchief into her purse and straightening a summer shawl on her shoulders. "If someone has an agenda item for the School Board," she said looking sideways at Henry, "they only need to submit a request with the superintendent's secretary."

"Oh."

"Her name is Ms. Arnold," added Mrs. Moss, "and she's a nice lady."

"Oh."

And Mrs. Moss left the library, side-by-side with Henry Haddock.

As it turned out, Myrtle Arnold, secretary to Superintendent of Schools Robert M. Ptaschnik, was quite a nice lady. After talking to Henry briefly the next day, she inserted into the School Board's next agenda, under New Business, an item that read, "H. Haddock, on the School Budget."

She also made Henry a copy of the agenda.

So, the next week, when Henry showed at the School Board meeting, along with Fantasia, he brought proof—in writing—of his right to address the four members of the Board in attendance that night. Mrs. Moss, who suffered from weak lungs, was absent.

Also present that night, after a vacation in the Carolinas, was Superintendent Ptaschnik, who seemed aware of Henry's intentions. Myrtle Arnold was seated beside the superintendent. They occupied a separate table, to the left of the School Board.

The August 24 meeting of the School Board was the last before school started, which meant there was a lot of New Business to cover. It was past 11:30 when, at last, Chairman McDuff nodded toward Randy Zink for a motion to adjourn.

Zink moved to adjourn. Darlene Gazelick seconded crisply. McDuff dropped the gavel. Henry gaped.

"Wait!" he cried, standing.

"What the HELL?" shouted Fantasia, who had exhibited more patience, throughout the long evening, than Henry had ever seen from her.

The Chairman turned toward Henry and Fantasia. He was shocked, *shocked* at Fantasia's outburst.

"Hey," said Henry, "what about me?"

Chairman McDuff smirked, looking down the full length of his nose at Henry. "What about you, son?"

Henry was irked. He almost replied, "I'm not your son, blubberface!" But he curbed his tongue and said, instead, "Mr. McDuff, I was on the agenda. I went to the office and—"

"Son," said McDuff. "It's the Chairman's job to approve every single agenda item. I didn't approve your request."

Henry, desperately, thrust his copy of the agenda at Chairman McDuff. "But I got it right here. See? I'm on the agenda."

McDuff shook his head piteously. "That's a preliminary agenda. It's not the final agenda. I approve the final agenda. You're not on it, son."

That did it for Henry. "I'm not your son, blub—mister!"

Visibly offended, Chairman McDuff rose to his full altitude, looming over Henry and Fantasia, glowering as he motioned his Board cohorts to depart the building.

"What the HELL is this CRAP!" said Fantasia.

The Board left, followed by the superintendent, who looked back once, his expression a mixture of curiosity and apology.

A second later, Fantasia had Henry by the throat, as she snarled at his face. "You brought me here, agendaface! And you made me sit here all night, bored out of my mind, for THIS?"

But Henry was angry, too. He snarled back, "Yeah, I did! And I'm comin' back next week! And you can do whatever you wanna do! Scooterface!"

"Oh yeah? Oh YEAH?" said Fantasia, kicking a chair so hard that it folded itself and fell over. "Well, I'll be here, boringface! You try and KEEP me away!"

CHAPTER 3

31 AUGUST

On his first day of middle school, Henry Haddock couldn't help but feel a thrill. He was finally out of grade school, liberated from elementary school, free from the mothering oppression of little-kid school. He was no longer stuck in the same classroom, with the same old teacher hour after hour, every day. With each ring of the bell now, he was on the move, hell-bent for a fresh subject, a different room, another teacher. He had his own locker, with a unique combination, which he could visit—if he wanted—before class, after class and even between classes in those five frantic minutes that every student had to rush and jostle from one room to the next. Of course, the first day was only a half day, and class only amounted to meeting his teachers, filling out attendance forms, getting desk assignments and all that jazz. But it included all the rushing and jostling of life in middle school, and it gave him the feeling that now, finally, he was growing up.

Beneath his excitement, though, Henry couldn't help noticing the absences at the Blackhawk Middle School. In every corridor, there were one or two classrooms dormant, their doors locked, no teachers there. Peering through the narrow window of Ms. Webster's art room, Henry could see dust motes drifting in shafts of sunlight among broad tables and upended chairs.

Other classrooms were packed to overflowing, like Henry's third-period American History class. All of Ms. Quaadman's students had been jumbled together with Mr. Kussow's students, because Ms. Quaadman had been "axed." Mr. Kussow roll-called more than seventy students, including Henry, and shouted—as the bell rang and everyone rushed from the room—that he would be assigning half of the group to "another section." Henry wondered what that was.

There were two gaping holes in Henry's schedule. In second period, which would have been gym class with good old Coach Abernathy three times a week and Study Hall on Tuesday and Thursday, there was no Coach Abernathy. Second period was just Study Hall all week long. And where Henry would have had art with the formidable but wonderful Alice Webster in sixth period, he had more dumb old Study Hall.

Henry especially lamented Ms. Webster's absence. His fifth-grade teacher, Mrs. Drummond, had sent Henry to Ms. Webster last fall when Henry volunteered to make posters for the Christmas pageant. "She has better art supplies than we do," Mrs. Drummond had said.

But secretly, Mrs. Drummond had contacted Ms. Webster with the information that Henry had "talent." So, instead of a lot of crummy 18x24 posters made with stencils and ink, Ms. Webster had put in more than an hour after school for ten days teaching Henry how to design and produce silk-screen prints. Henry had never been so excited about art. He had never anticipated a class as eagerly as he looked forward to middle-school art with Alice Webster.

But she was gone. She had actually moved away from Blackhawk. When he looked inside her unused art room,

Henry saw that it was starting to fill up already with non-art stuff, shoved inside by the janitors.

"This is unacceptable," said Henry to no one in particular. He was incensed all over again.

Other students were also incensed, or at least befuddled. These included the kids who thought they were going to take Mechanical Drawing and Woodworking with Mr. Schwartz, Art Metals with Mr. Gamble, Beginning French with Madame Seronde, Beginning Spanish with Señora Epstein, Keyboarding with Mrs. Gatewood, Music with Mr. Pringle ...

"And so on and so forth," grumbled Henry, who found Fantasia moping on the school steps after the dismissal bell.

"Decimated," said Fantasia, her face in her hands.

This was accurate, thought Henry. At least one in every ten teachers had disappeared, although—Henry had read this in the *Weekly Argument*—actual school enrollment in the growing town of Blackhawk had increased by just over eight percent.

"More kids, less teachers," said Fantasia, apparently reading Henry's mind.

"Fewer teachers," Henry—a stickler for grammar—said.

"Yeah, that, too," said Fantasia.

"RATS!" she added.

Henry Haddock sat down beside Fantasia and clenched his jaw. "We can't give up," he said.

"Oh yeah, decimationface? What the HELL can we do?"

"Try again, with the School Board."

Fantasia turned. "WHAT? You're really gonna go back?"

Henry was thinking about Lech Walesa and the Solidarity strikers in Poland who just kept coming back and coming back until they toppled the Communist regime.

"I'm on the agenda," said Henry.

"That doesn't matter," said Fantasia. "Ol' potatoface is just gonna erase you again."

"They've got to listen," said Henry.

"They ain't gonna," said Fantasia.

"Aren't."

"Neither one."

But that night, there was Henry, in the front row at the School Board meeting, hoping he might have finally cracked Scooter McDuff's agenda.

He had certainly done everything he could.

On Monday, Henry had gone back to the superintendent's office, where he politely asked Myrtle Arnold to put him on the next agenda. As before, Mrs. Arnold squeezed Henry into New Business (although, by now, Henry's presence was turning into Old Business).

True to her threat, Fantasia came to the meeting and plumped down next to Henry, ready to lend him moral (and vocal) support. This, however, was all the support Henry had. He'd invited other Blackhawk Middle School students—mainly the kids who played in the Blackhawk Independent Baseball Organization (BIBO)—to join him at the meeting, in united protest against the School Board budget cuts. Several kids said they'd think about coming. Exactly zero had actually shown up. So much for Solidarity!

Unseen by Henry, however, lingering in the shadows of the high-school library was Henry's eldest sister, Amy. Mainly, Amy was there to see what would happen to Henry. But she also shared some of Henry's ire over the disappearance of so many teachers and so many resources at Blackhawk High.

Henry did recognize one new face in the sparse crowd. Instead of the useless college kid usually sent to "cover" the meeting, Blackhawk *Weekly Argument* editor Darren Flack was making a personal appearance. He was seated beside Buzz Skelton, the teachers union "spy." The two men chatted in quiet tones as the School Board members arrived and took their seats.

From her place beside the Chairman, Annabella Moss

caught Henry's eye and subtly motioned him forward. Henry, cautiously, approached the head table, feeling with every step the chilly gaze of Chairman McDuff. Mrs. Moss showed Henry her copy of the agenda, where—as usual—Henry's name did not appear under New Business. Henry shrugged with resignation, turning toward his seat. Mrs. Moss cleared her throat.

Henry turned back.

"I'll see what I can do," she said. Henry smiled weakly.

When Henry told her he had been erased again, Fantasia squeaked, "WHAT?"

As the meeting began, Henry dug, from his backpack, his favorite 11x14-inch sketchbook. He loved to sketch, especially people, especially if they agreed to sit still while he drew. The School Board members, who sat still for hours, were perfect subjects. Henry tucked a selection of pens and pencils into his shirt pocket and got to work immortalizing Chairman McDuff.

This being the first day of the new school year, the Board had lots of business. They seemed to linger over every item. Eleven o'clock came during Old Business. Henry looked back toward Buzz Skelton and saw, with surprise, that Darren Flack was still around. The *Argument* editor covered three towns for three different weekly newspapers owned by some outfit called the Klaxon Group. This fractured schedule meant that Flack could visit the Blackhawk School Board only infrequently. When he did, he usually lit out by 10:30, driven—Henry assumed—by his "deadline."

By studying past issues of the paper, Henry had figured out that most of the Blackhawk School Board news published in the *Argument* was not the work of the stringer from Coulee Junior College. Darren Flack got most of his news from personal phone conversations, after each meeting, with Scooter McDuff and Buzz Skelton.

New Business carried the Board to the brink of midnight.

Chairman McDuff, looking at his watch, rushed through the last item—an upcoming fire alarm test at the elementary school by the Blackhawk Consolidated Fire Department. McDuff signaled Randy Zink to move for adjournment.

Randy Zink did so. Annabella Moss broke in, "Mr. Chairman, before we adjourn ... "

Chairman McDuff swelled in his chair, stiffening his back and looking down upon the small elderly woman seated at his left.

"Mrs. Moss?" he asked archly.

"Scooter, dear," replied Annabella Moss looking back pleasantly and speaking in maternal tones. "I know how busy we've been, and I know you have good reason to trim the agenda. But I really must point out that for three weeks now, a very bright and well-meaning young man has been—"

"You can stop right there, Annie," said Chairman McDuff warningly. "This Board has rules and procedures. We have to maintain order. Strict order. Or all hell breaks loose. The barbarians are at the gate, Annie."

"Barbarians?" said Mrs. Moss, pretending to be alarmed. "Scooter, this is a ten-year-old boy."

"You're eleven," Fantasia hissed into Henry's ear.

"Sssh," said Henry.

"Oh, balls!" whispered Fantasia.

Chairman McDuff said, "Joan of Arc wasn't much older, and look at all the trouble she stirred up."

Annabella Moss just laughed at this and said, "Mr. Chairman, I move that Henry Haddock, a student in excellent standing at the Blackhawk Middle School, be allowed—per his repeated requests—to address the Board."

"Oh, for Pete's sake," said Chairman McDuff.

"Hm. I think I'll second that motion," said Board member Randy Zink, with an unusually mischievous glint in his eye, "just for the sake of argument."

And so, they argued over Henry Haddock for almost fifteen minutes. Henry shifted self-consciously in his seat throughout the debate. Fantasia hung on the edge of her chair, drinking in the drama and muttering angrily at any remark that challenged Henry's right to speak. Henry glanced back and noticed that Darren Flack was very busy with his notebook and pen.

Annabella Moss advanced the position that letting Henry speak could not conceivably do any harm. She said it would make the Board look open and responsive to the schoolchildren in their charge. Chairman McDuff, with vehement support from Darlene Gazelick, contended that allowing the general public to "horn in, willy-nilly" on every deliberation undertaken by a duly elected body of representatives amounted to nothing less than "an invitation to anarchy, an opening of the thoughtful processes of public policy to the second-guessing of ill-informed dilettantes and the pressures of special interests."

Henry, on the margin of his book, next to a study of Lyle Lehnherr's close-set eyes and button nose, wrote down "ANARKY" and "DILLATAUNTS," followed by a question mark, so he could look both up later.

"Oh, applesauce!" replied Annie Moss. "Scooter, look at Henry. He's a little boy, not Attila the Hun. He's not even Joan of Arc!"

But the Board voted, four to one, against Henry. And swiftly adjourned.

"WHOA!" roared Fantasia. "This is SO bogus. Henry, you ... they ... OOOH, I'm so MAD!"

While Fantasia fumed, Henry noticed that Darren Flack was following Chairman McDuff out the far door of the library.

Two days later, a headline just below the fold on page one of the *Argument* read:

SCHOOL BD. GAGS PUPIL PROTESTING BUDGET CUTS

"Wow," said Henry Haddock. Darren Flack's coverage of the School Board meeting devoted only three paragraphs to Henry Haddock. But Henry read them at least forty times.

CHAPTER 4

7 SEPTEMBER

In its edition of September 2, the *Weekly Argument* quoted School Board Chairman Farrell "Scooter" McDuff as follows: "This Haddock boy is just a pawn. He probably doesn't even know what he's supposed to be protesting. There are people pulling this innocent youngster's strings. This is an organized campaign to subvert the democratic process here in Blackhawk ... "

McDuff went on: "I don't know who's behind all this. But I'll find out. I certainly have my suspects ... "

And he concluded: "But Henry Haddock? A sixth-grader? I feel sorry for the poor little kid ... "

Scooter McDuff was a stubborn man. He'd had to be stubborn, all his life, to get ahead. In grade school, he had been a goofy-looking, gangly boy whose nickname, Scooter, was a joking reference to his utter inability to either scoot, scurry, skip or skate. But he took his sardonic sobriquet to heart and threw himself into every test he faced, in class or in sports—but especially in sports. He ran and battled, he blundered and lumbered and plodded, all the time trying to scoot. And, although he never scooted, he won more games than he lost and he made people stop laughing at him. Eventually, despite his ungainly size and awkwardness, Scooter McDuff became a star athlete at Blackhawk High School. He was an all-conference tight end on the football team, the starting center for the basketball team and, in his senior year, the sixth-best shot putter in the state.

Likewise, as a grown-up in business, he had prevailed through dogged determination. When he took over his father's faltering truck repair shop, he decided to specialize in tires. In a few years, his little tire store had grown into McDuff's Monster Tire Depot. Step by plodding step, Scooter overwhelmed every small tire retailer in the nine towns surrounding Blackhawk. Along the way, he fought off challenges from J.C. Penney, Sears, Firestone and even Walmart. Scooter became the region's biggest supplier of tires by calling on every customer, personally. He promised—face to face—that he would give them better prices and service than anyone else, or he would kill himself trying.

Scooter's next crusade was local politics. He worked just as ferociously to get elected as he had worked at playing sports and selling tires. After failing four times in to win a seat on the Board of Aldermen, Scooter turned to the School Board. He lost three more elections before the exhausted voters gave him a seat. He was now in his fourth term on the School Board. He was the senior member of the Board and was serving as Chairman for the third time.

Scooter McDuff lacked charm. He had no sense of humor. He was not clever, not complicated, not subtle. He called himself a "plugger." He always got what he wanted because he just plain outplugged everybody else 'til they were worn to a frazzle.

Scooter McDuff figured that Henry Haddock, a "poor little kid," would be easy to outplug.

In his war on Henry, Chairman McDuff had ample help,

particularly in the form of Board member Darlene Gazelick, who regarded the Chairman as a strong leader, a devoted family man, a brilliant businessman and a militant Christian. She supported Scooter's every decision.

Mrs. Gazelick, who wore bifocals and dressed always in black, had a bleak and pessimistic view of human nature. She believed that people were inherently rotten and prone to make the worst choice nine times out of ten. She had spent her life stifling her own instincts and regretting her rare moments of pleasure. She knew that the only way to keep people from running wild and wreaking havoc was to impose rigid discipline. She believed you have to step on children at a very early age and then continue to crush them, squelching for the rest of their lives their natural impulse to do evil.

Naturally, Mrs. Gazelick was a very religious woman. She believed in the Ten Commandments, creation science, school prayer and, when necessary, the destruction of "indecent" books. She personally knew of more than a thousand books that deserved to be burned to a crisp, ideally in public.

The first time Darlene Gazelick spotted Henry Haddock at a School Board meeting, she smelled trouble.

Also loyal to Chairman McDuff were Randy Zink and Lyle Lehnherr. Randy Zink was a simple fellow who wanted to feel like a big wheel without having to actually work very hard at the job. He discovered that campaigning for School Board was a good way to achieve this goal. All he had to do was spend time in local coffee shops, restaurants and taverns talking to people. He would nod helpfully whenever a mother complained about a teacher who had wronged her child. Randy Zink's face would be wreathed in sympathy when an aggrieved homeowner lamented the tax burden imposed upon him by wasteful public schools and greedy teachers. He would scowl pensively when a senior citizen asked him why—why must I continue to pay for schools when neither I nor my children have been to school for 25 years? Why?

Randy Zink had been elected, and then reelected, without answering why. He rarely ever said a word to anyone about education. Randy Zink thought Henry Haddock was a cute kid, but he was also suspicious of Henry.

"That kid's up to something," he said to Lyle Lehnherr one night. "I just don't know what."

Lyle Lehnherr was a man of tight-lipped certitude. For example, although he had never said so, he did not believe at all in public education. His ideal world was a place where no public money—neither taxes nor bonds—could be spent on schools. Lyle Lehnherr felt that education was like a new car or a chicken dinner at Applebee's. If you couldn't afford to buy it, you shouldn't have it. In his secret heart, he believed that anyone who could not afford to pay tuition to a religious school, a private prep school or a military academy should teach their children reading, mathematics and history at home. If parents were too busy to do that, they should just let their kids go through life unschooled and illiterate.

Of course, if anyone had suggested to Lyle Lehnherr that these were his beliefs, he would have said, "No, I support the schools, but I just think they're wasteful." Lyle Lehnherr had often said that public schools should just teach kids a little reading and a little math, up to about third or fourth grade. After that, they should get a job or go to military school.

He saw little social value in trying to teach every single person all sorts of impractical knowledge about European history, mathematics beyond the multiplication tables or confusing scientific concepts like cell division and inertia. He believed that most people—like him—can't understand such things. They'd be happier not trying to learn. He believed, above all, that schoolteachers were spoiled. They were all terribly overpaid. They had lost all the idealism and self-sacrifice that teachers used to have, in the "good old days." Lyle often said that the public schools would be just as good—maybe better—if all the "elitist" teachers were replaced by volunteers.

However, Lyle Lehnherr's skeptical outlook on public schools allowed one exception. He was a big supporter of Blackhawk High School's award-winning band. He thought it fostered "community spirit."

Like Chairman McDuff, Darlene, Randy and Lyle didn't like Mrs. Moss very much. Of course, they would never say so to her face.

The five School Board members, at their regularly scheduled meeting on September 7, saw before them a slightly larger audience than usual. Henry Haddock and Fantasia Fulton were in their usual seats in the front row, right under Chairman McDuff's substantial nose. The gallery included Henry's sister Amy and her best friend, Tiff Melrose. Seated beside Tiff, with a dark and unwilling scowl on his broad but handsome face was Fantasia's big brother, and Tiff's boyfriend, Darnell Fulton.

Darnell, who was always the biggest kid in his class, had started out school with the nickname "Bullwinkle." Later, this was changed to "Moose." For a while, when people saw Moose with his little sister, they called them "Moose and Squirrel." But Fantasia developed a habit of beating the snot out of kids who called her Squirrel. As a result, Fantasia no longer had a nickname.

Moose, on the other hand, didn't beat anybody up. It had never bothered him when people called him Bullwinkle and he was equally tolerant of the nickname Moose. As names go, he figured it was way better than "Darnell."

Amy was at the School Board meeting—along with Tiff and Moose—because she was still curious about what would happen to Henry. She thought his little crusade was windmill-tilting. Nobody, she believed, could ever buck the Board, especially a little smartmouth like Henry, even if he had gotten his name in the newspaper and embarrassed the whole family in the bargain.

Tiff was there because Amy and Moose were there—the latter against his will. Tiff preferred not to let Moose loose among all the cute girls of Blackhawk. Moose, the best and most popular athlete at Blackhawk High, was highly sought-after by the school's female population.

Moose got steady B-minuses in school, just good enough to squeeze onto the Honor Roll. He could have gotten A's, like his prickly little sister Fantasia, but he didn't like to put himself above friends who were only sharp enough to get C's. So Moose slacked off a little, out of loyalty.

As for Moose's feelings about budget cuts, he had none. He thought everything in school was fine, as long as he could play football and basketball, and maybe a little baseball in the spring. The School Board—although Moose was unaware—had protected Moose's favorite sports by making big cuts elsewhere. While keeping the high-school football and basketball teams, the Board had wiped out physical education entirely, and had reduced sports at the middle school to just two—boys basketball and girls volleyball.

Also present in the high-school library that evening were Superintendent Ptaschnik and Myrtle Arnold, along with Buzz Skelton, who had to attend, and *Argument* editor Darrell Flack, who was starting to think there was a good story in Henry Haddock.

The Board had a short agenda. As Chairman McDuff hurried the members through their paces, he couldn't help noticing Henry Haddock as he drew pictures, with an unmistakable artistic panache, on the pages of his ever-present sketchbook. Every once in a while, Henry would show a sketch to the little Black girl beside him. The little Black girl nodded, smiled and, once or twice, laughed out loud. Her laughter got on Scooter's nerves.

In the first week of school, Henry had made two decisions.

The first was that, if he could not study art—which he loved—the way he was supposed to learn it in school, he was going to stay in practice by drawing whenever, wherever and whoever he could. Henry's second decision was that, if he wasn't allowed to talk to the School Board, he could at least *draw* the School Board. As Henry sketched and colored and shaded and altered the faces of the Board members, he came to enjoy these meetings more and more. The School Board members were great "models." Henry enjoyed tracing the contours of Scooter's mountainous bulk, his lantern jaw and his extra chins. Henry was fascinated by Mrs. Gazelick's sharp features and dark, beady raccoon eyes. Lyle Lehnherr's glasses and mustache were fun to draw. There was something about Randy Zink that made Henry think of Richard M. Nixon. And Henry realized that Mrs. Moss wore a different hat every Tuesday night ... And so on.

Fantasia whispered, "Henry. This is cool. You're freaking them out."

"No, I'm just drawing."

"Yeah, but it bothers them. Check it out."

It was true. Besides Scooter, Mrs. Gazelick cast frequent furtive glances in Henry's direction.

The meeting was winding toward an early adjournment (much to Moose Fulton's relief) when Henry set aside his sketchbook. He raised his hand.

Scooter McDuff scowled.

Henry waved his hand.

Scooter McDuff turned away from Henry and raised his gavel. "Okay then," he began.

"Mr. Chairman, sir," Henry piped up.

Scooter McDuff swung back toward Henry, leaning across the table and narrowing his eyes—like an owl with a chipmunk in its sights.

"Er, sir," Henry said, a little more meekly.

"Young man," said McDuff in a voice that set chairs in the

last row of the audience vibrating. "You are not permitted to address the Board. You are *not* on the *approved* agenda. I have told you this before."

As quickly as he could speak, Henry replied, "I know I can't address the Board, sir. I just had a question."

"Don't you dare split hairs with me, young man," said Scooter McDuff, who felt strongly that he had already said too much to this impertinent brat. "You can't address the Board and you can't *question* the Board."

Even more quickly, Henry said, "Oh, no, that's not right, sir. I can."

McDuff actually rose to his feet, towering over Henry Haddock. "WHAT?" he growled. "You can WHAT?"

Somewhere in the vicinity of Scooter McDuff, Henry heard the whispered voice of Lyle Lehnherr. "Scooter, ssh. The press."

McDuff, surreptitiously, beneath his eyebrows, glanced at Darren Flack, who was aiming a camera at him. "Oh, hell," said McDuff to himself.

Henry was undeterred. He spoke again. "According to the state Open Meeting Law, sir, members of the public are allowed to ask about points of information ... sir."

McDuff paused at this, staring down at Henry. As he did, Darren Flack's camera flashed.

"Oh, God," said Lyle Lehnherr.

In the moment of silence that followed, the voice of Moose Fulton could be heard whispering to his girlfriend, Tiff. "Jeez, why doesn't the great dictator let Henry ask a question?"

Tiff blushed a lovely shade of pink. "Moose, not so loud," she said. "Ssh!"

Scooter McDuff noticed that he was standing up. He didn't remember how he'd gotten there. He sat suddenly and addressed Superintendent of Schools Robert Ptaschnik. "Bob," he asked, "is that right?"

Superintendent Ptaschnik, a harried man who maintained

a stoic demeanor, cocked his head and shrugged. "Honestly, I don't know," he said. "I haven't read the Open Meeting Law since, well, ages ago. And I don't have a copy with me."

He turned toward Myrtle Arnold, the Board's secretary. "Myrtle?" he said.

Myrtle Arnold, who wanted no part of this argument, simply shuddered.

"Well, I read it!" said Henry. "Yesterday. At the Public Library."

"Young man!" Scooter McDuff whanged the table with his gavel, causing Amy and Tiff to jump in their seats. "That will be enough from you!"

"But I read it!" Henry protested. "I read the Open Meeting Law."

"Yeah," said Moose, not very quietly. "The kid read it."

Moose was fearless on the football field, but the look he got from Scooter McDuff sent a chill down his spine.

"Young man, I don't care what you've read. I am not going to violate this Board's procedures and disrupt our deliberations on your say-so," Scooter McDuff said, glaring at Henry. "Out of courtesy, we will take your request under advisement. Bob?"

The superintendent looked up.

McDuff said to him, "Will you consult the Town Counsel on this matter?"

The superintendent nodded.

But Henry wasn't backing down just yet.

"Hey, why don't we just look it up? We're in the school library. I bet there's a copy right here."

McDuff ground his teeth and waved his gavel, menacingly, in Henry's direction. "Young man, we don't have time to go rummaging through this library in search of some dusty old law."

"No, no, it's no trouble. I can find it in a minute," said Henry. "It's on the computer, right there."

Scooter McDuff slammed the gavel. Without seeking a

motion or second, he ended the meeting. "This meeting is adjourned. Good night!"

"Well," said Moose, "that wasn't fair."

Smiling like the Cheshire cat, Darren Flack slipped out the door, his fingers already itchy for the keyboard.

The following Saturday evening, the Haddock household was holding its weekly pizza party. The "usual gang" consisted of the Haddock and Fulton families. Lately, Tiff Melrose—blessed by her association with Moose—was included. Also present, and observing the scene with deep fascination, was one of Fantasia's friends, Merrilee Pheeters, who was doing a sleepover at the Fulton household. Sarge, the Fulton dog, policed the floor for fallen food and assisted anyone who didn't like to eat the crust.

Two subjects dominated the conversation. One was Blackhawk High School's victory in its first football game of the season, 45-7, over Loganville. Moose, the quarterback, had accounted for five touchdowns, three running and two passing.

The subject, however, that commanded most interest was Henry's second appearance in the Blackhawk *Weekly Argument*. It was seven paragraphs long. Darren Flack had used the word "quixotic" to describe Henry's effort to address the School Board and had depicted Scooter McDuff as a great big bully, although not in so many words. Best of all, in Henry's view, was that the *Argument* editor had bothered to look up the Open Meeting Law. In a box beside his story, the editor had printed a section of the law that guaranteed any citizen's right to query an elected municipal board on a "point of information."

"Y'see?" said Henry. "I was right."

"Right, shmight, pizzaface!" replied Penelope Haddock. "You're making trouble. For everybody!"

"Oh yeah? How'm I doing that? Anchovyface!"

(This was a low blow. Penelope despised anchovies.)

"You made 'em mad, Henry," said Penelope. "Now, even if they wanted to give you back your dumb old Ms. Webster, they won't do it 'cause they're mad at you."

Henry was amazed at the foolishness of Penelope's argument. "Penny, that's just stupid!"

Helen Haddock broke in. "Henry, that'll be enough of that. You can have a discussion without calling your sister names."

"Stupid's not a name," said Henry. "It's a pathology."

At this, Henry's father, against his better judgment, laughed. Causing Henry's mother to laugh and spread the merriment. Fantasia's parents joined in. The laughter drowned out Penelope, who was asking, "It's a what? What did he call me?"

By and by, everyone—except poor Merrilee, who wasn't sure *what* everyone was arguing about—had taken a position on Henry's war with the School Board. Penelope and Fantasia stood at opposite poles. Penelope, mostly because Henry had called her a word she didn't understand (even though she got better grades than Henry), was firmly opposed to Henry's campaign. Fantasia supported Henry wholeheartedly, mostly because Henry was her best friend but also because she thought Henry was right and he shouldn't be stopped from speaking out.

Henry's parents were both proud and worried. Ralph Haddock, a biochemist who spent his life in research, was very pleased that Henry was delving into libraries and index cards and reading law books to support his convictions. But he was worried that Henry, after losing a fight he couldn't possibly win, would end up with a broken heart.

Helen Haddock wished she could stand up in public and support Henry's crusade to save the teachers. She thought her son was extraordinarily brave to challenge Scooter McDuff. But she knew that the Board's animosity toward Henry might affect the whole Haddock family, especially her. If Helen Haddock lost her job, Amy—now a junior in high school—

might not be able to afford college.

Amy Haddock thought Henry's little war was fun. But she also knew it was hopeless. Amy believed that politics—at least for regular folks—was a waste of time. The people who ran the world, she thought, ran it for their own benefit. Once they got into office (mostly by cheating), they did anything they felt like doing. They ignored most of the people who elected them. They only listened to big shots with lots of money. And whenever they did something cruel and terrible—like firing all those teachers and ruining the whole language program at Blackhawk High—they never, ever changed their minds.

So, there!

Fantasia and Moose's father, Lt. Col. Lafayette Fulton, was a military man. As such, he might be expected to support the authorities, namely the School Board. But Lt. Col. Fulton—who was called "Colonel Fate" around the house because, when she was very small, Fantasia couldn't pronounce "Lafayette"—had grown up admiring the Rev. Martin Luther King, Jr. As a result, he believed deeply in every citizen's right to stand up and question what he called "the status quo."

Fantasia and Moose's mother, Delia, always stood by her husband, except when she didn't (which was often). But, in this case, they both agreed with Henry. Besides, Delia Fulton had always thought Henry was a sweetheart.

Moose and Tiff had almost no opinion on Henry's situation. They held hands under the table when they weren't eating pizza. They did a little discreet kissing. Moose thought Henry was getting the shaft from the School Board, but he also figured it was none of his personal beeswax. He had other concerns, mainly the football team from Castle Rock—Blackhawk's next opponent.

"So, Hank," said Moose, "are you goin' back again next week? Into the lion's den?"

Fortunately, thought Henry, Moose was the rare person who called him "Hank."

"Of course," said Henry. "But first, I'm going to see the Town Counsel."

Ralph Haddock was surprised. He ended up talking through a mouthful of pizza. "You're gon' see Cha-ee Muh-gay?"

"Wha'd he say?" asked Fantasia.

"Dad," said Penelope, "don't talk with your mouth full!"

Ralph Haddock swallowed and tried again. "Henry, you have an appointment with Charlie Mulcahy?"

"Yeah," said Henry. "After school."

"Well, I'll be hornswoggled," said Henry's father. "Good for you."

"I'm gonna ask him to come to the School Board meeting," said Henry. "You think he will?"

"I think he'd be a dope if he did," Penelope offered.

"Penelope," said her mother warningly.

"You know, I think he might come," said Ralph Haddock. "Since you started showing up at meetings, Henry, the School Board has gotten to be pretty entertaining. If I know Charlie Mulcahy, he'll drop in just to see what all the excitement's about."

"What about you, Dad? Can you come?"

"Oh, I'd love to. But on Tuesday, I have my late class at the university."

"Oh, right," said Henry. Henry knew he should probably resent his father for missing important events in his life. But he understood that his father was a pretty important scientist—which made him a very busy man. Henry was proud of having an important dad. So, a few paternal absences were easy to forgive.

He asked his mother if she planned to come. She shook her head. "I'll get reports from Amy and you," she said. "Meanwhile, I think it's better to keep myself out of range of Mr. McDuff's holy wrath."

Henry understood this, too. "Yeah, he can be pretty scary."

"And mean," said Fantasia.

"Too much so, maybe," said Ralph Haddock, thoughtfully.

Everyone turned toward Henry's father.

He said, "You know, Scooter's just one member of the Board. One vote out of five. But somehow, he has gotten everyone but Annie Moss to follow his lead on every little thing. He's an emperor and he's turning the school system into his personal fiefdom."

"Fiefdom?" said Penelope.

"Ain't fair," said Moose.

"What's a fiefdom?" said Penelope.

"Well, you know what President Carter said," replied Henry, ignoring Penelope.

"What?" asked Moose.

"He said life isn't fair."

"Oh yeah?" said Moose. "President Carter said that?"

"Yup," said Henry.

"Where does the little pipsqueak find this stuff?" said Amy.

"I read," said Henry.

CHAPTER 5

14 SEPTEMBER

The riot at the School Board meeting came unexpectedly. Afterward, nobody knew for sure who had started it all.

Some blamed it on Scooter McDuff, whose obstinacy had powers to drive a saint, eventually, to mayhem.

Others blamed it, logically, on Henry Haddock, for being the thorn in Scooter's paw.

A faction among this group found fault with Henry's parents, for failing to teach him a proper respect for authority, not to mention decent manners.

A few keen observers placed the onus on W.C. "Wally" Wilcox, director of the Blackhawk High School "Thundering Three Hundred" Marching Band. They thought Wally had barged into a volatile situation and injected a fresh source of disagreement.

Many folks—with great reluctance—blamed Darnell "Moose" Fulton, star quarterback for the Blackhawk High School Blackhawks, who, everyone agreed, threw the first punch.

A larger contingent blamed Blackhawk Police Department Officer Billy Karkle, who "provoked" the fight by waving a nightstick carelessly in Moose's vicinity.

Charlie Mulcahy, Blackhawk's agreeable Town Counsel, blamed himself for all the trouble, because if he had not come to the meeting and spoken his peace, probably nothing would have happened. In retrospect, he concluded that he could have avoided poking his nose into this whole can of worms by just sending Scooter McDuff a memo that clarified the Open Meeting Law.

Charlie Mulcahy was being too hard on himself. No one else saw Charlie as even slightly responsible. On the other hand, Board member Darlene Gazelick deserved some measure of blame, according to at least one bystander, for bringing God—unnecessarily—into the dispute, specifically by telling Henry that he was a "bad seed," unloved by God Almighty.

Looking back, *Weekly Argument* editor Darren Flack saw an outburst by Fantasia Fulton—who defended Henry by calling Darlene a "wicked old hatchetface"—as the tipping point that set off the fracas.

(Not that Darren Flack disapproved of the fracas. It provided the most exciting School Board story in his entire career.)

Of course, almost everyone agreed that if Darren Flack had not started showing up at School Board meetings, reporting on the clash between Scooter and Henry and turning Henry's little stunt into a big fat *cause celebre*, there would have been no blow-up at all — because the school library would have been empty as usual.

Hardly anyone pegged Amy Haddock as the troublemaker. But she was the one who silently pecked away at her smartphone, messaging her many friends. She invited them to "join the fun" at the School Board meeting. Amy's friends eventually swelled the crowd in the library from about two dozen people at the start to more than sixty when the fur began to fly.

Finally, there was the matter of Paul Lamartine, who stayed far back in the room. He had slipped quietly away at the first hint of conflict. Yet, many of those who attended the September 14th meeting seemed to sense his presence, especially the members of the School Board.

Henry, however, did not notice Paul Lamartine. He had no idea who Paul Lamartine was. Such is often the way with politics.

Despite a much larger audience than usual, including a contingent of Henry Haddock's sniggering, whispering sixth-grade classmates, Scooter McDuff presided masterfully over the evening's agenda. He disposed crisply of everything from the Approval of the Previous Minutes to nine items of New Business. He sat back in his chair at 10:15 pm, scanned the swaying sea of humanity before him and poised his gavel.

"The agenda is complete, except for a matter to be discussed in executive session, to which we must adjourn. Do I have a motion to—"

"Mr. Chairman, sir."

The kid.

"Oh, hell," said Lyle Lehnherr.

"Young man," said Scooter McDuff, with surprising force. He rolled his chair forward and leaned, glaring, at the boy in the front row. "I will tolerate no disturbance. I warn you. The police are here."

With this, everyone in the high school library turned to stare at Officer Billy Karkle, the newest member of the Blackhawk Police Department. Billy flushed crimson.

"But sir," replied Henry, undeterred.

"That's enough!" responded Chairman McDuff, slamming the gavel. "Silence, child."

"Sir," Henry persisted, "I have a point of info—"

"I said! Silence!" This came out as a veritable roar that froze everyone—except Moose Fulton, who stood up, right behind Henry. Moose crossed his arms, scowling at Chairman McDuff.

"Excuse me. Scooter?" The voice of Charlie Mulcahy gently broke the ominous silence.

"Oh, hell," whispered Lyle Lehnherr.

"What is it?" The Chairman's voice was lower, but still angry and impatient.

Charlie Mulcahy had been sitting quietly through the meeting, at the same table as Superintendent Bob Ptaschnik and Myrtle Arnold.

Now, the Town Counsel stood.

"Well, Mr. Chairman," said Charlie Mulcahy, speaking with lawyerly formality, as befitted his station. "I did review the Open Meeting Law, as requested by Superintendent Ptaschnik. As I understand the law, it seems clear that if a member of the public does have a legitimate question, on a point of information, the Board has a duty to allow—"

"Allow?" cried Scooter. "Allow that little pest, that little—"

Here was the moment when Darlene Gazelick disputed Scooter McDuff's use of the word "pest." She contended that Henry Haddock was far, far worse than a pest, that he was, in fact, in cahoots with the Devil. And so forth.

Her speech, condemning Henry, also went unfinished. Darlene was interrupted by Fantasia, leaping to Henry's defense. After calling Mrs. Gazelick an unfortunate name ("underwearface"), Fantasia, bristling and sparking, advanced on the head table.

Chairman McDuff, his judgment impaired by emotion, shouted, "Seize that child!"

Seeing his duty, Officer Billy Karkle then rushed forward, taking Fantasia by the arms and trying to hold her back. He was laboring to restrain the little girl as gently as possible, but Fantasia had grown up listening to her parents tell stories about nonviolent civil rights protesters beaten by police in Birmingham and Selma. Officer Karkle's touch triggered in

Fantasia a flaming righteousness. She squirmed and wrestled in Billy's grasp.

"Get your DAMN hands off me," shouted Fantasia, "you Nazi thug!"

Fantasia's resistance, naturally, caused Billy to squeeze her tighter, motivating Fantasia's big brother, Moose Fulton, to hurdle several rows of chairs in a single bound. Moose ordered Billy Karkle to unhand his sister. Billy did so but mainly for the purpose of facing Moose. Then, the young policeman dexterously—but unwisely—drew his nightstick from his belt.

There ensued a tense confrontation, during which Billy Karkle held his nightstick between himself and Moose, its tip inches from Moose's nose. Moose pushed the police baton away several times, only to see it return to its prior position. Meanwhile, Billy was softly but resolutely warning Moose to "Back off, kid." Moose, for his part, kept replying, "No, *you* back off!"

Inevitably, Officer Karkle's nightstick touched Moose's nose, inciting a fateful response. With one hand, Moose grabbed the baton. He placed his other hand in Billy Karkle's face and with the Herculean strength of an all-conference linebacker, flung the policeman to the floor.

The incident might well have ended there. Indeed, most people were so shocked that they stood motionless, staring breathless as Moose stood over the fallen lawman. But Scooter McDuff reverted to his own high-school football days. In an act of swift agility that seemed improbable even to those who were there to witness it, the Chairman of the School Board dropped his gavel, mounted the table and launched himself toward Moose.

Scooter's flying tackle sent Moose and himself crashing and tumbling into a tangle of folding chairs and innocent bystanders. As they continued to scuffle, Officer Karkle, unhurt, got to his feet and tried to intervene. But Tiff Melrose, who disapproved of two-against-one, particularly when her boyfriend was the minority party, jumped onto Billy Karkle's back.

Band Director W.C. "Wally" Wilcox, whose presence that night was a mystery, suddenly pushed people aside, charging toward Billy Karkle, who was flailing blindly as Tiff's fingers dug into his eyes. Wally Wilcox, a large man, knocked over a half dozen of Amy Haddock's BFFs before they even saw him coming. This prompted retaliation. Seeing the Band Director suddenly swarmed over by angry teenage girls with razor-sharp nails, three more School Board members—Darlene, Lyle and Randy—plunged into the fray.

Meanwhile, *Weekly Argument* editor Darren Flack retreated strategically and found a safe vantage point from which to take pictures. He flashed away contentedly while a general melee unfolded. The donnybrook raged awkwardly for at least two minutes and only lost steam when someone noticed that Tiff Melrose was bleeding slightly from a cut above her eye.

Several members of the audience, who had been grabbing at one another's clothing, let go. Darren Flack, tastefully, ceased to take photos. Sheepishly, the people sprawled on the floor—including Moose, Scooter, Billy Karkle, Amy Haddock and the Band Director—got to their feet. Wincing from a painful ankle, the Chairman made his way back around the table. Mrs. Gazelick groped around the carpet, searching for her glasses.

Billy Karkle decided to arrest Moose. He proceeded to do so.

"No!" cried Amy.

"Not fair!" added Tiff, who was holding a handful of tissues against the cut on her head.

Nevertheless, Moose was arrested. Billy Karkle led him from the high-school library, to spend the night in jail. Tiff and Amy followed all the way, pestering Officer Karkle and objecting vigorously.

Mrs. Gazelick, still without her glasses, tried to point at Henry, but actually pointed at an empty space three feet to Henry's right. She called him a "bad seed" again and said, "You see? You see what you've started, you little incubus?"

"Aw, shuddup, pruneface," growled Fantasia.

Moments later, with a much smaller audience, Scooter McDuff tapped the gavel, restoring the meeting to "order." Before Henry could object or Charlie Mulcahy could rule in Henry's favor, the flustered Board had agreed—Annabella Moss in dissent—to adjourn to an executive session.

"Mr. Wilcox," Scooter said to the Band Director. "Please stay. Everyone else has to leave."

"Leave? Why?" asked Fantasia.

"My glasses! Where are my glasses?" said Darlene Gazelick.

On his way out, Henry found himself beside the Town Counsel. So he asked, "Mr. Mulcahy, what's executive session?"

"It's a secret meeting, Henry."

"Secret? They can do that?"

"Well, yes," said Charlie Mulcahy. "But only for very special reasons."

"Oh."

No one noticed Paul Lamartine. He had quietly reentered the library through another door. He stood, mostly in shadow, until everyone departed the room.

Next day, Moose was arraigned at the courthouse in Wilton, his offense reduced from assaulting a police officer to something called "malicious mischief." Afterward, Moose was released from custody and ordered to face a judge two weeks later. He missed a half day of school and was dismissed from the football team by Coach Grammus.

On the day after that, the football staff at St. Croix University found out that one of their prized recruits had been arrested for public rioting and subsequently kicked off his high-school team. The university immediately withdrew its scholarship offer to Moose Fulton.

When she heard the news, Fantasia Fulton wept and raged, but she didn't blame Henry. Neither did Moose.

But Henry blamed Henry.

ROUND II:

HENRY HITS THE BOOKS

CHAPTER 6

22 SEPTEMBER

Henry Haddock knew when he was licked.

In the days after the School Board riot, he slunk around the halls of Blackhawk Middle School avoiding social contact, especially with his best friend, Fantasia. Her mere appearance filled him with guilt and remorse.

The Blackhawk Independent Baseball Organization (BIBO) continued play, but without its unofficial "commissioner," who couldn't bring himself to show his face on a sandlot.

Henry turned off his little-used mobile phone entirely. Not even his mother could track him down.

Henry's withdrawal from society became much more troublesome on Thursday the 16th. That was when a big story—with a page-one picture of Moose battling Officer Billy Karkle—appeared in the *Weekly Argument*. Editor Darren Flack fingered Henry as the "instigator" of the brawl, because Henry had (reportedly) driven Chairman Farrell "Scooter" McDuff to "frustration and rage" over his "relentless effort" to "openly repudiate" the Board's budget cuts and teacher dismissals.

On Friday night, without their banished star quarterback and linebacker, Darnell Fulton, the Blackhawk High School Blackhawks lost for the first time that season, 20-12, to the Castle Rock Walleyes. Henry did not attend the game but learned of the result when Amy, a member of the cheerleading squad, came home crestfallen.

Amy, to her credit, did not blame Henry for the defeat.

But Henry knew better. This, too, was his fault.

Henry was relieved when Saturday arrived, ending the longest week of his life. He spent the weekend in his room, emerging only for nourishment and trips to the bathroom. On Monday, to his relief, Henry sensed that his fame around the middle school was beginning to wane. But among some peers, he still sensed a smoldering resentment over the banishment of the town's football hero.

Henry skipped the next School Board meeting, thus signaling his surrender. He conceded that he would have to adjust his ambitions and adapt to a more ignorant school career. He would accept the reality of an illiberal education, without art, without music, without freedom of speech. There were, after all, millions of Third World children who did not even have school, much less a school that enhanced their cultural sophistication.

By Wednesday, the School Board riot story in the *Weekly Argument* was a week old and fast fading in public memory. There would be no follow-up story because Henry had missed the next meeting. From now on, Henry was skipping every School Board meeting. He was beginning to think that the whole catastrophe would pretty soon blow over.

He was mistaken. On his way to the kitchen that afternoon, he encountered Moose Fulton, who happened to be hanging out at the Haddock home with Amy and her best friend, Tiff Melrose.

Henry saw Moose sprawled in Ralph Haddock's favorite

easy chair. Henry stared for a moment, then dropped his eyes. He could find no words anywhere in his brain. It was a total blank. Henry wanted to shrivel up right there, like a salted slug, and soak disgustingly into the carpet.

But Moose would not cooperate with Henry's shame. "Hey, Hank!" he said cheerily, "'Sup?" He reached a fist toward Henry, forcing Henry to respond, tapping Moose's huge paw with his own puny fist.

"Hi, um," said Henry. "Moose."

"How ya doin', Hank?"

"Um, okay, I guess."

"Yeah, me, too," said Moose. "Doin' fine. Gettin' a fresh outlook and all that. Lemme tell ya, kid. Life without football is weird!"

Henry raised his eyes, getting a full view of Moose's broad, infectious smile. Henry managed to lift one corner of his mouth.

"Jeez, Moose," Henry began, "I'm really sor—"

"I hear you missed the School Board meeting last night, Hank," said Moose. "What's up with that?"

"Um, yeah, well, I ... "

"Man, that's too bad. We needed you there, Hank, You could've asked a few questions."

"Wait," said Henry, surprised. "You were there?"

"Yeah, man," said Moose. "I've got loads of time on my hands these days. Remember? No football. And I wanted ol' Scooter—I mean, Mr. McDuff—to know he couldn't scare me off that easy."

"I've been wondering why you weren't there, Henry. You should've come to the meeting," said Amy. "You'll never believe what happened."

"What?" said Henry.

"They put French back."

Henry gaped. "They did what?"

"They voted to reinstate the whole French program, Henry.

I mean, we didn't get Italian back. Or Herr Haushalter, the German teacher. But they're going to rehire Mme. Celestine and Mlle. Brady and they're even bringing back Mme. Seronde at the middle school. The whole French program. Isn't that great?"

Henry's mind actually boggled.

"French?" asked Henry. "Why?"

"That's the thing, Hank. Nobody said. *Je ne sais quoi!*"

"We might've found out more, Henry. But you weren't there to ask questions," said Tiff.

"Yeah. Not one word of explanation. It was so *odd!* They just voted to put French back in, five to zero," said Amy. "Just like that."

"Just like that? No talking?"

"Nothing," said Amy.

Henry scratched his head, adding a tangle to his anarchic hair.

"That's weird," said Henry, sitting down on the couch opposite Moose.

"Well, I think they did it because of you, man," said Moose. "'Cause of all the trouble you made."

Henry hung his head.

"I dunno," said Henry. "Why French?"

"What's the difference? You did it, man! You made 'em flinch. You're the Che Guevara of BMS."

Henry's curiosity was taking hold of his mind, forcing him to exit his cozy cocoon of apathy. He said, "No, it's not that simple, Moose. Why not phy ed?"

He went on. "Why not manual arts at the middle school? Why not art, or music? Huh?"

Tiff shrugged. Amy shrugged, too.

"Why just French?" Henry asked again.

"No idea," said Amy.

"We didn't think to ask," said Tiff.

"Aw jeez," said Henry, now frustrated over the dearth of

data.

"Tiff's right, man," said Moose. "You should've been there, Hank. You could've asked."

"Aw, c'mon, Moose," replied Henry, finally meeting Moose's gaze. "They wouldn't've let me talk."

"Yeah, but they would've been nervous, man. They might've told us what was up, man. They might've said why French."

"Or else," said Amy, "you could've asked Mrs. Moss. She really likes you, Henry."

Henry scowled, suddenly deep in thought. He felt his fighting spirit rising up, but he still wanted to lower his profile, to slink back into obscurity and be quiet. He had already done too much damage.

After a while, Moose stood, gesturing to Tiff, who started putting on her coat. "We'll be gettin' goin'," said Moose.

Henry looked up. Moose said, "So, man. You givin' up?"

"I dunno," Henry muttered.

"Be too bad if you did, man," said Moose. "We needja, bro."

"Yes," said Tiff Melrose. "It would be awful to see all your effort go to waste, Henry."

Amy nodded in agreement. Henry felt both flattered and bewildered. He and Moose tapped fists again before Tiff and Moose departed.

Henry pondered his quandary all that evening and the next day. Through all his reflections, one phrase kept repeating itself. By the next afternoon, he couldn't stand it any longer. He had to know.

So, after school on Thursday, Henry found himself facing Evelyn Grant, the receptionist at Charlie Mulcahy's law office on Main Street.

Charlie served as Town Counsel at the convenience of the Aldermen and School Board, but he had a real job. His private law practice kept him busy twelve hours a day.

Ms. Grant, remembering Henry from his previous

appointment, smiled. She said Mr. Mulcahy was busy but he might be able to talk to Henry for a minute if he could wait. Henry waited.

Twenty minutes later, Charlie Mulcahy ushered Henry into his office. He and Henry sat down. They faced each other across the attorney's desk.

"What can I do for you, Henry?"

"Well, Mr. Mulcahy—"

"Better you should call me Charlie, Henry. Only judges call me Mr. Mulcahy. And they rule against me half the time."

"Well, okay."

"Now, what is it?"

"I guess you didn't go to the School Board meeting Tuesday night, Mr. Mulc—er, Charlie."

"No, wasn't there. Were you?"

"No, I didn't go."

"Ah."

"Okay, but I have a question about something from the meeting before," said Henry. "We were both there."

"Oh, we certainly were," said Charlie Mulcahy, grinning. "And we both survived without a scratch."

Henry squirmed at this reference to his personal riot. But he continued. "At the end of that meeting, after the ... you know ... Um, they went into an executive session, right?"

"Yes."

"And that's a secret meeting."

"Right, Henry."

"Okay, so I was wondering. I mean, how can they do that? Doesn't the Open Meeting Law say they gotta do everything out in the open?"

"That's absolutely true, Henry. But there are certain exceptions to the rule—mainly to protect someone's privacy or reputation."

"Oh." Henry looked uncertain, so Charlie continued.

"For example," said Charlie Mulcahy. "Let's say there's a

teacher who might have to take time off from the job because of a personal issue—like having a baby, getting a divorce or maybe there's a death in the family. None of this is public business. So, the School Board doesn't have to discuss it publicly. They can call an executive session."

"Oh, I see," said Henry. "Well, I guess that makes sense. When else can they have a secret meeting?"

Charlie Mulcahy smiled and leaned forward. "Okay, I get it, Henry. You're not going to let me get away with one example."

Charlie Mulcahy stretched out an arm and pulled a heavy dark-blue volume from a row of books on his desk. "Let's read that section of the law, shall we?" he said. "I could probably use a refresher anyhow."

So, in a swift ten minutes, Henry got a primer on the concept of "executive session." He learned the exact situations that permitted secrecy by a local board. Henry found out that a board had to restrict its secret discussion to just the one item in question. Henry also learned that written results of executive sessions had to be made available to the public—on request—after thirty days.

"Hm," said Henry. "But if the information is public after thirty days, what about that teacher's privacy?"

"Good question," said Charlie Mulcahy. "The Board has to release any decisions they've made, but they're allowed to withhold details that might be private, including the names of people involved, if they think it's necessary."

"I see," said Henry. He did see.

But Charlie Mulcahy wanted to make sure. He said, "For instance. Maybe Mr. McDuff orders an executive session just so he can call in Henry Haddock and yell at Henry for making trouble."

"Could he do that?"

"Sure, as long as it was just talk."

"Okay, but I hope he doesn't."

"He won't, Henry," said Charlie with a smile. "Because he

knows you'd talk back."

Henry smiled.

"Anyway, Henry, after thirty days, the minutes of your executive session would be available to the public. But they probably wouldn't mention your name or what Scooter—I mean, Mr. McDuff—said to you. It would just read something like, 'The Board met with a student on a disciplinary matter. No action was taken.'"

"Just a little yelling," said Henry.

"Yes, a little friendly yelling."

"And they didn't mention my name, so my reputation is still okay, right?"

"That's right, Henry."

"But everybody would prob'ly know about it anyhow."

Charlie Mulcahy smiled. "Well, there aren't many real secrets in a town as small as Blackhawk."

The next day after school, Henry climbed on his bike and headed straight to the Superintendent's office. Myrtle Arnold beamed as Henry entered.

"We missed you Tuesday night, Henry."

"Oh, I don't think so."

"I certainly did, Henry," said Mrs. Arnold. "Don't you contradict me."

"I'm sorry."

"Don't be silly. Nothing to apologize for," said Mrs. Arnold. "Now, I assume you're here to catch up on what you missed."

"Well, yeah," said Henry.

"I typed up the minutes just this afternoon. I can run you a copy or you can read them right here."

"Here is fine."

In a twinkling, Myrtle Arnold produced minutes of the School Board meeting of September 21st. Henry pored through Mrs. Arnold's highly condensed prose. He looked for the discussion about the French-language program. It was the first item under New Business.

All it said was, *"Chairman McDuff moved for restoration of French language in MS and HS. Supt. to contact F. Celestine, J. Brady and L. Seronde to propose rehire. Second, member Zink. Approved 5-0."*

Henry raised his head. "Um."

"Yes, Henry?"

"When they brought back French, they didn't say why?"

"No, not Tuesday night. They just up and voted, Henry."

"Just up and voted."

"That's right."

"Oh."

Henry had a thought and dismissed it. But then it popped right back into his head. So he gave in to his brain and asked a question. "They didn't talk about it at all?"

"No, Henry," said Mrs. Arnold patiently.

"But what if they did?" Henry followed. "Would that be here, in the minutes."

Mrs. Arnold smiled. "Not necessarily."

"Really?"

"Yes."

"Why?"

"My orders, Henry, are to record only the votes, not the discussion."

"Oh," said Henry.

But another thought immediately sprang up.

"Um," he said.

"Yes?"

"Who says?"

"Who says I should write down just the votes, not the discussion?"

"Yeah. Who?"

Myrtle Arnold folded her hands and turned off her face, showing no expression. "I work for the School Board, Henry, but most of my guidelines come from the Chairman."

Henry went back to studying the minutes. He felt sure there had to be something missing there. The minutes hardly said *anything*. He raised his head, and caught Myrtle Arnold's eye.

"Yes, Henry?"

"What about the money?"

"Money?"

"For French. Where did they get the money to pay for it?"

"Hm," Mrs. Arnold cocked her head curiously. "Henry, I don't know. They didn't discuss that at all."

"Really?"

"Yes," said Mrs. Arnold. "Not a word."

"Oh.

Henry skimmed the rest of the minutes. Except for the "French miracle," nothing was terribly interesting. He lay the minutes back on Mrs. Arnold's desk and thanked her very much. He was just leaving the office when yet another thought halted him.

"Mrs. Arnold?"

"Yes, Henry."

"I was wondering about the minutes from, um, executive sessions."

"Yes."

"Can anybody read them?"

"Anybody?"

"I mean," said Henry, "can I?"

"Yes, you can."

"Wow."

"Did you have a particular executive session in mind, Henry?"

"Um, no," said Henry. "Well, I'd like to see the one from the other night, you know, when there was ... "

"The big fight?"

"Yeah," said Henry embarrassed. He hurried on. "But I know it hasn't been thirty days for that one. Mr. Mulcahy said."

"That's right," said Mrs. Arnold with an air of approval. She was partial toward well-informed children.

"So, I guess I want to see other executive sessions. Are there any?"

"Oh, yes, Henry. Quite a few."

"Oh, good."

"Perhaps," suggested Mrs. Arnold. "The last six months or so?"

"Oh. Yeah. That'd be great."

"Very well then, Henry. But I don't want you sitting here in my office in that uncomfortable chair for the next hour. I'll make some copies. You just sit tight."

Mrs. Arnold extracted a folder from a file cabinet and disappeared into another room, leaving Henry alone until Superintendent of Schools Robert Ptaschnik popped out of his office. He looked at Mrs. Arnold's empty chair.

"Oh," he said. Then he noticed Henry. "Henry!"

"H'lo, Mr. Ptaschnik." Henry felt small, although Bob Ptaschnik was not that much taller than he was. The superintendent was a mostly bald, roly-poly man with a prominent lower lip and fuzzy hair. He maintained a constant air of equanimity. Now, he remained typically calm, and seemed actually pleased to see Henry.

"We missed you the other night," he said, stepping all the way into the outer office with Henry.

Henry slipped from the chair and stood, respectfully. "Really?"

"Oh, of course," said the superintendent. "You have to remember that all that fuss and bother wasn't your fault. No, sir. You just came to ask a question. And you were entitled, young man."

"Really?"

"Really!" The superintendent cocked his head. "Did you want to see me?"

"Oh no. I just came in for, you know, the minutes."

"Oh, good. Catching up. And Mrs. Arnold is helping

you out?"

"Oh, yes sir. She's great."

"That she is, Henry. You have excellent taste in women."

Henry blushed, Bob Ptaschnik smiled, looking like an elf.

"Will I see you next Tuesday night, Henry?"

Henry thought for a moment. Finally, he said, "I think so."

"Good. The more the merrier!" said the superintendent, and he was gone.

A while later, Henry was walking home with a slim file of minutes from School Board executive sessions. He had a lot on his mind.

CHAPTER 7

28 SEPTEMBER

As usual, the first School Board member to take her seat at the big table in the high-school library the following Tuesday was Annabella Moss, whose hat was a close-fitting dove-gray felt number with a red silk rose above the ear. Mrs. Moss kept her hat on, but removed her matching dove-gray gloves and laid them on the table beside her microphone.

Henry Haddock approached Mrs. Moss. He was in a hurry to talk with her before the other members arrived. Before asking his first question, he told Mrs. Moss that he liked her hat.

"Henry," said Annabella Moss, "are you buttering me up?"

Henry's face registered genuine shock. "Huh?"

Mrs. Moss smiled over her little joke. "Never mind, Henry. How are you tonight?"

"Oh, I'm fine."

"Well, it's good to see you back."

"Oh, thank you," said Henry. "Um, I was wondering something."

"Aren't you always?"

Henry paused. "Um, I guess so."

Mrs. Moss prodded Henry. "All right then. What were you wondering, Henry?"

"Oh," said Henry. "Well, I was reading minutes of meetings, you know, and some of the executive sessions."

"Yes?"

"And, well, I was just wondering. Who's P. Lamartine?"

Mrs. Moss' eyebrows rose an entire inch. "Ah," she said.

Henry tried for a moment but could not fathom the meaning of this lonely syllable.

"Um," said Henry.

Mrs. Moss cut him off. She said, "Henry, I think you're starting to catch on."

"Catch on to what?"

"Oh, I think you'll figure that out, Henry," said Mrs. Moss. She paused for one beat and said, "The person you're wondering about is Paul Lamartine."

"Oh." Henry crinkled his brow. "Who's that?"

Mrs. Moss sighed. Her eyes flickered very slightly, as though she was looking around for eavesdroppers. Then she said, "Paul is a general contractor and property developer, Henry."

Henry was still a little confused. "Um, what's that?"

Mrs. Moss shrugged and smiled, then replied just above a whisper: "Henry, Paul Lamartine is the richest man in town."

"Oh," said Henry.

Henry saw other Board members arriving and he began to back away from Mrs. Moss. But she halted his retreat by saying, "I think his daughter is in your class, Henry."

Henry quickly ran his classmates, most of whom he had known since kindergarten, through his memory banks. He came up empty. "I know every kid in my class, and there isn't any girl named Lamartine," he said. "Unless she's new."

"Oh no, she's not new. She grew up right here in Blackhawk. She was one of my students and a pleasure to teach. She has a beautiful name. Gabrielle."

"Gabrielle?" said Henry, surprised. "You mean Gabrielle O'Connor?"

Mrs. Moss nodded. "There you go."

"Oh," said Henry. Chairman Farrell McDuff was bearing down. His face was dark with disapproval. Henry fled to his seat.

There, Henry considered Gabrielle O'Connor, daughter of Paul Lamartine. Henry wasn't terribly surprised that their names didn't match. It simply meant Gabrielle's parents were probably divorced—like Henry's aunt Molly and uncle Jeff. Henry knew other kids whose parents had split up. Often, their last names got changed to match their mother rather than their father.

Gabrielle was an Honor Roll student, like Henry, but she spoke up very rarely in class. She was polite and serious, always well-dressed and exceedingly clean.

There was one other important thing about Gabrielle O'Connor. She was so pretty that Henry had always been afraid to talk to her.

As he sat beside Fantasia and thought about Gabrielle, Henry checked out the audience. He spotted all "the usual suspects," including Amy, Moose and Tiff, Buzz Skelton from the teachers union and Darren Flack from the *Weekly Argument*, plus a few curious people he didn't know by name. There were also two—rather than the usual zero—police officers standing in the back of the room, flanking the doorway. To his surprise, Henry noticed, seated beside Amy and looking highly skeptical of the whole situation, his sister Penelope. He waved at her. She crossed her arms and looked elsewhere.

Just before turning his back on the crowd, Henry took one last look around, hoping to spot the mysterious Paul Lamartine. He didn't know what Paul Lamartine looked like, but he thought he might be able to guess who he was.

Nobody in the library looked the least bit like the richest man in town.

"Oh, well," he said, sitting down.

"What?" asked Fantasia.

"Nothing," said Henry.

The meeting then dragged along. Henry passed the time with his sketchbook. He was getting especially adept (he thought) at capturing the permanent sourpuss expression on Lyle Lehnherr's solemn, bespectacled face. The more he drew Lyle Lehnherr, the more Henry imagined that he looked like Silas Marner.

Henry had gotten a copy of the agenda from Myrtle Arnold, allowing him to track the meeting's progress. He laid aside his sketchbook when he knew that Chairman Scooter McDuff was near the moment of adjournment. Henry had to be alert because, week by week, Scooter McDuff had gotten into a progressively bigger hurry to end the meeting and hightail it out of the library.

However, on this night, McDuff didn't have a chance to bang the gavel and run. Barely had the Board voted unanimously to approve the next week's school lunch menus (the lowlight of which, next Wednesday, was what the kitchen ladies called "pizza" and what the kids called "barf on a shingle") when Henry was on his feet, hand raised.

Chairman McDuff's dark expression grew darker, not in the least because Henry's quick move drew a smattering of applause.

"Oh, for God's sake," said Scooter McDuff.

"I have a point of information," said Henry.

"Well, fine, young man. You can have whatever you want. I'm adjourning this meeting," said Chairman McDuff. He stood up, apparently to indicate his readiness to depart but really to intimidate Henry. "Do I have a motion?"

As Randy Zink, timidly, raised a hand to move for adjournment, Superintendent Bob Ptaschnik cleared his throat.

"Excuse me, Scooter," he said.

McDuff settled a baleful gaze on Superintendent Ptaschnik.

"Perhaps," said the superintendent, "we should consult the Town Counsel?"

"The Town Counsel?" growled Chairman McDuff.

"Here!" said Charlie Mulcahy, raising his hand. He was clearly visible, sitting beside Myrtle Arnold.

Chairman McDuff sized up Charlie Mulcahy, who smiled back amiably. "I was wondering why you were here, Charlie," he said.

"Well, it seemed like I might be needed," said the Town Counsel.

"Because of *him?*" asked Scooter. He indicated Henry Haddock without looking at Henry.

Charlie Mulcahy nodded, still smiling.

Scooter McDuff scowled at Charlie and—gesturing toward Henry—said, "Do I have to let the kid talk?"

Charlie Mulcahy wiped the smile off his face and stood, addressing Scooter McDuff formally. "Mr. Chairman," he said, "by law, if a member of the community —and Henry here qualifies, I've checked his address. If a member of the community has a legitimate question on a point of information, the Board is required to listen, and to respond as completely as possible. And—"

"There's more?" said Chairman McDuff impatiently.

"Yes, Scooter," said the Town Counsel. "If this inquisitive citizen asks you a question you can't answer right away, the Board must provide the answer at its next available opportunity."

"Is that it?" asked McDuff.

"That's the law," said Mulcahy.

"Fine," said the Chairman. He swung toward Henry Haddock. "All right, young fella. What's your question?"

Henry flinched at the suddenness of Scooter McDuff's

demand. His mind went momentarily blank.

"What's the matter, kid?" the Chairman said. "Cat got your tongue?"

"Give him a chance!" said Fantasia, standing up beside Henry. This prompted several voices in the audience to agree with Fantasia. Scooter McDuff waved his gavel threateningly.

In the meantime, Henry recovered his cool.

Henry's original purpose in coming to the School Board was to ask why the members had so ruthlessly fired Ms. Webster and all those other teachers. But for weeks, Scooter McDuff had banned Henry from opening his mouth. This taboo ended up snowballing one little question into an avalanche. If on that very first night Scooter had been a little cleverer, he would have fielded Henry's question and answered with a lot of hogwash that Henry didn't understand. Henry would have probably gone away frustrated and ignorant. He wouldn't have returned.

Instead, Chairman McDuff had stubbornly prolonged the battle. Weeks of delay gave Henry time to hit the books and study the Board's past proceedings. Bit by bit, Henry Haddock became a pint-size maven of local politics.

So, when Henry finally got his chance to ask a question, he posed one he wouldn't have been informed enough to ask six weeks before. He said, "Mr. Chairman, when you call for an executive session, who's allowed to be there with you, besides Mr. Ptaschnik and Mrs. Arnold?"

"Huh?" said Scooter McDuff.

Charlie Mulcahy chuckled out loud.

"Well," said Henry, pleased with the opportunity to speak after all those weeks of being told to shut up, "I know you have to kick out the audience. But who can stay? Who gets to be in on your secret meetings?"

"Secret?" huffed Scooter McDuff. "Young man, that's a loaded word."

"But they are secret, aren't they?"

"They're *executive* sessions," McDuff insisted.

"*Secret* executive session," Henry retorted. "'Executive' means 'secret.' Right?"

"Oh, for God's sake!" The Chairman's chest was swelling dangerously and his eyes seemed to be bulging from his face.

"The boy's right, Scooter," said Charlie Mulcahy, helpfully.

"What?" roared McDuff.

"There's nothing wrong with secrecy, Mr. Chairman," said the Town Counsel, in a voice as soothing as he could manage. "An executive session is supposed to be secret. It's perfectly legal, Scooter."

The Chairman paused, twisting the gavel in his hands. "Well, I don't like the kid's implication," he replied. His chest was receding, his eyes began to unbulge.

"I'm sure that Henry meant to imply nothing," said Charlie Mulcahy.

"I didn't," said Henry. "Honest."

The Chairman turned toward Henry and glowered. He took a deep breath. Then a bewildered look crossed his face.

"Dammit," said McDuff. "I forgot the kid's question."

Myrtle Arnold came to everyone's rescue, hastily reading from her notes, "Henry wanted to know," she said, glancing at Henry, "who is allowed to be present during an executive session, besides Board members, the superintendent and the secretary."

"Oh, right," said McDuff. He paused to think.

"Well!" McDuff went on, rather loudly. "Well, anybody I say. I'm the Chairman, dammit!"

"Really?" said Henry.

"Yes! Now, you've had your question—"

"Excuse me," said Charlie Mulcahy.

Scooter turned again toward the Town Counsel. He was starting to swell up again. "Dammit, Charlie! What now?"

"Scooter," said Charlie Mulcahy gently, "what you just said—about your authority. That isn't strictly true."

"Isn't true? What's not true?!" bellowed McDuff. "Are calling me a liar?"

At this accusation, Charlie Mulcahy recoiled. With a hint of anger, he shot back, "Of course not, Mr. Chairman. I wouldn't suggest such a thing. I'm simply trying to advise you on the details of the law. That's my job, Mr. Chairman."

"Oh, well, of course," said the chastened Chairman, who was unaccustomed to displays of emotion from the normally cool Town Counsel. "I didn't mean—"

Charlie Mulcahy, calm again, replied, "I understand Mr. Chairman."

"Okay then," said McDuff. "You were saying?"

"I was saying, Scooter, that you don't have the authority, even as Chairman, to invite just anyone into an executive session."

"I don't?"

"No."

"Well, then, who the hell does?"

"Actually, no one, Scooter."

"What! What are you saying?"

Charlie Mulcahy took a deep breath. "Scooter," he said, "according to the law, the only parties allowed in an executive session of any local board are members of the board, their administrators—like Superintendent Ptaschnik, their secretary—that would be Mrs. Arnold, and people who have specific business before the Board for which the executive session is convened."

"Say what?" asked McDuff.

A hum of voices arose in the library as members of the audience attempted to interpret, for one another, Charlie's ruling. The Town Counsel heard people muttering. He tried to simplify.

"The only outsiders allowed at a secret meeting," said Charlie, "are people who are in on the secret."

"Oo-o-oh," said the audience, in unison.

Myrtle Arnold patted Charlie on the arm. "Lovely, Charlie," she said.

Henry seized his opportunity. "So, Mr. Chairman," he said, taking a step closer to Scooter McDuff, "that means—"

"That doesn't mean a damn thing!" roared Scooter McDuff. "You've had your question, son. This meeting is over."

And with that, the Chairman pounded his gavel and walked out of the high-school library.

"Wow," said Henry.

"For a fat slob," said Fantasia, "he really moves fast!"

Moose was suddenly beside Henry, talking into his ear. "You want me to get him back, Henry? I'll go get him. I'll drag that lard-ass right back in here."

Henry thought of Moose's history. He cast a quick glance toward the two policemen. One of them was the infamous Billy Karkle. "Nah, that's okay, Moose. Thanks."

"Big fat bully," said Amy.

"He's not so bad," said Henry placidly. "He told me what I wanted to know."

"He did?" said Fantasia.

"Really?" said Moose.

"Oh yeah."

"Excuse me, son." Here was a new voice.

Henry looked up into the face of Darren Flack, editor of the Blackhawk *Weekly Argument*. It was a fairly young face for a grown-up, but it was tired-looking under a thinning patch of mousy hair. Flack's scrawny mustache only served to strengthen the mouse impression. But Henry also saw a keen intelligence in Darren Flack's eyes, like several of Henry's favorite teachers—who also looked pretty tired most of the time.

"Oh, hi," said Henry. "Mr. Flack."

"Just Darren," said the newsman. "Hey, is that Randy Zink?" He pointed at the exposed page of Henry's sketchbook.

"Uh, yeah."

"That's great," said Flack. "You're a real artist, Henry."

Henry noted that Moose, Amy, Tiff and even Penelope were looking very suspiciously at Darren Flack, the man who had made Henry infamous.

"You're not buttering me up, are you, Mr. Flack?" said Henry.

"Call me Darren," said Flack. "You don't happen to have a sketch of old Scoots in there, do ya?"

"Mr. McDuff? Sure," said Henry. He flipped a few pages, to his best rendering of Chairman Farrell McDuff.

"Aw, that's terrific," said Flack. "I'd like to use that in the paper. Would you mind?"

"I guess he's not butterin' you up," murmured Fantasia.

"Mind?" Henry looked around. Amy and Tiff were nodding. A second ago, they were suspicious of the *Argument* editor. Now they were on his side.

"Girls!" thought Henry. But then he said to Flack, "No, I guess not."

"Great," said Flack. He nudged Fantasia over, and sat down where she'd been sitting. Fantasia glared at Flack dangerously, but the editor paid no heed. "Listen, Henry. I think it's time you and I talked."

"About what?"

"Well, how about those executive sessions you just threw in Scooter's face?"

"Oh," said Henry. "Well ... "

A moment later, Henry and Darren Flack were alone in the high-school library, huddled in deep conversation. Just outside the library, Henry's posse waited for him to finish with Flack. After about twenty minutes, Charlie Mulcahy—who had been elsewhere in the building—passed through the library. He noted the dialog between editor and boy. He nodded genially toward Amy, Tiff, Fantasia, Penelope and Moose as he left the high school.

Ten minutes later, Myrtle Arnold fluttered into the library, ordered the room cleared and—to emphasize her point—flicked off the lights as she exited. Darren Flack shook Henry's hand, said thank you and followed Henry out of the library.

The lead paragraph of the *Weekly Argument*, landing Thursday morning on doorsteps all over Blackhawk, began:

Diligent research by a student at the Blackhawk Middle School has revealed possible illegal secret meetings conducted by the School Board and involving a powerful local developer. Records clearly show that these meetings were attended by Paul Lamartine, a frequent benefactor to school activities but not a member of the School Board.

Contacted on Wednesday, School Board Chairman Farrell McDuff declined to explain the purposes of these secret sessions, nor would he comment on the role of Lamartine ...

Reading the news over his breakfast that morning and studying with fatherly pride Henry's page-one drawing of Scooter McDuff, Ralph Haddock looked over at his son. He said, "Holy smokes, Henry."

Henry, his mouth full of oatmeal, said nothing.

"It's official, Henry," said Amy. "You're famous."

"Oh, I don't think so," said Penelope, who was kneeling on a stool so she could read the front page over her father's shoulder. "They don't even have Henry's name in there 'til the —let's see—one, two, three. The fourth paragraph. That's not so famous!"

Henry shrugged. Helen Haddock smiled. She said, "Penelope, maybe you should read us the headline."

Penelope Haddock scowled at her mother and climbed off the stool. "I don't wanna," she said.

The headline was:

HENRY HADDOCK CHALLENGES SCHOOL BD. SECRET SESSIONS

CHAPTER 8

5 NOVEMBER

As he sat in third-period American History, Henry Haddock's mind wandered from the French and Indian War. He kept thinking about his letter to the state Attorney General. Henry had written it a month ago but still had no answer. In his letter, he had asked if the Blackhawk School Board had violated the law when it allowed an "outsider," Paul Lamartine, to sit in on its executive sessions.

Henry understood that the Attorney General had bigger crimes to prosecute than a few possible public-meeting irregularities in the little town of Blackhawk. But still, how hard would it be to send Henry a postcard?

As day after day passed with no answer from the Attorney General, Henry had stayed busy investigating the strange case of Paul Lamartine. How come he got invited to the School Board's executive session on September 28th? What was he doing there?

Henry solved the mystery unexpectedly while talking to another sixth-grader, Briana Ringgold. Their topic was the beautiful but unapproachable Gabrielle O'Conner. Briana mentioned that Gabrielle O'Connor went to France every summer to visit her great-aunt Genevieve, the sister of Paul Lamartine's mother.

"Gabrielle just loves French," said Briana. "She was really looking forward to sixth grade because she was gonna be the best student in Mme. Seronde's French class. But then, poof! No more French in the middle school. And no Mme. Seronde!"

But then, poof! On September 29th, French was back, along with Mme. Seronde.

Henry, of course, had no actual evidence that Paul Lamartine had secretly met with the School Board and influenced—maybe even bribed!—them to restore his only daughter's favorite subject. Henry could only surmise.

Henry thought about writing a postscript to the Attorney General, further explaining the Case of the Reappearing French Program. But this was a letter he dared not write, for fear of getting Mme. Seronde—and all the French teachers—in trouble. They might get fired all over again. Henry decided that having French back in the curriculum was a good thing and shouldn't be jeopardized—even if it took a shady deal to turn the trick.

Henry couldn't help wondering if Gabrielle O'Connor had been wise to the subterfuge. He thought so for a while, but changed his mind. Henry wasn't giving Gabrielle the benefit of the doubt just because Gabrielle was so terrifyingly pretty. She was also very nice and—although Henry was personally afraid to talk to her—she wasn't stuck-up at all. Henry concluded rationally—that Gabrielle was not the sort of girl who would ask her rich father to throw his weight around.

Henry would have continued to think pleasantly about Gabrielle O'Connor all the way through third period, except for the sound of cornets, glockenspiels and bass drums seeping into his brain. This happened often during third period. Besides being Henry's history class, this was the hour for the Blackhawk High School Thundering Three Hundred to practice on the middle-school football field, just below Mr. Kussow's classroom. Mr. Kussow closed all the windows during third period. Even then, when the Three Hundred started to thunder, a few panes of single-ply glass proved a poor defense against all that brass and percussion.

Like every kid in class, Henry had gotten used to the sound of band practice. Besides third period, there was also fifth period, when the "junior band" stumbled around on the same field, banging into one another and hitting a lot of bad notes. All this took place under the tutelage of legendary Band Director W.C. "Wally" Wilcox. Wally was over seventy years old but, according to the *Weekly Argument*, he was "still going strong."

Throughout Henry's life and even his parents' lives, Wally and the band had been a community constant, always marching to and fro, always the "pride and joy" of little Blackhawk. Everyone agreed that Wally Wilcox—who had started the Thundering Three Hundred 42 years before with a tone-deaf handful of teenage pimple-pusses—had put Blackhawk on the map. The Thundering Three Hundred had won hundreds of band competitions and had appeared in dozens of football stadia. The band had been invited to major parades all across the country, including St. Patrick's Day in Chicago, Macy's on Thanksgiving in New York and the Tournament of Roses on New Year's Day.

Still in a thinking mood, Henry found himself pondering the band—which was strange. Nobody really thought about the band. It was always just *there*. But Henry started wondering, for the first time, why the band practiced during regular schooltime, even though it also practiced—for hours—after school, and sometimes even in the morning before the sun came up. Wasn't the band an "extracurricular activity," like basketball or Future Nurses of America, which kids normally did after school?

As long as he was wondering, Henry also wondered why the high-school band rarely showed up at its own high school's events—like football games? Band Director Wilcox often explained (proudly) that the Thundering Three Hundred was in tremendous demand throughout the region and the nation, even internationally. It received so many invitations to perform on America's grandest stages that it didn't have much spare time for hometown appearances in dinky old Blackhawk.

On the other hand, Henry continued wondering, why couldn't Mr. Wilcox peel off twenty or so of his Three Hundred members (or even some of the slightly off-key junior band kids) to stay home and play easy stuff like "We Will, We Will Rock You" for football and basketball games?

Henry had another question: With so many kids in the band, why didn't Blackhawk High School also have an orchestra? Henry's father once asked why—with three hundred "musicians" in school—the only accompaniment for the annual high-school musical was Mrs. Braithwaite, the chorus director, playing the piano all by her lonesome. "Why"—Ralph Haddock wondered—"couldn't the best high-school band in the whole world learn to play the score of *West Side Story*?"

While all these questions coursed through Henry's overworked cranium, the band outside the window was launching into a 300-instrument arrangement of "Dancing Queen." This is the moment when Henry hit upon the $64,000 question.

How come the band hadn't shrunk? Why hadn't the School Board trimmed it down to the Thundering Two Hundred-Seventy Or So?

Ever since the budget crunch hit, everything else in every school had gotten smaller. Even the sacred football team was smaller.

Everything but the band.

They even had new uniforms. According to the *Weekly Argument*, Homecoming—coming up that day—would be the first chance for the people of Blackhawk to see the Thundering Three Hundred in their brand-new threads.

Henry wondered how much three hundred band uniforms cost.

$64,000?

When the bell rang, Henry hurried to the window to catch a glimpse of the Thundering Three Hundred as they blasted the last few ear-splitting bars of "The Girl from Ipanema." Looking down from the second floor, Henry was amazed—he always was—at how big a three hundred-member band really was. He looked for his sister Penelope but couldn't find her in the milling mob of clarinetists, trombonists, trumpeters, flute players, French-horners, sousaphonists, drummers and other music makers as they scattered toward their next class.

"Wow," said Henry to himself, "that's a lot of kids."

"Certainly is," said Mr. Kussow, leaning over Henry's shoulder.

As the last straggling piccolo player scurried back into school, Henry realized there was more to the band than meets the eye. He was beginning to sense that there was something about the band, and the School Board, and Paul Lamartine, that all came together.

Henry attended the parade after school and went faithfully to the Homecoming game that night. It was a chilly evening with stars in the sky. As usual, he sat with Fantasia and her family. This included Moose—who, after the notorious Billy Karkle incident—could only watch helplessly.

Henry was impressed with Moose's good spirits. Moose wasn't allowed to set foot on the field, but he kept attending games, cheering for his teammates and showing no hard feelings toward Coach Grammus.

Naturally, his teammates still loved Moose.

"We're gonna beat these guys," said Moose. He had said the same thing before each of the Fighting Blackhawks' previous six games. Without Moose, however, the Blackhawks had lost them all.

As the game began, Henry noticed that even the Blackhawk cheerleaders, including his sister Amy and Tiff, seemed to be stricken with a pale cast of fatalism. Henry sighed guiltily as the Blackhawks kicked off and some fast kid from the visiting team, the Necedah Night Owls, returned the kick for a touchdown.

The Blackhawks, however, bounced back for the Homecoming crowd. They trailed Necedah by only 20-7 at halftime. Then, for the first time that year, the Thundering Three Hundred performed for their hometown crowd. The show featured all the songs Henry had heard during third period for weeks, so he knew the routine by heart, including the finale, a Village People medley that ended with the rhythm section dropping their drums and spelling out the chorus of "Y.M.C.A."

Henry had to admit it. "That was fun," he said to Fantasia.

As though inspired by the Thundering Three Hundred, the home team fought their way back after halftime. Led by Anton Wojczyk, the little sophomore who had replaced Moose at quarterback, the Blackhawks rallied for a 27-26 victory. Moose was so excited that he charged the field afterward, lifting Anton Wojczyk to his shoulders and carrying him into the locker room.

Watching the scene on the field, Henry felt a little better. The football team swarmed around Moose, slapping his back and helping him carry the little hero. Even Coach Grammus smiled.

Henry had also been inspired—with curiosity—by the Thundering Three Hundred. He spent Saturday at the

Blackhawk Public Library, one of his favorite haunts, along with Fantasia and librarian Peg Bradner, one of his favorite people. Henry pored through years and years of school budgets, which were all carefully stored, under a coat of dust, in the library's least popular corner, the "public- records room."

"Damn! I know why nobody comes in here," said Fantasia. "It smells!"

On Monday, Henry headed for the superintendent's office, where he enlarged his collection of the minutes of School Board executive sessions. While he was using the photocopy machine, he asked Myrtle Arnold an important question. He said, "Mrs. Arnold, I was just wondering. I noticed that the minutes don't really tell much about what happened during the meeting."

"You got that right, Henry."

Myrtle Arnold had been recording School Board meetings for seventeen years. In past times, the Board's minutes were sometimes ten pages long. Recently, they barely covered a single sheet of paper.

Myrtle Arnold looked over her glasses and replied, "It's just as I told you before, Henry. *Short* is how the Chairman likes his minutes."

"But what about exec—"

"And that goes double," said Myrtle Arnold, "for executive sessions."

This caused Henry to think of another question: "So, Mr. McDuff doesn't want you to write down everything that everybody says?"

Mrs. Arnold smiled at this. "No flies on you, Henry Haddock."

Henry smiled back.

"But you listen to everything—during the meetings. Right?"

"I do more than that," said Mrs. Arnold. "I take shorthand."

“So, even though—”

“Nothing gets past me, Henry,” said Myrtle Arnold. “Nothing.”

Henry nodded, satisfied. He started to leave, but then ...

“Wait,” he said.

“Yes?” said Myrtle Arnold.

“Um, shorthand—that’s kind of like code, right?” asked Henry.

“Yes, Henry,” said Myrtle Arnold. There was a glint of pride in her eye. “Not many people know how to do shorthand anymore. But I keep up.”

“So,” said Henry, his mind churning away, “since the stuff you write in shorthand is during meetings, that means it’s a public record. Right?”

“It certainly is,” said Myrtle Arnold. “Every jot and tittle, Henry.”

“So I could ask you questions about what you wrote down in shorthand, and you could tell me exactly what everybody said, right?”

“No flies on you, Henry.”

“So, if it’s okay, could I ask a few questions now?”

“Why not?” said Mrs. Arnold.

For another forty-five minutes, Henry sat with Myrtle Arnold. While she shuffled and flipped through old steno books, Henry riffled through his library notes, asking questions and thanking Mrs. Arnold repeatedly.

Henry had skipped four straight School Board meetings. On the Tuesday after Homecoming, he was back. Henry took his customary seat in the front row. By now, his posse had dispersed. No Moose, no Amy, no Tiff, no newspaper editor—just Fantasia. Buzz Skelton was there, of course, but he had to be.

Henry wasn’t planning to ask any questions. He was just there, like Mr. Skelton, to observe. Of course, he also worked in his sketchbook, concentrating on Mrs. Moss, whose hat was a vintage skimmer with a yellow silk chrysanthemum tucked in the band.

Henry's pen stopped suddenly when Scooter McDuff, in the New Business portion of the meeting, proposed that the Board officially commend Band Director Wally Wilcox for the Thundering Three Hundred's "tremendous show" at Homecoming. He also announced that the band had been invited to play at halftime of the Texas vs. Texas A&M football game on Thanksgiving, "a rare honor for a non-Texas high-school band."

The vote to commend the band was unanimous. Henry took a few notes on the back of a sketch of Darlene Gazelick, in which Henry had slightly exaggerated Mrs. Gazelick's nose.

On Wednesday after school, Henry was back at the library, scrounging dustily in the public-records room. That evening, he placed a phone call to John DeSimone, the current president of the Band Parents Association. The BPA was the most powerful civic group in Blackhawk. John DeSimone's son, Robbie, was drum major for the Thundering Three Hundred and one of the worst pills at Blackhawk High School. Henry was acquainted also with Brytannee DeSimone, a fellow sixth grader and first-chair flutist in the junior band.

"Mr. DeSimone," Henry said, "this is Henry Haddock."

"Who?"

"Henry Haddock, sir. I go to the middle school. Brytannee is in my class."

"Oh, yeah," said Mr. DeSimone. "Your mother's a teacher."

He made it sound like an accusation.

"Yes, sir. Second grade."

"Uh huh," said Mr. DeSimone. "I hated second grade."

Henry wanted to say that Mr. DeSimone would have loved second grade if the brilliant Helen Haddock had been his teacher. But he stifled the urge.

A silence fell over the conversation. After about twenty seconds, Henry gave forth with an "Um."

"Yeah?" said John DeSimone with a note of impatience.

Henry, who had strategized this interview, said, "Mr. DeSimone, I heard last night that the band is gonna play on Thanksgiving in Texas."

"Yeah, they are. Texas vs. Texas A&M. You may not know it, son, but that game is huge in Texas."

Henry had researched the game. He said, "Oh yeah. I know. Yippee ki-ay."

"Say what?"

"Oh, nothin'. Just, um ... "

Silence returned for a while. Henry wasn't accustomed to talking on the phone with grown-ups.

"So," Henry pressed on at last, "I was just wondering."

"Yeah?"

"Those Texas people. Do they pay—like transportation and stuff—for the band to come there and play?"

Henry listened to a moment of deep quiet. "Some of it," said Mr. DeSimone finally. "Why do you ask?"

Henry was ready for this. "Oh, jeez, didn't I say? I'm doing a report, for school, on the history of the band."

"Oh, well, good for you. Good," said Mr. DeSimone. His voice turned suddenly friendlier. "That's a great story. An *American* story! You know, son, people don't appreciate this band the way they should. They just take us for granted. We put this town on the map, you know."

"Oh, I know. They were great at Homecoming!" Henry enthused.

"Absolutely! said John DeSimone. "Heckuva show!"

Henry didn't want to get too far off the subject. "So—just to make sure—you're saying the Texas people don't pay everything. That means you're gonna have to pay some of what it's gonna cost to go to Texas, right?"

"Oh yeah. It's always a struggle, son."

"I bet it is."

"Oh, boy. You have no idea!" Mr. DeSimone was warming to the topic. "We're out there fundraising 365 days a year. The expenses for a band this size? Well, you wouldn't believe it."

Henry, in fact, would have believed it. He had been reading school budgets.

"I guess so, Mr. DeSimone," said Henry. "Um, but, for instance, on this trip to Texas—"

"Say, there's an idea! You wouldn't like to take the trip with us, wouldja, son? If you're writing a report, well, you oughta see what it's really like, in person."

"Well, jeez," said Henry. "Could you afford to take me along?"

"There's always room for one more, Harry."

"Henry."

"Sorry, son. Henry."

"Well, maybe I'll come," said Henry.

"Great. Well, just tell Mrs. Plink, our travel coordinator. Tell her you're going along. She arranges all those things."

"Oh, okay," said Henry. "But I'm not sure—"

"So, son. We all done?"

"Oh. Um, just one thing, sir."

"Yeah?"

"Well, I was wondering, sir. How much does it actually cost for the band to go to Texas for three days?"

"You'd be surprised, Henry."

"Yeah, I prob'ly would," said Henry. "That's why I'm tryin' to find out. For my report."

"Well, I'd like to tell you. But this whole dollars-and-cents business, well ... it's actually pretty confidential, son," said John DeSimone. "Wally—Mr. Wilcox—well, that's how he likes it."

Henry knew this. In all of his research, the hardest numbers for him to find were the actual costs of keeping the Thundering Three Hundred in full thunder. The Philosopher's Stone was easier to dig up.

"Oh, I understand," said Henry. "I know it's not polite to ask. But, well, I really want to get an A on this report. I have to keep my grades up, or I'll never get into Ohio State."

"Ohio State?" said John DeSimone. "Now there's a great band."

"Oh, I know," said Henry. He had done the research on Mr. DeSimone's college alma mater. "Best Damn Band in the Land. Right, sir?"

"Henry, you're quite a band fan," said John DeSimone.

Henry, who was too stricken with guilt—over his own deceitfulness—to respond, said nothing.

After a moment of silence, John DeSimone said, "Henry, I tell you what. "Since it's only for your report. And if it'll get you an A."

"Oh, it will."

John DeSimone, lowering his voice, revealed—just between Henry and him—the price of flying the Thundering Three Hundred to Texas and back.

"Wow," said Henry. "That much?"

"Oh yeah," replied Mr. DeSimone.

"But you can do it, huh?"

"Oh, you bet we will, son. Our people always come through."

"They do, huh?"

"They sure do."

Henry instantly thought of another question, but he didn't ask it: Which people?

Henry thanked John DeSimone profusely for his help. He promised to give him a copy of the report, as soon as he finished it. Of course, this was a lie. There was no report and never would be. Henry felt a fresh wave of guilt.

He also wasn't going to Texas.

After saying goodbye, Henry spent ten minutes writing notes on his interview with Mr. DeSimone. On his computer, he transcribed them into his "Band" file. He wasn't sure what to do with all this information. He certainly wasn't going to write the history of the band. And he didn't believe the Band Parents were dishonest. At least, they didn't *mean* to be dishonest. But he was starting to worry about the Thundering Three Hundred and its effect on everybody in Blackhawk.

CHAPTER 9

13 NOVEMBER

It was pizza night at the Haddock house, with a few absentees. Moose Fulton, a regular participant, had been invited to the football team's end-of-season party. The Blackhawk High Blackhawks had finished the season with a flourish, following their Homecoming win by beating their archrivals, the Wolf Creek Werewolves, 12-7.

Also missing from pizza night were Amy and Tiff, who were tagging along with Moose.

Almost missing was Henry, who sat at the end of the Haddock dining table gnawing a leathery pizza crust and reflecting on his past week of political research. He was facing a serious decision. He had no idea what he was going to do. He looked down into his lap, where Sarge the dog was resting his head, his big brown eyes looking up hopefully. Henry gave Sarge the pizza crust.

Henry's dilemma came from knowing too much. He had spent days in the Blackhawk Public Library. He had reviewed every school budget for the last twelve years. Beyond that, he knew a lot more from pumping Myrtle Arnold about what she had recorded in her scribbly notebooks.

Henry had discovered that, year after year, one big budget item kept popping up. Henry knew that cutting this item could solve a lot of the school system's budget troubles. But he also knew that this item was a "sacred cow." Anyone who threatened it was asking for open warfare.

If the war broke out, Henry's opposing general would be Scooter McDuff.

Henry didn't think he could defeat the Chairman in battle. So, one day that week, Henry went over Charlie Mulcahy's office, hoping for a little advice. Henry explained his research findings to Charlie. He asked one question.

"I can't answer you, Henry," said Charlie Mulcahy. "As Town Counsel, I represent the School Board."

Next, Henry thought about seeking advice from Superintendent Robert Ptaschnik. But Henry gave up without asking because the superintendent, just like Charlie Mulcahy, worked for the School Board.

There was always Fantasia, Henry's best friend. She would definitely have an opinion. But the trouble with Fantasia was that she *was* Henry's best friend. He didn't need to ask her advice. He knew exactly what she would say before she ever said it.

Henry was stuck.

On Saturday night, he remained stuck. Henry looked around the table, at Fantasia and his sister Penelope, at his parents and Fantasia's mom and dad. He also glanced at Sarge, who had returned to Henry's lap, hoping for more. The pizza party had fallen silent in one of those strange moments when everyone simultaneously pauses to gather new thoughts.

Henry seized the opportunity.

"Okay," he said. "I'd like to pose a hypothetical question."

"A what?" snapped Penelope.

Henry's mother interpreted. "He wants to play 'let's pretend,' Penelope."

"I knew that!" Penelope insisted. "I'm in high school, y'know!"

Henry laughed. Penelope made a rude gesture at Henry.

"What's your hypothetical, Henry?" said Ralph Haddock, pushing his plate aside.

"Yeah," said Penelope. "What's on your mind, hypodermicface? Hypnosisface? Hydrophobiaface?"

Henry paused, glaring at Penelope. Penelope grinned.

Helen Haddock, sensing Henry's mood, intervened. "Henry, is something bothering you?"

"Oh no, Mom," said Henry. "It's just something I have to decide."

"Really?" said Penelope. "What?"

"None of your business, mozzarellaface," said Henry.

"Oh no. Not fair, Henry," Penelope rejoined. "You know the rules! It's Saturday night."

One of the traditions of Saturday night pizza at the Haddocks' was complete candor. Anyone who admitted a problem had to go ahead and confess. For one night, there were no secrets—and no consequences. Clamming up—as Henry had just done—was the only sin.

"Penelope's right, Henry," said Ralph Haddock. "You brought up your mysterious hypothetical. You can't stop now."

"Yeah, you didn't shut up," taunted Penelope. "So you gotta put up! Punk."

Henry didn't really hate his sister, except when she was right.

"Well," said Henry.

Henry didn't think his family, or Fantasia's family either, had an answer for his dilemma. He had spent a lot of time studying pages and pages of obscure, boring municipal records that no one here had even seen. If he tried to explain everything, it would take hours. And even if everybody understood his problem, they couldn't do anything to help. Henry would still be stuck making his decision all alone.

"Henry," said Helen Haddock, "if you have a problem, you've got to tell us."

"Yeah," said Penelope, "even if it's a hypothalamus."

"Hypothetical," said Fantasia Fulton.

"Yeah, well, whatever," replied Penelope. "It's Saturday night. C'mon, upchuckface. Spill it. Spit it out, Henry. Cough it up!"

While Penelope embellished her demands with barf sounds, Henry wondered if maybe his problem wasn't so complicated after all. He didn't really need to say anything about school budgets or executive sessions or any of that stuff. He just needed to pose an example.

"Okay," he said, "let's say there are these two pirates."

"Aha!" Ralph Haddock leapt in. "This is no mere hypothetical, Henry. It's an allegory."

Henry knew what an allegory was. He said, "Well, no. It's more of an analogy, dad."

"What're you guys talkin' about?" Penelope complained.

"They're drawing a comparison, sweetie," said Delia Fulton, Fantasia's mother, who was always the peacemaker.

"Oh, a comparison," said Penelope. "Well, why don't they say so?"

"As I was saying," said Henry.

"Proceed," said his father. "With names."

"Oh, right," said Henry. "Names."

Another rule of the Haddock household was that all stories—whether real-life or fiction—required characters with names. Stories about "this girl" or "that guy" were forbidden to continue.

"And you can't just call 'em Pirate A and Pirate B, stuffedcrustface," said Penelope. "We want real names!"

"I know the rules, pepperoniface," said Henry, thinking fast. "Okay, two pirates. Um ... "

A parade of pirates, swashbucklers and buccaneers tumbled through Henry's brain (with notes of advice from Henry's dad): Captain Kidd, Captain Flint, Long John Silver, Billy Bones, Henry Morgan, Jean LaFitte, Sir Francis Drake, the Dread Pirate Roberts, Captain Hook, Sinbad, Jack Sparrow, Davy Jones, Edward Teach ...

"Okay, I got it," said Henry. "Cap'n Blood and Cap'n Blackbeard."

"Good! Blood and Blackbeard," Penelope said. "Now, let's go, Henry. What about 'em?"

Henry sat back, thinking about the school budget. "Okay, so there's a buried treasure. It belongs to Cap'n Blood, and his crew."

"Why'd he bury it?" asked Fantasia.

"Because he was being chased by the Spanish fleet," said Ralph Haddock. "Right, Henry?"

This was good. Henry, who realized that in this analogy he was the Spanish fleet, nodded. "Yeah, he was. The Spaniards were closing in. So he buried the booty on a desert island, okay? Except, it's not buried anymore. After they got away from the Spanish fleet and landed in Far Tortuga, Cap'n Blood snuck away from his crew. He sailed back to the desert island all by himself, and he dug up the treasure chest."

"Dug it up? Why'd he do that?" asked Fantasia.

"What's Far Tortuga?" asked Penelope.

Henry answered Fantasia's question. "Well, that's 'cause as soon as Cap'n Blood got to Far Tortuga, he runs into his old buddy, Cap'n Blackbeard. And Blackbeard says he needs a loan. And Cap'n Blood says okay."

"Just like that?" asked Fantasia, who was pretty stingy and didn't believe in lending money to anybody.

"Yeah, just like that."

"Why?" asked Fantasia.

"'Cause they're best friends," said Henry.

Lt. Col. Lafayette Fulton, Fantasia's father (also known as

Colonel Fate), was getting into the spirit of the analogy. "I see. Captain Blood had all this money in the treasure chest, just sitting there, doing nothing. He figured why not loan it out, and maybe he could collect a little interest, right, Henry?"

"I guess," said Henry.

"And he assumed," continued Colonel Fate, "that Blackbeard would pay him back before the heat was off from the Spaniards, when the crew would expect to go back to the desert island and dig up the treasure."

"Okay," said Henry.

"But Captain Blood didn't tell the crew about how the treasure ended up with Blackbeard," said Colonel Fate. "Right?"

"Nope, not a word. He only told his parrot."

"So, this is a big secret," said Penelope.

"Wait! Name!" said Ralph Haddock.

"Name? For who?" asked Henry.

"The parrot!"

"Oh, the parrot. But the parrot's not gonna be in the story anymore."

"Doesn't matter, Tortugaface," snapped Penelope. "A rule's a rule."

Henry sighed

"Okay, let's see." Henry thought. He looked around the table. "Diet Coke!"

"A parrot named Diet Coke?" said Penelope. "That's stupid!"

"That's his name," said Henry. "Like it or lump it."

"Where in heaven's name were we in this story?" asked Delia Fulton.

"It's more of an allegory," said Ralph Haddock.

"Analogy," said Henry.

"Whatever!" cried Delia Fulton.

"Okay, Cap'n Blood just cheated his crew out of a fortune, loaning it to Cap'n Blackbeard, with not so much as an IOU between them, right?" Ralph Haddock said to Henry.

"No, not exactly," said Henry, thinking fast. "That's the whole problem. Cap'n Blood is friends with Blackbeard. But Blackbeard keeps asking for money and treasure and stuff. but he never pays Cap'n Blood back. After all, they're pirates! They take stuff. It's not normal for a pirate to give anything back, right? So, yeah, Cap'n Blood gets an IOU."

"Aha!" said Colonel Fate. "A buccaneer's IOU, written in blood!"

"But whose blood?" interjected Ralph Haddock digressively. "Blackbeard's blood or Blood's blood?"

"Stop that, you two!" cried Delia Fulton.

A moment of laughing and giggling interrupted Henry's analogy.

Henry began again. "So, anyway, Cap'n Blood worries about losing Blackbeard's IOU. If he does, he can't get the treasure back. So, he can't just carry it around in his pocket. So, he slips it into his ship's log, which is always on his desk, on the poopdeck, where anybody could walk in and read it."

"Well, that's a stupid place to put it," asked Penelope, "if it's s'posed to be a secret?"

"Well, maybe not so stupid at all, Penelope," said Helen Haddock.

"Oh yeah? Why not?"

"Mom's right. The captain's the only one who really uses the log," said Henry. "Plus, most of the crew couldn't read. And even the ones who could read, they weren't interested in reading the ship's log."

"Why not?" asked Ralph Haddock.

"'Cause it's boring," said Henry, remembering how he almost fell asleep reading school budgets.

"Well, I think this is quite clever, Henry," said Helen Haddock. "Captain Blood hides the fateful IOU right out in plain sight."

"Wait a minute," said Fantasia. "You left out somethin'."

Henry sighed. "What?" he asked.

"You left out what the loan was for," said Fantasia. "Why'd Blackbeard need all that money?"

"A boat," said Henry.

"Of course," said Colonel Fate. "A pirate ship—The Golden Hind, The Black Pearl! To sail the wine-dark sea and prey on Spanish galleons!"

"Well, no," said Henry.

"Oh," said Colonel Fate, visibly disappointed.

"No, y'see," said Henry, thinking about the Thundering Three Hundred. "Cap'n Blackbeard wanted to get out of piracy and go into show business."

"Show business?" said Penelope.

"Really?" said Helen Haddock, smiling at this unexpected twist in the tale.

"Yeah," said Henry. "All the time he was growing up, the thing that Cap'n Blackbeard really wanted was a riverboat. So he could paddlewheel up and down the Mississippi, stopping along the way to put on musical shows."

Colonel Fate, who had a fine singing voice, began to hum the tune to "Ol' Man River."

"But the trouble was," Henry went on, warming to his analogy, "nobody ever really makes money in showbiz."

"*... Dat 'ol Man River, he mus' know sumpin', but don't say nuthin' ...* " crooned Colonel Fate, gently.

"Really?" said Fantasia, who'd been studying dance. She had her own dreams of show business.

"Oh, absolutely," said Delia Fulton, who would rather that Fantasia study medicine. "Show business is wonderful fun, but it's hard to make a career."

"Oh, Mom," said Fantasia. "You always say that."

"... He don't plant taters, he don't plant cotton ... "

Ralph Haddock broke in again. "Name!"

"What?" asked Henry.

"Blackbeard's riverboat!"

Henry was stumped for a moment. Then he said, "The

Domino!"

"The Domino?" said Ralph Haddock. "Hm. Not bad."

"Oh, Daddy!" cried Penelope. "He's just reading the pizza box!"

Henry ignored this. He continued his analogy. "So, of course, Cap'n Blackbeard couldn't pay back his friend, Cap'n Blood. Actually, pretty soon, he needs more money, to keep the riverboat going."

"... Tote dat barge, lif' dat bale, git a little drunk ... "

"The show must go on," said Colonel Fate, who had just "landed in jail."

"So Blackbeard sends a telegram to Cap'n Blood asking for more treasure."

"Yeah, but Cap'n Blood doesn't send Blackbeard the money, does he?" asked Penelope.

"Fish got to swim, birds got to fly, I got to love one man 'til I die ... "

For some reason, Colonel Fate had changed his tune, from "Ol' Man River" to "Can't Help Lovin' Dat Man."

"Well, he sends him as much as he can. He has to. They're best friends," said Henry. "Besides, if he doesn't send the money, Cap'n Blackbeard might go broke. If he did, he'd lose his big star, Nell Truelove, who's the most beautiful dance-hall gal on the whole Mississippi."

"Who?" said Penelope.

"... Tell me I'm crazy, maybe I know, can't help lovin' dat man of mine ... "

"So Blood sends more treasure to Blackbeard?" said Ralph Haddock.

"He has to," said Henry. "Because besides being best friends, Cap'n Blood and Cap'n Blackbeard are actually, secretly, brothers."

"Wait a minute," Delia Fulton tried to protest.

"The Blood brothers?" said Ralph Haddock.

"Jake and Elwood?" said Colonel Fate, suddenly ending his

solo.

"Oh, for Pete's sake," said Penelope. "This story's getting stupider and stupider."

"You're absolutely right, young lady," said Henry's mother. "Henry, as much as I enjoy watching your flights of imagination, I must tell you."

"Tell me what?" asked Henry.

"Your metaphor is running amok?"

"It's not a metaphor," said Henry, ignoring his mother and addressing Penelope. "It's an analogy. Well, more of an allegory, I guess."

Penelope turned up her nose.

"Never mind that, Henry," said Helen Haddock. "if you don't get down to brass tacks and speak literally, nobody will understand who you're talking about."

Henry sighed and surrendered. His analogy had failed. For a moment, he considered trying to explain his discoveries from reading all those School Board minutes (represented by the Blackbeard IOU hidden in the ship's log of Cap'n Blood). But he still wasn't sure about what to make of all the intelligence he had collected. He didn't really know what was inside the treasure chest that Cap'n Blood (played by Scooter McDuff) had buried on the desert island.

So, Henry settled back. He needed to figure how how to tell the crew—otherwise known as everybody in town—how Cap'n Blood funneled their taxes (the buried treasured that got unburied) over to Bluebeard (Wally Wilcox), so he could buy a riverboat (the Band). While Colonel Fate led everyone in a sing-along of "The House of the Rising Sun," Henry just sat there, thinking quietly and scratching Sarge behind an ear.

Henry Haddock didn't say much at all for a few days. On Tuesday after school, he walked past Mr. McCloskey's classroom.

Ray McCloskey was a young, energetic teacher with lots of

facial hair. Henry had first encountered him in fourth grade, when Mr. McCloskey substituted for a week for Mrs. Murdo. After that, Mr. McCloskey kept showing up in Henry's classes, always as a substitute teacher, through fourth and fifth grade.

Henry got a kick out of Mr. McCloskey because he asked a million questions. He was the askingest teacher Henry had ever seen. He figured Mr. McCloskey should go around with a giant question mark painted on his shirtfront, like The Riddler. But the funny thing was, the more Mr. McCloskey asked questions—about the Civil War, or long division or the periodic table of the elements—the more everybody else started asking questions, all the way through the school day. Even after the last bell, kids would still be hanging around Mr. McCloskey's desk, asking and asking.

So, when Henry passed by a classroom in the Blackhawk Middle School and saw in there the new eighth-grade history and social studies teacher, who just happened to be good old Ray McCloskey, Henry thought that here, at last, was the person to ask his big question—without need of any dumb analogies.

Or even allegories.

"Excuse me?" said Henry timidly, poking his head into the classroom.

Mr. McCloskey looked up from his gradebook.

"Henry!" he shouted. "My old buddy!"

Henry beamed. There's no feeling quite as good as being remembered enthusiastically when you're not sure you'll be remembered at all.

Mr. McCloskey said, "Henry, I've seen you around school, but never got a chance to say hello. How've you been? Come on in!"

After ten minutes with Mr. McCloskey, Henry had his answers and knew what he had to do, about Cap'n Blood and Cap'n Blackbeard and even Nell Truelove. At first, Henry's solution seemed a little crazy. But Mr. McCloskey insisted it wasn't crazy at all.

Henry also thought he might "get in trouble."

"Well, you might," said Mr. McCloskey. "But if you're worried about that, you should take your sister Penelope's advice and keep your mouth shut."

"But I can't do that," said Henry.

"Then you can't worry about getting in trouble, Henry," said Mr. McCloskey.

"Besides," added the teacher, "I've got your back."

CHAPTER 10

16 NOVEMBER

Henry Haddock believed, with deep conviction, that the school budget was unjust. It was, in fact, the greatest injustice that had ever touched his life. He knew that if he did not battle this misfeasance with all his strength and ingenuity, he would be ashamed of himself (at least a little bit) forever. It didn't matter so much if he lost this struggle. Henry knew the odds were against him. The important thing was to keep fighting.

Henry had recorded all his notes, minutes and library research in a spiral notebook stuffed with photocopies that he carried always in his backpack, along with his sketchbook, his pens, a Swiss Army knife, an emergency Milky Way bar, a bug-collecting jar with holes in the lid, a pair of spare socks, several dried horse chestnuts, his lucky sand dollar, the cell phone he almost never used (but it made his mother feel better because it had GPS and she could track his wanderings), along with 68 cents in loose change and one tarnished 1892 silver dollar, three laminated vintage football cards depicting Ray Nitschke, Dan Marino and Jerry Rice, his current reading (lately, he was working his way through the complete works of Jim Kjelgaard) and an extremely dog-eared paperback copy of *Webster's Collegiate Dictionary*.

As recorded in his spiral notebook, Henry had proven—beyond the shadow of a doubt—that the school budget was unjust, because

a) it required the firing of good teachers who had done nothing wrong, and

b) it eliminated programs and classes that were absolutely necessary to a good, well-rounded education, and

c) it was passed by the School Board in the middle of the summer while no one was looking, and

d) worst of all, there were parts of it that had been discussed and decided in secret meetings, hidden away from everyone except the School Board and a few privileged people—namely Band Director W.C. Wilcox and local plutocrat Paul Lamartine.

Henry didn't just believe these things. He knew.

Absolutely.

Henry's problem was that, aside from the perpetrators, he was the only one. Nobody else at the Blackhawk Middle School, except for his best friend Fantasia Fulton, knew the first thing about this spectacle of corruption.

However, as Ray McCloskey reminded Henry, people—especially middle-school kids—don't have to know anything to raise a ruckus. It's pretty easy to convince 11-year-olds, 12-year-olds and teenagers to make mischief, for pretty much no reason at all. Especially if you have a "smart" mobile phone!

So ... when Henry and Fantasia at the middle school—joined by Henry's sister Amy, along with Tiff and Moose at the high school—urged and coaxed and tweeted their friends to come out on Tuesday night to a "Save Our Schools" rally, sure enough, they found about thirty kids who said, "Why not?" It helped that Henry, the previous summer, had launched the Blackhawk Independent Baseball Organization (BIBO). All the kids who'd played baseball with Henry were glad to join in the demonstration—even though none of them knew what they were supposed to do, or why they were there.

But there they were!

Henry was immediately anxious, because he had only made twenty signs.

But these were great signs. He had made them in the art room, which had been locked up after Ms. Webster was fired and art became a forbidden subject at the Blackhawk Middle School. Henry got into the room, anyway, because Mr. McCloskey was buddies with Curly, the custodian. Curly was happy to help Henry because he didn't like the School Board. Besides firing all those teachers, the Board had also dismissed two custodians, two cafeteria ladies, six bus drivers and Earl the electrician. These now-unemployed people were all Curly's friends. He was concerned that he might be next on Scooter's hit list.

So, Curly unlocked the art room.

The storeroom there had everything Henry needed—sheets of heavy white butcher board, huge rolls of poster paper, jars of tempera paint in a rainbow of colors, dozens of brushes.

Henry had put a lot of thought into slogans to paint on his protest signs. Slogans now covered several pages in his spiral notebook. But when Mr. McCloskey saw the list, he rubbed his beard pensively and said, "Henry, you've read about the great protests of the past."

"Oh, yeah. I have," said Henry eagerly.

"I'm trying to remember," said Mr. McCloskey, "what did those signs say, when the mineworkers walked out, or when the autoworkers sat down?"

Henry thought about this, remembering photos of the greatest strikes and protests in American history.

"Were the messages long?"

"No," said Henry.

"How many words?"

Henry saw it in his head. And he smiled. "Just one, Mr. McCloskey."

"Which one?"

And so, every sign that Henry and Fantasia painted on Tuesday after school in Ms. Webster's art room said the same thing, one word, in bold, capital letters—either black or red.

UNFAIR!

"What's unfair?" asked a middle-school girl named Callista Blume when Henry handed her a sign.

Henry began to explain the injustices of the school budget and the tyranny of the School Board's closed-door decision-making. Henry emphasized the Chairman's habit of making everybody shut up. As Henry talked, more students arrived and received signs from Fantasia. They heard Henry explaining but hadn't heard him from the beginning. So, Henry started over several times. Eventually, every one of his protesters had a rough idea of what they were picketing about.

Fortunately, they all seemed to agree that they were joining a good cause. At least nobody walked away.

In fact, more kids kept coming. He spotted five loyal charter members of the Blackhawk Independent Baseball Organization (BIBO). Henry greeted them boisterously and made sure they all had "UNFAIR!" signs. Henry had expected a handful of protesters, but when he tried counting heads, he lost track at around forty. Some of these kids had made their own signs, with messages like "Save Our Schools" and "We Want Our Teachers Back NOW!" A seventh-grader named Christenson was waving a cardboard placard that read, "Scoot THIS, Scooter!"

Among the last wave of arrivals were Amy and Tiff. They

were late because they came in Moose's car and Moose had to finish basketball practice. By the time Moose showed up, all the "UNFAIR!" signs were taken. But Henry gave up his sign because Moose, at six feet, eight inches, was the tallest protester. He could hold his sign highest, which was important because, according to Mr. McCloskey, there would be a TV news crew on the scene that night, from Channel 8.

"TV? Really?" said Callista Blume. "I'm gonna be on TV?"

Henry looked around. There must have been more than fifty—or sixty—"protesters," mid-schoolers, high-school kids, even some grown-ups, all bundled against the cold, everyone shouting, cheering, laughing, whacking each other with signs and completely disorganized. "What have I done?" said Henry to himself.

Just after 7 pm, things started happening fast.

First, Annabella Moss, who was usually the first School Board member to show up, arrived—to a big cheer from Henry's crowd of protesters. To Henry's surprise, this turned out to be a very orderly and well-synchronized cheer, thanks to the presence of Amy and Tiff, both cheerleaders at Blackhawk High. It went like this:

"Who ya gonna call?
"Annabella Moss!
"Who ya gonna call?
"Annabella Moss!
"Who ya gonna call?
"Annabella Moss!
"Ca-a-a-a-a-a-all ANNIE!"

This ended in a lot of jumping and shouting "Yay!" and such. Henry immediately started worrying that the kids were having too much fun. It also ended up with Mrs. Moss grinning with great pleasure and leaning down toward Henry.

"Good for you, Henry," she whispered. Of course, Mrs. Moss then regathered her dignity and went inside the library.

Next to arrive were Mr. McCloskey and a man Henry had never seen before. The stranger was wearing a purple satin Los Angeles Lakers jacket, black slacks, two-toned shoes, dark glasses and a fedora with a feather in it.

"Henry," said Mr. McCloskey, "I'd like you to meet my dear friend, Dexter D. Lee. He's the one with the connections at Channel 8."

"Oh! Hi," said Henry.

Dexter D. Lee extended a hand. "It's entirely my honor, dear Henry, dear Henry. It's entirely my pleasure, dear Henry. It's mine!"

As weird as this greeting was, it made Henry laugh, and he shook hands with Dexter D. Lee.

By the time, a moment later, when the Channel 8 news crew hit the scene, Dexter D. Lee had mobilized Henry's chaotic demonstrators into a well-oiled dissent machine. Sixty-odd middle- and high-school students (plus adults) formed a picket line, marching in a neat circle that blocked the rear entrance of the high-school library. They were chanting in perfect unison.

"School Board unfair, School Board unfair," they intoned, and the Channel 8 light man fired up his lights.

Ray McCloskey put an arm on Henry's shoulder. "Dexter's a very organized guy," he told Henry. "He does interiors for office buildings."

"Oh," said Henry, watching his motley crew march in perfect order.

"Save our schools, save our schools, save our schools," they chanted, as the Channel 8 cameraman flicked a switch and started to roll video.

And then, just when School Board Chairman Farrell McDuff pulled up in his Mercedes-Benz and popped out of the car, looking befuddled and vexed, every protester stopped marching and chanting. They turned to face the Chairman and, reading from little slips of paper handed out by the resourceful Dexter D. Lee, they began a new chant:

"We want music!
"We want art!
"Come on, Scooter!
"Have a heart!"

As the protesters began repeating this chant and marching again in a circle, the Chairman slammed his car door and charged toward the library entrance. He didn't make it there.

Channel 8's locally famous on-the-spot reporter, Melissa McFarland, intercepted him. The picketers took up another of Dexter D. Lee's compositions.

"We want phy ed!
"We want shop!
"'Til we get 'em,
"We won't stop!"

At the instant Melissa McFarland pushed a microphone into Scooter McDuff's face and opened her mouth to speak, Dexter D. Lee ran his finger across his throat. The protesters—immediately—fell silent.

"Mr. McDuff," said Melisa McFarland mellifluously. "A moment, please."

Scooter puffed out a great chestful of air and said, "What the—"

"Mr. McDuff, what's your response to this spontaneous—"

Scooter cut off Melissa McFarland, sweeping her aside so suddenly that she teetered on her high heels and fell to the ground.

Chairman McDuff actually did answer the question. He announced that his response to this "unlawful and riotous mob" was to go inside and call the police. However, the Channel 8 sound woman didn't record this rejoinder. Scooter had knocked the microphone to the ground with Melissa McFarland.

Scooter barged inside, groping in his overcoat for his telephone. Melissa McFarland regained her feet, with help from Moose Fulton. Although her hair was mussed and she had somehow acquired a smudge on her cheek, she seemed quite pleased with herself.

One by one, the School Board members arrived and braved the gauntlet of protesters, each of them surprised and annoyed. None agreed to an interview with Melissa McFarland. But Darlene Gazelick stopped long enough to bend down, look Henry Haddock straight in the eye and hiss into his face, "This is all your doing, you little Bolshevik."

Henry found this encounter somewhat frightening. But balancing his discomfort was vocabulary pride. He knew what a Bolshevik was.

To Melissa McFarland's delight, every word of Darlene Gazelick's utterance was audible and on tape. The Channel 8 newswoman now knew, also, who the real troublemaker was. At first, she had thought that the demonstration's ringleader was the flamboyant fellow in sunglasses and purple satin. Henry Haddock, small and clearly precocious, provided a much better protagonist for Channel 8's viewership. Melissa McFarland closed in on Henry.

She was interrupted by the Blackhawk Police Department, who arrived in force (two squad cars, four cops), led by Officer Billy Karkle. He spotted Moose Fulton towering above a group of circling, chanting schoolkids. Billy headed for Moose like a bloodhound after a ham hock.

He never saw Melissa McFarland approach, attended closely by her sound woman, Debbie, her cameraman, Bernie, and her blazing light man, Speed.

Melissa McFarland stopped Billy Karkle cold.

"Excuse me, officer. Your name?"

"Huh?"

"Your name, officer. Who are you?"

"Who am I? Me? Well, I'm ... I mean, I'm Officer William Lorenzo Karkle of the Blackhawk Police Department. That's who! Who're you?"

"Now then, Officer Karkle, what is your purpose here this evening?"

"My purpose? My purpose? Who the hell are you?"

"Melissa McFarland. Eyewitness News. Channel 8," replied the newswoman crisply.

"Oh. What? Huh? Really?" Billy Karkle, obviously, had never been on TV before. His eyes grew larger. His fellow officers, terrified of suffering the same exposure as Billy, backed away and clammed up.

Silence reigned over the scene. Chanting stopped. Henry's picket line, and the camera, gathered around and pressed close to Melissa McFarland and Billy Karkle. The newswoman and the cop were side-by-side, between them Melissa's microphone and behind them, a sea of faces and signs that said: "UNFAIR!" and "Scoot THIS!"

"Officer Karkle, what is your purpose here?"

"Purpose? They called us."

"Who called you?"

"Um, the School—um, Scooter. Scooter called."

"You're speaking of Mr. Farrell McDuff, Chairman of the School Board?"

"Yeah, him."

"Chairman McDuff called you? For what purpose?"

"Well, um, to break it up."

"To break up ... what?"

Billy Karkle was flummoxed. He took his eyes off Melissa McFarland for the first time. He looked, furtively, at the crowd surrounding him. He waved his hands toward the circle of protesters.

He said, "Well, this, I guess."

"You mean this peaceful, legal demonstration? These young people expressing their First Amendment rights, Officer Karkle?"

"Legal? Who says it's legal?"

"Who says it's not legal, Officer Karkle?"

"Ooh, that's a good one," Ray McCloskey whispered to Henry. "She's tough."

It was a cold November night, but sweat had begun to appear on Billy Karkle's upper lip. "Who says?" he repeated.

"Yes, Officer Karkle. Who says this demonstration is not lawful? What law has been violated?"

Billy Karkle stared at the microphone.

"Yeah, Billy!" cried out Fantasia Fulton. "What law, you big fat blueface!"

Beads of sweat emerged on Billy Karkle's brow. The brow itself turned a vivid shade of pink. Melissa McFarland inched the mike closer to Billy Karkle. She said, "Officer Karkle?"

Billy Karkle spoke, "Yeah, well, they're, um ... they're creating a disturbance."

"A disturbance?" said Melissa McFarland. As she did she looked into the camera. "Whom are they disturbing?"

"Um." Billy Karkle chewed a damp lip. Blackhawk's high school and middle school stood side-by-side on a vast swath of municipal property, surrounded by playing fields, adjacent to a small woods. Across School Street was the Blackhawk Elementary School, which was currently locked up and empty. The nearest residence was a quarter-mile up the street.

"Officer Karkle, seriously," said Melissa McFarland. "Unless these peaceful young people, exercising their First Amendment rights, are disturbing each other, I don't see a disturbance here. Do you?"

"Well, I, uh ... " But no further words came to Billy Karkle's mind. His mouth moved. No sound came out.

Still, the Channel 8 inquisitor kept her microphone in Billy's face. She gazed expectantly into his eyes. A thin rivulet of sweat coursed between his eyes and down his nose. Just then, Ray McCloskey edged through the crowd and nudged Billy Karkle. He whispered in Billy's ear.

Suddenly, Billy Karkle seemed to relax, just a little. He turned toward Ray McCloskey and said in a loud but slightly shaky voice, "Well, okay, Ray. But you tell 'em they better hop to it, okay? We don't want a disturbance here!"

With that, Billy Karkle and the other BPD officers broke free from Channel 8, escaped the crowd and hurried to their squad cars.

The crowd cheered.

By the time Billy and the police had disappeared, the circle was moving and Dexter D. Lee's chant was ringing through the November air.

"We want music!
"We want art! ... "

Melissa McFarland captured Henry Haddock.

Henry hesitated to answer her. He had seen what she did to Billy Karkle. But Mr. McCloskey jostled Henry back into microphone range, saying softly, "Henry, this is what you signed up for. This is politics."

So, Henry submitted to Melissa McFarland. Of course, since this was his first television interview, Henry tended to ramble. But later that evening, after Channel 8 had edited his remarks, two turned out to be successful "sound bites."

"The School Board," said Henry, looking deathly pale and bug-eyed on the 10 o'clock news, "fired some of our best teachers. Behind our back. Nobody got a chance to say anything. They don't let people talk. It's not fair."

Even more significantly, Henry was quoted as follows: "They did stuff in secret, um, executive sessions, that they're not supposed to do."

"You mean," asked Melissa McFarland, whose face was so close he could smell her makeup, "the School Board broke the law?"

Here, Henry hesitated. So the newswoman just bored right in on him, as she had done to Billy Karkle.

"Henry, did Chairman McDuff and the Blackhawk School Board break the law?"

"Well ... "

"Did they, Henry?"

"I think so," said Henry Haddock. Here, he had added hurriedly, "Except for Mrs. Moss."

But this part was edited out.

Not edited out, however, was Fantasia, pushing her face into the camera and shouting, "Henry doesn't THINK so. He KNOWS, dammit!"

"He does?" asked Melissa McFarland, turning the microphone on Fantasia.

"DAMN right!"

"Oh my goodness," said Delia Fulton that night, as she watched her only daughter cursing on the 10 o'clock news.

The Channel 8 report ended with Fantasia sharing Speed's dazzling lights with Melissa McFarland. Henry was seen receding hastily into the background.

The protest scene at the school entrance was only half of Channel 8's report. The other half was filmed inside the high-school library. Cameraman Bernie's viewfinder circled the room, lingering first on the audience. All the protesters had trudged inside. They were standing in a semicircle—directed, of course, by Dexter D. Lee. He put the two prettiest girls, Amy and Tiff, in the middle, with Moose right behind them, holding his "UNFAIR!" sign. Everyone else was arranged by height, tallest in the middle, shortest on the edge, all holding their "UNFAIR!" signs.

The Channel 8 shot ended up behind the School Board as Scooter McDuff conducted his meeting. Bernie zoomed slowly past the back of Scooter's neck, toward the front row of the audience, where side-by-side sat Henry and Fantasia. Henry was drawing in his sketchbook. Fantasia was partly concealed behind a sign that read, "UNFAIR!"

Suddenly, Chairman McDuff stood and turned toward the camera. He shouted, "All right. That'll be enough of that."

The Chairman lunged toward the camera. The last split second of the shot showed Scooter McDuff's face rushing toward the camera, out of focus, as his hand reached out and covered the lens.

CHAPTER 11

19 NOVEMBER

Long before halftime, a group of Blackhawk fans in the bleachers had lost interest. This was the first basketball game of the season, Blackhawk High versus Koshkonong, a nonconference opponent. The Blackhawks had a twenty-point lead. Except for the dominant play of the Blackhawk center, Moose Fulton, there was not much reason to pay attention.

The least attentive group in the Blackhawk bleachers was probably Henry Haddock and friends. They were busy proofreading Henry's petition. It proposed the "recall" of four members of the School Board.

Recalling one public official is a very big deal. The impeachment of four borders on—Henry had looked up the word—"insurrection."

But Henry believed recall was the right thing to do. He was sure he could prove that the four members of the Board—not counting Annabella Moss—had broken the law.

That's what it said on his petition. It read:

"Whereas ... "

(Henry had discovered that almost all good petitions began with "whereas.")

"Whereas four members of the Blackhawk School Board, Farrell McDuff (Chairman), Darlene Gazelick, Lyle Lehnherr and Randolph Zink, have violated the state Open Meeting Law by deliberating in executive session on matters of public concern, to wit, line items of the school budget, and

"Whereas, these four members of the Blackhawk School Board have further violated the state Open Meeting Law by consulting in executive session with private parties on matters of public concern, to wit, line items of the school budget,

"Therefore, be it resolved that these four members are subject to a recall election to be held no later than ... "

On the advice of Town Counsel Charlie Mulcahy, Henry had not filled in the date. Since he served as the School Board's lawyer, Charlie had barely said a word to Henry about his recall petition. But Charlie did look it over. After that, he nodded.

Henry figured Charlie's little nod meant that his draft—for which Henry had also gotten help from Mr. McCloskey—was pretty much "legal." The only entire sentence that Charlie Mulcahy uttered was, "Henry, if you get your signatures by the end of the year, we'll schedule the election on the 30th of January."

"Whoo-ee!" said Lt. Col. Lafayette Fulton, reading over Henry's draft. "You are a pistol, Henry."

"Wait a minute!" said Penelope Haddock. Does this mean you wanna kick out the whole School Board?"

"Except for Mrs. Moss," said Henry.

"But what for? Wha'd they do? I don't get it," said Penelope.

"Well, that's 'cause you're a moron," said Henry.

"I am not—"

"Wait! Stop!" said Helen Haddock She was conveniently located, within bopping range, one row above Henry in the bleachers. She bopped him sharply on the head with her program. "Henry, explain the petition to your sister—nicely."

Rubbing his head, Henry acquiesced. "Okay, it's simple, Penny."

"Penelope!"

"Yeah, right, Pennyloopydoopy. Okay, so, the School Board—actually, any elected board in town—they have to do everything out in the open. In public meetings, where people can go and watch them. Okay?"

"Transparency!" intoned Colonel Fate. "The cornerstone of the republic."

Henry continued. "The School Board didn't do that. They had secret meetings about public business. That's against the law."

"What law?" asked Penelope.

"The Open Meeting Law."

"Oh," said Penelope. "How do you know they did that?"

"I looked it up. I read lots and lots of public records. Anybody can look it up. Hardly anybody ever does."

"Oh," said Penelope.

"Aha! So that would make you Billy Budd, the cabin boy, poking through the ship's log," said Colonel Fate, remembering Henry's pirate analogy.

Henry smiled. "Yeah."

"And you were afraid nobody would believe you."

"Right."

"So Scooter McDuff is—"

"Cap'n Blood!" said Fantasia. "Cool!"

"Okay, wait," said Penelope. She was peering at Henry's petition. "What about this part? Where were they having secret parties?"

"No, they weren't having parties, pennyface. They invited 'private parties'—that means people—to their secret sessions."

"They can't do that?"

"Collusion!" intoned Colonel Fate.

"That's right. Henry's accusing them of collusion," said Ralph Haddock. "The Board can only meet with private parties if these people have private business with the Board. For instance, Penelope, if the high-school principal decided to expel you from school—"

Penelope leapt in her seat as though jabbed with a cattle prod.

"Oh no! Expel me? Why? I didn't do anything?"

Ralph Haddock said, "Sweetheart, this is a hypothetical."

"Oh," said Penelope, remembering the word. "One of those."

"Good. Well, Penelope, let's say you were being expelled. Your mom and I don't want that to happen. So, we come to the School Board to argue in your favor. Now, you see, whatever you've been accused of doing, and whatever the principal and your mom and dad say about you, that's all personal. Your behavior in school is not public business. We don't want everybody in town to know about it, and everybody in town isn't entitled to know. You got that?"

"I guess," said Penelope.

"Hypothetically," said Colonel Fate, "you did something privately bad in a public school."

"Oh, I get it," said Penelope, smiling up at Colonel Fate.

"So, because the bad thing you did is personal and private," Ralph Haddock continued, "it's okay for the School Board to close the meeting and talk with us in secret."

"So nobody else knows why I'm getting expelled," said Penelope.

"Right," said Ralph Haddock. "Hypothetically."

"But if we're talkin' public business, like the budget," said Henry, "then everything has to be public!"

"Henry," said Delia Fulton, leaning over from her seat beside Henry's mother, "you say here in the petition that there were 'private parties' in these secret meetings. But you don't say who they were."

"No," said Henry.

"Why not?"

"Prudence," said Ralph Haddock with a smile.

"Oh my God," lamented Penelope Haddock. "What's *that* mean?"

"It means that if you don't have to say something, you maybe should not say it."

"Oh, okay," said Penelope. "You mean Henry's not saying somethin'. What's he not saying?"

"I'm not saying the names of those people," said Henry.

"The private parties," said Penelope.

"Right," said Henry.

"Why not?" asked Penelope. "Didn't they break the law, too?"

"That's a good question, Penelope. And the answer is no. They didn't break the law," said Ralph Haddock. "Because the Open Meeting Law only applies to the people who were elected."

"Oh." Penelope scratched her head.

For a moment, the Haddocks and the Fultons sat thinking.

"For instance," said Henry, suddenly, to Penelope, "let's say you're being expelled, okay?"

Penelope snorted in an unladylike way and said, "Why don't we say *you're* being expelled, petitionface?"

Henry shrugged. "Okay, fine, I'm being expelled. I'm there. Mom and Dad are there. Mr. Holling, the principal, is there, 'cause he needs to tell the School Board why he's expelling me, okay? And we're all talking in secret."

"Are you whispering?" said Penelope.

"No," said Henry. "But it's a secret meeting. And I'm saying, please, please, please, don't expel me. I'll be a good boy."

"Yeah, fat chance," said Penelope. "What you did was rotten."

"Wha'd he do?" said Fantasia.

"Hush," said Helen Haddock.

"Now, so far, it's all legal," said Henry, ignoring Penelope's interruption. "And the Board says, you're not expelled. But then, at the end, I tell them they ought to fire Mr. Holling for picking on me. And they say, hey, good idea! And they fire Mr. Holling. Is that legal?"

Everyone stared straight at Penelope.

"What?" asked Penelope.

"Firing Mr. Holling," said Henry. "Is it legal?"

"Um," said his sister. "No?"

"Right!" said Henry. "Why?"

"Jeez, legalface! I dunno," said Penelope.

"Penny, it's *not* legal 'cause hiring, or firing, the principal of the middle school, that's public business. He's a public official."

"Oh, right," said Penelope. "Yeah. I knew that."

"Very good, Henry," said Delia Fulton. "Now, who are they?"

"Who?" said Henry.

"Henry. The private parties!" said Delia Fulton. "The School Board's been sneaking around talking to these people, right? So who are the unindicted coconspirators in this scandal?"

"The *what?*" said Penelope.

Henry looked around evasively. He noticed that the two basketball teams were about to start the second half.

"Henry, don't be rude to Mrs. Fulton," said Henry's mother.

"Oh, he's not," said Delia Fulton. "Are you, Henry?"

"Oh no, Mrs. Fulton. I just didn't want to put their names in the petition."

"You thought they'd be embarrassed?" asked Delia Fulton.

"No, that's not the problem," said Ralph Fulton. "Henry left out the names of the School Board's coconspirators because, if everybody in town knew those names, Henry might not get anyone to sign his petition. Right, Henry?"

"Well," said Henry.

"My goodness!" said Delia Fulton. "Who are these shadowy figures?"

"Delia, they're not shadowy at all," said Colonel Fate. "Henry found their names in the public record. Right, Henry?"

"Yes, the names were right there. I found them in the summaries of the executive sessions that Mrs. Arnold wrote up," said Henry.

"Fine! If they're not secret," demanded Delia Fulton, "then for heaven's sake, tell me!"

Henry sighed.

Ralph Haddock spoke. "Well, for one thing, you've got the richest man in town."

"Paul Lamartine?" said Delia Fulton.

"Right, Henry?" asked his father.

Henry nodded.

"Oh, Henry," said Helen Haddock. She sounded just a little frightened. "He's a very powerful man."

"Oh, but that's not the best part, honeybunch," Ralph Haddock continued. "The other one is Wally Wilcox."

"Wally Wilcox?" said Delia Fulton.

"The band director?" said Helen Haddock.

Henry nodded.

"Wait a minute!" said Penelope. She stood up, her face flushed with alarm. "Is this *thing*—" She grabbed Henry's draft petition and waved it at him, "—about the *band*?"

Henry said, "Sort of."

Penelope gasped. She clutched her chest. Suddenly, a cheer went up all around them as the second half began. Penelope pressed her nose right up to Henry's nose.

"Henry, you weasel-nosed snakeface! What are you trying to do to *my band*?"

Blackhawk beat Koshkonong that night, 77-48. Moose scored 26 points. But the next night, during pizza time at the Haddocks', no one was even thinking about basketball.

Henry was planning to launch his petition drive—to recall Scooter McDuff and three other School Board members—the next morning, Sunday. He had printed fifty copies of his petition. He had bought a dozen clipboards and a lot of plastic ballpoint pens. He had recruited Fantasia to help him solicit signatures. Amy and Tiff also volunteered. Moose said he would help when he wasn't practicing, and he would definitely get signatures from all the parents of the basketball team. Mr. McCloskey told Henry he couldn't join the petition drive, because he was a teacher. Mr. McCloskey feared retaliation from the School Board. On the other hand, Dexter D. Lee was fearless. He insisted on manning one of Henry's clipboards.

On Henry's invitation, Mr. McCloskey and Dexter D. Lee were guests at the Saturday night pizza party. They had brought along a bottle of Italian wine, which pleased Henry's parents. Everyone seemed to be having a good time, except Penelope. She ate pizza, of course, and drank soda, but didn't join into the spirit of the evening. She was still mad at Henry for plotting to destroy the band.

Band was Penelope's favorite subject.

Henry had told his sister over and over again that wasn't trying to destroy the band. But Penelope just said he was a rotten, lying spitvalveface.

So Penelope sat glaring (and spying for Wally Wilcox) while everyone else was busy planning strategy for Henry's petition drive.

"The picket line was a very smart opening gambit," said Lt. Col. Lafayette Fulton, who was well qualified to discuss tactics. "You framed the battle on your terms and you got a lot of public attention. And when Scooter flattened that newsgal? Terrific. He comes out looking like the heavy!"

"Heavy?" said Fantasia.

"Bad guy," said Ray McCloskey. "By the way, the picket line? Dexter's idea."

Everybody (except Penelope) applauded. Dexter D. Lee

took a bow.

"Wait," said Ralph Haddock. "Does anybody—Henry! Do you understand what you're up against?"

"Up against?"

Ralph Haddock paused and looked around. He caught the eye of Ray McCloskey, who had a knowing smile on his face. Ralph Haddock said, "Shall I explain?"

"I think you'd better," offered Helen Haddock.

"Henry, what's the rule on recall elections?"

"The rule?"

"How many signatures do you need on your petition?"

"Oh, well," said Henry. "Charlie—Mr. Mulcahy—said I have to get ten percent of all the registered voters in Blackhawk."

"Which is how many?"

"Well, there are about 7,000 people in town, but only 4,211 are registered voters. I guess the rest are kids and stuff."

"So, you need 421 signatures?"

Henry shook his head. "No, because all the signatures have to be certified by the City Clerk, and if I got 421 and he rejected just one, then I wouldn't have enough."

"So, how many do you really need?"

"At least 500. Maybe 600."

"Good," said Ralph Haddock. "Doesn't sound too hard, right? Five hundred citizens, good and true."

"Yeah," said Henry, warily. He knew his dad was hiding bad news up his sleeve.

"Here's problem number one, Henry," said Ralph Haddock. "All four of the School Board members you're going after—Scooter and Darlene, Lyle and Randy—they all have supporters who voted for them. Scooter got more than 2,000 votes the last time he ran. Now, most of those people are going to stick with whoever they voted for. They're not going to sign."

"Yeah, but, Dad," said Henry, who loved history almost as much as he loved art, "a lot of people who voted for Jimmy Carter in 1976 voted against him in 1980. And Ronald Reagan won. And then in 1992—"

Ralph Haddock raised a hand. "Okay, good point, Henry. Voters are fickle. But what about the Band Parents?"

Henry looked puzzled. His father said, "Henry, you could have named Wally Wilcox in your petition. But you left his name out. Tell me why?"

"Well," Henry said, "I guess I wanted to make the petition really simple."

"Hah! That's a crock!" said Penelope. "You're a big fat lying fibface!"

Ralph Haddock smiled. "Penelope's right, Henry. It's a crock."

"Well, okay," said Henry. "I left out Mr. Wilcox because of the Band Parents."

"Aha," said Colonel Fate.

"Henry," said Ralph Haddock, "do you know many people there are in the Band Parents Association?"

"A lot?" said Henry.

"Counting all the former band members and their parents, there are more than a thousand in town. And they stick together. They think Wally Wilcox is Superman," said Ralph Haddock. "Your biggest problem is that almost every member of the Band Parents is a registered voter and none of them—except your mother and me—are going to sign your petition. Without the Band Parents, your pool of 4,200 possible petitioners is more like three thousand."

Ray McCloskey said, "That means—to get 500—you need signatures from one out of every six people who aren't loyal to the Thundering Three Hundred."

"That's a pretty tall order, Henry," said Colonel Fate.

"Aw, we can do it," said Fantasia.

"No, you're gonna lose, Henry," growled Penelope. "We're gonna crush you. Like a wet nightcrawler."

Everyone looked at Penelope.

"Hold it," said Moose. "The School Board broke the law, right? Like Henry said. They had secret meetings they weren't supposed to."

Everyone turned to Moose. Henry said, "Yeah, that's right. They broke the Open Meeting Law. I wouldn't make up something like that."

"Okay then," said Moose. "People will see that! They don't want cheaters on the School Board. They'll sign the petition. I'll make 'em sign."

Moose reached out and slapped palms with Henry. "We start tomorrow!" he said.

"Well, I guess that's settled," said Helen Haddock, smiling. "Who wants ice cream?"

On Sunday, Henry deployed his forces to the churches of Blackhawk. He stood outside Faith Episcopal, waiting for Episcopalians to come out and sign his petition. Fantasia covered the Baptists. Amy and Tiff ganged up on the Catholics at Immaculate Heart. Moose, who manned the Methodist Church and then caught late services at St. Paul's Lutheran, collected the most signatures. He got six.

On Sunday afternoon, Henry looked over his collection of clipboards. They contained fifteen signatures, including Reverend Dade, the Baptist pastor, who only signed after Fantasia agreed—after three years' absence—to come back to Sunday school.

"Fifteen down," Henry said to himself, disconsolately. "Four hundred eighty-five to go."

Penelope appeared. She looked over Henry's shoulder and counted the fifteen pathetic signatures.

"Like a wet nightcrawler," she said.

ROUND III:

HENRY HITS THE STREETS

CHAPTER 12

23 NOVEMBER

By midday on Monday, Henry Haddock was beginning to feel as though the corridors of the Blackhawk Middle School were enemy turf. Kids who belonged to the junior band were giving him a regular parade of dirty looks. It wasn't hard for him to guess why. His treacherous sister Penelope had spread the word among the Thundering Three Hundred—who were everywhere at the high school and middle school—that her rotten little brother was out to sabotage the band.

Not that he was.

Henry had to admit that if his school budget campaign succeeded, it would affect the band. Maybe the band would be smaller.

But sabotage? No.

But how could he explain this to every angry band member in the whole school? There were dozens—hundreds—of them.

Henry simply resolved to keep a stiff upper lip.

Meanwhile, the story of Henry versus the School Board had stretched beyond the Blackhawk *Weekly Argument* and made the Sunday paper. The headline, on page one of the Regional section, read:

SIXTH-GRADER LEADS BLACKHAWK IMPEACHMENT EFFORT

"Yeesh," said Henry.

"Henry!" roared his father. "You publicity hound! You shameless headline grabber!"

Reading the article about himself, Henry learned a few things he didn't know. For example, although Henry had sent letters to the state Attorney General and the county's District Attorney, he was not aware that the D.A. had sent his "complaint" upward to the state Education Commissioner. Reading on, Henry found out that the Education Commissioner had "referred" the "issue" of an "alleged" Open Meeting Law violation in Blackhawk to a judge in the state capital.

"Henry," said Ralph Haddock, "think of it. Right now, there's a state judge reading your letter."

Henry went pale. "Jeez, Dad, I didn't mean to start any trouble."

Ralph Haddock laughed out loud. "Oh yes, you did, Mister Celebrity!"

"Mr. Haddock," said Fantasia, who happened to be reading the newspaper over Henry's shoulder, "this judge. Could he send the School Board to jail?"

"Jail?!" squeaked Henry.

Ralph Haddock laughed. "No," he said. "You can't go to jail for secret meetings. But you might get kicked out of office."

"Kicked out? Even without Henry's petition?" asked Fantasia.

"Possibly," said Ralph Haddock.

"Great!" said Fantasia. "I hate this petition stuff."

"Well, if I were you, I wouldn't give up on the petition,"

said Henry's father. "The judge might take the School Board's side."

"Dumb judge," said Fantasia.

By Tuesday afternoon, Henry had added eleven signatures to his personal clipboard, reaching a total of fourteen. On the advice of Mr. McCloskey, Henry went, after school on Tuesday, to an old folks' home called Monmouth House.

"Believe me," said Ray McCloskey, "the old folks out there are so glad to get a visitor that they'll sign anything for you."

Mr. McCloskey was right. Henry ended up hanging out at Monmouth House for two hours, chatting with dozens of senior citizens. Three of them thought he was their great-grandson. But he came away with seventeen new signatures from real live registered voters. He couldn't wait to get home and talk to Fantasia, Amy, Tiff and Moose, and get on the phone with Dexter D. Lee, to see how many they'd gotten.

About two blocks from home, Henry heard voices behind him. Someone called his name. He turned. He saw a group of high-school boys. And a dog. He didn't recognize the kids at first, but Henry knew Wagner (pronounced, for some reason, "Voggner"), the Wilcox family dog. Wagner was a German shepherd.

Henry was well-acquainted with Band Director Wally Wilcox's four grandchildren. They lived on Cady Avenue, a couple blocks from Henry's house. All the Wilcox kids—and sometimes their father, Wally Wilcox, Jr.—took turns walking Wagner.

Peering through the November dusk, Henry finally saw that the boy holding Wagner's leash was Wally the Third, eldest child of Wally, Jr. Wally III was a sophomore at Blackhawk High. He played first trombone in the Thundering Three Hundred. Among Wally III's companions was Marty DeSimone, first bass drum in the Thundering Three Hundred and son of John DeSimone, president of the Band Parents.

After a moment, Henry recognized each of the six high-school boys. They were all band members. They did not look genial.

Henry tried to conceal his clipboard inside his coat.

Now, Henry had always felt that he had a good relationship with Wagner the German shepherd. When they met in the neighborhood, he would rub Wagner's coat and scratch his ears. Wagner, in return, would lick Henry's face, which was easy for him because Wagner was tall enough—almost—to look Henry straight in the eye. Wagner, however, had a reputation for being dangerous if provoked. Henry had never seen Wagner provoked, nor did he have any idea what sort of stimulus might expose Wagner's dark side.

"Hey! Haddock!" This was Wally III, shouting at Henry from half a block away. Usually, Wally III called Henry "Henry," not "Haddock." This was a clear sign of unfriendliness.

Wally III shouted, "Whaddya got against the band, ya little creep?"

Wally III's five human companions muttered and grumbled behind him, providing a sort of chorus. Wagner, meanwhile, sat on the sidewalk, his mouth open and his tongue hanging out. He didn't look provoked.

"I like the band," said Henry, barely audible.

"You what?" yelled Wally III.

"You got me wrong, Wally. I *like* the *band*," said Henry, louder. This met with hoots of derision. Wagner stood up, excited by all the commotion. But the dog looked more curious than irate.

"You do *not!*" replied Wally III hotly. "Or you wouldn't be tryin' to fire the School Board!"

"No, you don't understand," said Henry, stepping toward Wally III and his gang. Seeing Henry move, Wagner started to wag his tail.

"No, we understand! We understand that you're a rotten little sack of crap! You wanna wreck the best band in the whole state. You're jealous, Henry! We're famous! We're great!

And you're nothin' but a punk!"

"Oh no, that's not it!" Recalling his recent appearances in several headlines (not to mention Channel 8), Henry almost said that he, too, was famous. But he sensed that bragging wouldn't defuse the tension.

"Y'know what?" shouted Wally III.

Henry had a feeling the conversation was going nowhere. But he said, "What?"

"The band," said Wally III, his voice less angry, "is like the nicest house in town."

Not another analogy, thought Henry.

"Yeah, yeah, it is, that's true, he's right," murmured all the other kids, agreeing with Wally III.

"But it's not safe!" said Wally III. "From little firebugs like you, Haddock. You wanna burn it down."

More agreement from the group.

Henry started to say, "No," but was drowned out by Wally III.

"And you!" Wally III went on, pointing at Henry. "You're like a *trespasser*!" With the last word, Wally III's voice took on a sinister tone. Wagner's ears pricked up and his tail froze.

Bending close to Wagner's ear, Wally III said, "Trespasser!" He pointed at Henry, "Wagner! Look! A *trespasser*!"

Well, there it was.

Henry finally knew the secret to provoking Wagner. Just say the magic word: *trespasser*. Wagner was suddenly squirming with territorial vigilance. He began barking at Henry, making little growls between every woof. He leapt forward, reaching the end of his leash and staggering sideways. He spread his legs, barking and growling, straining to be freed.

Wally III made matters worse, repeating the magic word as his companions began to chime in.

"Trespasser, *trespasser,* TRESPASSER! ... "

"Wait a minute," shouted Henry. "I'm not—"

That was when Wally III reached down, said, "Wagner!

Trespasser! Sic'm!" and unhooked the leash.

Knowing Wagner as well as he did, Henry had good reason to assume that when the dog got close enough to smell and recognize him, Wagner would think twice about ripping Henry to shreds.

On the other hand, Henry had never seen Wagner provoked. He had no idea what Wagner might do while provoked—even to an old ear-scratching pal like Henry Haddock.

So, it was uncertainty, rather than cowardice, that motivated Henry to turn on his heel and run.

As Henry fled Wagner and Wagner chased him, Wally III and his friends followed, at a more leisurely pace, shouting encouragement to the dog and jeering at Henry.

Henry covered a block and crossed one street with Wagner hot on his dungarees. But he was still two blocks from home. He was wearing his school backpack, a ten-pound burden that Wagner did not have to bear. Besides, Henry knew that even an old, slow German shepherd (unfortunately, Wagner was young and light on his feet) could outrun any kid in town.

Henry was going to be caught, and possibly eaten.

So, suddenly, Henry lurched to his right, into the front yard of the Murchisons—Stan and Bessie—where stood an enormous oak tree. Henry put the tree between himself and the barking, snarling, slobbering German shepherd.

This stratagem worked momentarily. Wagner skidded to a halt, backtracked to the tree and stood staring at it, growling softly.

"Now, Wagner," said Henry. "Good boy. Good Wagner."

This seemed to be working. Wagner stopped barking and made no advances on the tree, behind which Henry continued to make soothing noises.

The truce lasted less than thirty seconds because, galloping up to the Murchisons' yard came Wally III and his crew.

"Where is he, Wagner? Where's the *trespasser*?" said Wally III. True to form, Wagner responded by barking at the tree. He encroached on Henry threateningly.

Henry looked upward for a branch or some toehold. But the Murchisons' mighty oak was smooth and unclimbable for at least twelve feet. Henry whimpered once.

Amidst shouts of "Trespasser!" and "Sic'm!", Wagner was suddenly after Henry again, growling and snapping his tooth-filled, drippy jaws.

"Oh, jeez!" And Henry began to run, in circles, around the tree. Wagner followed, lunging at Henry's pants, his feet, his tender flesh, briefly getting hold of Henry's backpack. Henry's only protection was his clipboard, which he clutched, with both hands, to the seat of his jeans.

As Henry fled, around and around, Wally III and his friends—unmoved by Henry's plight—cheered Wagner, who was as blameless in this situation as Henry.

On his fifth circuit, Henry remembered—for some reason—last year's Blackhawk Fourth of July Festival. Specifically, Henry recalled the Frisbee-catching contest, which had been won by Donny Friedl's Jack Russell terrier, Spanky—who had caught up to a speeding Frisbee after a 60-yard run, jumped eight feet and snatched it from the air, executing two complete somersaults before landing on his feet. This was a doubly dramatic moment because—until Spanky's otherworldly performance—the front-runner for the trophy had been none other than Wagner.

Which was an idea!

Suddenly, shocking everyone—even Wagner—Henry skidded to a stop and confronted the vigilant trespasser-killing German shepherd. As he halted, Henry assumed the unmistakable Grecian pose of the Frisbee-thrower. His clipboard, metaphorically, became a Frisbee.

Just as suddenly, Wagner's entire personality changed. From watchdog extraordinaire, he turned instantly into the champion Frisbee retriever that he knew himself to be. His eyes lit up, his tongue came out, his tail began to wag furiously.

Henry gave out a sigh for all those signatures about to be lost. Then, he reared back and—applying the expert wrist-English of a Frisbee veteran—let fly his clipboard, all the way across the Murchisons' snowy yard, over the Murchison fence and into the distant premises of the Sullivans'—Bob and Brenda.

Wagner took off as though launched from a catapult.

Henry remained at the Murchisons' oak, still outnumbered by a corps of angry band bullies. It was only reasonable for him to assume that Wally III and Company would take up the terrorizing of Henry where Wagner had left off. So, as Wagner lit out for the amazing airborne clipboard, Henry took off for home.

A shout of dismay from Wally III was the last Henry heard from him. After putting a block between himself and his antagonists, Henry turned. He saw Wagner with the clipboard clenched in his jaws, carrying it to Wally III, as bits of torn petition swirled around the dog's head and drifted in the breeze.

Thirty-one signatures, thought Henry, down the gullet of an illiterate pooch. As Henry reached home, he tried to take consolation from the thought that he'd be doing an encore at Monmouth House, making all those lonely old folks happy for two days in a row.

That night in the school library just before the School Board meeting, Henry huddled with Amy and Tiff, Fantasia, Moose, Mr. McCloskey and Dexter D. Lee—with Buzz Skelton, from the teachers union, kibitzing. Subtracting Henry's 31 eaten signatures (which he planned to recover), they were now up to 28.

"Yeesh," said Henry.

"Don't worry, Henry," said Dexter D. Lee. "We have not yet begun to fight."

"I'll help," said Buzz Skelton. "A lot of our teachers live here in town. If we all sign, we'll have safety in numbers. They can't fire all of us."

Henry pulled an extra clipboard from his backpack and gave it to Mr. Skelton.

The banging of Scooter McDuff's gavel signaled the beginning of the meeting. Henry, as usual, went to the front row with Fantasia, his sketchbook and an "UNFAIR!" sign. Henry spent the meeting quietly drawing sketches of Randy Zink, who had a very interesting nose and nervous lips. Henry did his best not to make eye contact with the Chairman, who regularly cast malevolent looks in Henry's direction.

Fantasia noticed this. She waited patiently and—every time Scooter McDuff glared at Henry and Henry looked innocently elsewhere—Fantasia stuck out her tongue.

And waggled it.

When the meeting ended, Chairman McDuff raised his gavel and gave Henry one last look, expecting that Henry might raise his hand to speak. But Henry was busy putting the cap on his pen, paying no heed. So, the gavel fell, the Chairman fled, the meeting broke up.

That's when it happened.

As he headed toward the door, Henry almost ran smack-dab into a tall man in a shiny gray suit. His thick but well-groomed hair, his mustache and his eyes were also gray—the color of stainless steel.

Henry looked up. Fantasia stumbled sideways.

"Henry Haddock, I presume," said the tall man. His smile was cool and princely.

"Huh?" said Henry.

"You *are* Henry Haddock?" said the great gray eminence.

"Oh, yeah," said Henry. "That's me." Henry backed up a step so that the man would look less like the Empire State

Building.

"Well," said the stranger offering a hand, "I thought we should make each other's acquaintance, young man. My name is Paul Lamartine."

Henry took the hand, felt it squeeze his, but not hard, and said, "Oh."

"Henry, you're a go-getter and I like that. I'm impressed with your efforts," said Paul Lamartine. "Although I'm quite certain they won't amount to much in the end."

"Oh yeah?" asked Henry, in a voice more curious than bellicose. Henry's team was standing in the background staring, doing nothing. Ray McCloskey was wearing a big grin.

"Yes," said Paul Lamartine. "But I wish you luck, Henry."

Then he added. "You'll need it."

Paul Lamartine turned to leave. Henry watched silently until the richest man in town was almost out of the high-school library. Then Henry said, "Hey. Mr. Lamartine!"

Paul Lamartine turned. He said, "Please, Henry. Call me Paul."

"Yeah. Okay, Paul," said Henry. He held up his clipboard. "How'd you like to sign my petition."

Dexter D. Lee laughed.

Paul Lamartine's face betrayed a glimmer of surprise before breaking out again in that cool smile. Paul Lamartine said, "That's a good one, Henry."

And he was gone.

CHAPTER 13

DECEMBER

By the time of the annual Blackhawk High School holiday basketball tournament, just before Christmas, much had changed.

Of course, many things hadn't changed at all. Among these was Wally Wilcox III, whose band guerrillas had mounted a steady campaign of harassment against Henry's petition drive. Most of this was just name-calling. Once, they chased Amy and Tiff out of the Blackhawk Shopping Center—but didn't steal their clipboards.

The petition drive got a break during Thanksgiving week, when the whole Thundering Three Hundred—Wally III included—went to College Station for the halftime performance at the Texas-Texas A&M battle. This prestigious performance prompted heavy coverage in the *Weekly Argument*, including a two-page spread of color photos that were printed only slightly off-register.

But Thanksgiving was over. From Mr. Kussow's classroom during third period, Henry Haddock could once again hear the band at practice, marching back and forth, around and about, trampling the snow under the gimlet eye of Band Director W.C. Wilcox, perched high above the middle-school football field in a specially designed observation tower (donated by the Band Parents). The tower put Wally Wilcox just about at eye level with Henry in his history class. But Henry figured the maestro probably wasn't peeking into Mr. Kussow's class or worrying about little Henry Haddock. W.C. Wilcox certainly had greater concerns than Henry's moribund petition drive. The Thundering Three Hundred was preparing now for a parade and halftime show at the renowned Christmas Day Kaopectate Bowl in balmy Fort Smith, Arkansas.

Henry had long since recovered all the signatures eaten by Wagner. He'd gotten a petitioning boost from the teachers union. Amy, Tiff, Fantasia, Moose and Dexter D. Lee, along with Amy's Facebook legions and Henry's baseball buddies, were out canvassing every day. But Henry's recall petition totaled fewer than a hundred signatures by the end of November.

There were rumors around Blackhawk that Henry's petition was a secret plot to "liquidate the band." After the Texas triumph and the announcement that Wally had scored a national TV appearance in Fort Smith, there was an upswell of enthusiasm for the Thundering Three Hundred. In the first week of December, Henry increased his signature total by exactly four.

Just about three weeks before Christmas, Henry gathered all his clipboards and did a recount. "Ninety-seven down, four hundred three to go," he said disconsolately. The crusade looked hopeless.

That was a Thursday. That evening, the undefeated Blackhawk High basketball team, with two games scheduled on the weekend, had a big rally and bonfire behind the high school. Moose Fulton provided the gathering's climax.

For a moment, Moose stood staring up at a disorderly tower of logs, brush, plywood, loose paper, cardboard boxes, wooden crates, cable spools, construction rubble and various flotsam and jetsam gathered by Blackhawk High School students. All the way at the top of the bonfire pile was an ancient, wind-weathered outhouse. The rickety pile was thirty feet high and it swayed a little in the westerly wind.

Stuffing a wireless microphone under his belt and moving as nimbly as a big cat, Moose clambered up the teetering heap and found a foothold next to the old gray outhouse. He waved. The crowd gave him a huge roar. Moose, star of the basketball Blackhawks, was averaging almost thirty points in the first four games of the season. He waited for the cheering to stop. Then he spoke—softly at first because he was a little shy about public oratory. He talked about the team, and his voice grew louder. He said the Blackhawks were going to beat Mill Bluff on Friday and then he shouted that they would crush Sextonville on Saturday. The crowd went ape and started dancing around the bonfire pile.

Moose waited a moment. The crowd settled down. Moose looked a little cross-eyed.

"Jeez, y'know what I wish?" he said.

And the crowd, full of high-school students, little kids and parents, all of them bursting with enthusiasm, hollered back, "Mooooose!"

This made no sense, but it's how mobs communicate.

And Moose said, not very loud but loud enough (because he had a microphone), "I think we have the greatest band in the world here in Blackhawk."

Huge cheer.

"But I wish they played at our games."

No cheer.

"I mean," said Moose.

The crowd began to mutter confusedly.

"I mean," said Moose louder, quieting the crowd, "there's a petition going around right now to recall some of the School Board, and a lot of you think the petition is against the band."

The crowd was getting restless again, but Moose was rolling.

"Well, it's *not*!" Moose was raising his voice noticeably. "I *know* what's in the petition, and it's NOT about the band!

"My friend Henry Haddock is not against the band. My parents, who signed the petition, are not against the band. I'm not either. Nobody's against the band. I like the band so much I want them to play more. Right here! In Blackhawk! For our games! Not for some stupid Pepto-Bismol Bowl a thousand miles away!"

Everybody in the crowd was looking at one another nervously.

"I love the band!" shouted Moose. "Do you?"

Here was a question well-suited for a mob.

"Yeah!" the mob cried.

"And I want the band back here! In Blackhawk! Don't you?"

Another "Yeah!"

"Not in Texas!"

"No!"

"Not in Arkansas!"

"NO!"

"Right here! In Blackhawk!"

"YEAH!"

"Hey!"

"HEY!"

"You know what else?" roared Moose. "I want our teachers back, too! Don't you!"

Without thinking about it, the mob agreed. "YEAH!"

"All of 'em!"

"ALL OF 'EM!"

Amy and Tiff, professional cheerleaders, knew a cue when they heard one. Instantly, they started up Dexter D. Lee's protest lyric.

"We want music!
"We want art!
"Come on, School Board!
"Have a heart!"

This spread through the throng and went on for almost five minutes, everyone circling the bonfire. Moose stood next to the outhouse, thirty feet in the air, swaying treacherously, shaking a fist and grinning into the darkness.

"We want phy ed!
"We want shop!
"'Til we get 'em,
"We won't stop!"

Henry looked up, worried that the tower of tinder might collapse and break every bone in Moose's body. But Moose didn't seem anxious at all. "Weird," Henry said to Fantasia.

"What's weird?" said Fantasia.

"I've never seen your brother act like this."

"Hey, me neither," said Fantasia. "I'm glad my mom's not here."

"He's like a wild man."

"Mom would kill 'im."

"I kinda like it, though," said Henry.

"She'd still kill 'im."

Finally, the uproar settled down enough that Moose could be heard.

"Okay!" shouted Moose. "Let's go!"

Pandemonium broke out all over again.

"Let's go, Blackhawk! Let's go, Blackhawk!"

The crowd continued to chant as Moose climbed down. The bonfire was set alight and for the next half hour, Moose and his Blackhawk teammates led everybody in a pagan snake dance around the old outhouse's blazing sacrifice.

Henry, circulating among the festive basketball fans, filled five pages on his petition. When he got home, he had 110 new signatures.

"Holy bonfire, Batman," said Henry.

Moose's bonfire speech was an inspiration. It turned around the recall campaign. Instead of "Throw the rascals out," Henry's new theme was: "Bring our band home! Bring our teachers back!" People were suddenly more willing to sign his petition. Henry didn't quite understand the change in the public mood until one day after school when he talked to Mr. Kussow, his history teacher.

"Henry, sometimes in politics, the most important thing is how you frame the issues," said Mr. Kussow.

Henry knitted his brow. Mr. Kussow continued: "Henry, you know a great deal about the school budget because you've studied it. But you can't expect everyone in town to do the work you've done."

"No," said Henry.

"That means you need to share your knowledge in a way that's true, but simple," said Mr. Kussow. "You can't tell people everything. But you can tell them the most important points. In a few well-chosen words."

"Didn't I do that?" said Henry.

"No, you didn't, Henry. You rambled and explained. It was Moose who put his finger on the right message," said Mr. Kussow. "He framed the issue for you."

"Well, then, maybe, maybe Moose should be—"

"No Henry, I can see where you're going," said Mr. Kussow. "Who's the one who read all that boring budget material and studied all those School Board minutes? Moose?"

"No," said Henry.

"That's right, Henry. You did the grunt work. You lifted the curtain. You exposed what was going on back there in secret. And then, when you told Moose what you knew, Moose understood the two most important things," said Mr. Kussow. "Moose understood, first of all, that teachers were getting fired while the band was still hip-deep in money. And second, Moose understood that the band—our town's band—was out of town ... most of the time."

Henry nodded.

"It all comes down to those two ideas," said Mr. Kussow. "For Moose to see those two simple points, and be able to express them, well. That was political dynamite."

"Jeez," said Henry. "Moose is pretty smart."

"Still not as smart as you, Henry."

Another big basketball rally took place just before the big December tournament, the Blackhawk Invitational. Eight teams from two states were invited. In fourteen years, the home team had never won.

Henry worked his petition at the rally and during the tournament, at halftime of every game. He stubbornly wormed his way through the crowd, telling people whose mouths were full of hot dogs and popcorn that he was fighting to bring the band home and save the teachers. The crowd, full of good cheer in a school full of teachers (but no band playing, because the band was in Fort Smith, Arkansas), signed agreeably on Henry's dotted line.

Meanwhile, Moose Fulton scored 36 points on Friday night and Blackhawk won. On Saturday afternoon, in the semifinals, Blackhawk won again. Moose had 27 points. In the finals that night, the Blackhawks faced an undefeated out-of-state team from Sinnissippi High. They were losing until the final two minutes, when Moose took charge. He scored a basket while being fouled, then made the free throw. Seconds later, he stole a pass and flipped the ball to teammate Brian Flinders for another basket. On Sinnissippi's next possession, Moose blocked a shot, grabbed the rebound, passed the ball, ran downcourt and scored on the fast break. With seven straight points in twenty seconds, Blackhawk was behind by one point.

With ten seconds left in the game, Sinnissippi had possession. Moose was guarding the in-bounds pass under Blackhawk's basket. He lunged to block the pass and tipped the ball as he crashed to the floor. The ball flew high in the air, almost straight up. Moose got to his feet, spotted the ball and outleaped everyone. As he came down with the ball, the crowd was screaming "Shoot! Shoot!" Time was almost up.

Moose smiled. He could see the clock above the backboard. He had two seconds. Plenty of time. Moose set his feet and settled the ball in his right hand. He jumped, flicked his trusty shooting wrist and came down, still smiling, as the ball went through the net. Blackhawk 71, Sinnissippi 70.

Moose's crowd, on cue, went stark raving bananas.

After the game, the only person calmer than Moose was Henry Haddock, who cornered ten more jubilant Blackhawk fans (two of them Band Parents) and got their names and addresses on his petition.

The pizza party that night was later than usual, but also happier, because the pizzas on the Haddocks' dining-room table were sharing space with Moose's Most Valuable Player trophy.

Henry had started his petition with a dozen clipboards, but ended buying more of them. Wagner had eaten one clipboard. Tiff Melrose had one that she was going to turn over to Henry after Christmas, but first she needed to squeeze a signature from her Aunt Effie who always came into town from the farm for Christmas dinner. Fantasia had three clipboards, but could only account for two. She had lost the third, but told Henry she thought it was somewhere in her school locker mixed up with a month's supply of brown-bag school lunches packed by her mother that she had never eaten because she hated egg salad. (Fantasia's locker smelled a little funky.) Moose was also missing one of his two clipboards, because he had given one to Mr. Finkel, the basketball coach, who shared Moose's conviction that it would be nice if the band played for basketball games. Henry controlled several clipboards, of course. Ray McCloskey and Dexter D. Lee each had one. Amy was responsible for about twelve clipboards and had collected all but one from her Facebook BFFs. One clipboard remained missing because Penelope had stolen it and hidden it somewhere. She might have burned it. Henry had provided clipboards to a couple of BIBO friends, Danny Messerschmidt and "Marvelous" DeSean Marvelle.

The day of gathering clipboards was the day after Christmas. By 4 p.m., Henry's crew had arrived at the Haddock house with all their petition sheets. Fantasia's lost clipboard had been fished up from the depths of her school locker. Henry's mother immediately threw the clipboard away and ran the petition pages through the clothes dryer to deodorize them.

Missing only was the clipboard swiped by Penelope.

If Penelope had made the "traveling team" for the band, she would have been in Fort Smith and the missing clipboard might have stayed missing 'til too late. But Penelope was a freshman, and freshmen rarely traveled with the Thundering Three Hundred.

Penelope was home.

Her father called her into the Haddock dining room, where she faced the cold glare of thirteen tired petition gatherers who were now looking down the barrel of a five-day deadline.

"What?!" she squealed before her father could even open his mouth. "You want me to betray the band?"

"No," said Ralph Haddock. "All we want is fairness."

"Play fair," was the Haddock family's unspoken motto. Everyone knew what was fair and what wasn't fair. There was no arguing.

Penelope knew she had swiped Amy's clipboard. She also

knew there were sixteen precious signatures on it. Above all, she knew what was fair.

"Aw, rats," she said. "It's not *fair*."

"No," said her mother. "It is."

Penelope skulked back to her room. Sulkily, she retrieved the clipboard from inside the box spring on her bed, where the fabric covering had torn just wide enough to hide Penelope's deepest secrets.

She turned the sixteen signatures over without a word and went back to her room, to pout.

Henry had acquired from Town Clerk Al Disney a revised copy of the official Blackhawk voting list—which was a public record. (Henry had grown strangely fond of public records.) According to the most up-to-date numbers, there were exactly 4,309 registered voters, thus requiring a rock-bottom minimum of 431 correct, legible signatures on the recall petition. For two hours, Henry and his team sat around the Haddocks' dining-room table, counting signatures and matching them up with names on the voter list.

They had to discard 28 signatures that did not match any names on the voter list.

They also had to disqualify two people whose penmanship was so awful that neither their signatures nor their printed names were remotely readable. The closest anyone got to translating one was "Jahm Ynrklxeey," but there was no one who had ever lived in Blackhawk named Ynrklxeey. The other illegible name was simply a straight line with three loops.

Eleven people had signed petitions with names like "Alfred E. Newman," "Petunia Poopsey" and "Rufus T. Firefly." These, too, they scratched off.

Around 6:30 p.m., finally, it came time for Henry to add up all the red-circled numbers scrawled on the bottom of all 42 petition pages that everyone had gathered all over Blackhawk, despite hostility from the political allies of Scooter McDuff and notwithstanding the active opposition of the band and

Band Parents Association—not to mention Wagner the dog.

Henry went through every page, tapping his calculator and speaking each number aloud. After the last page, he hit the "equals" sign and saw the number pop up. He scowled.

Henry said, "Wait a minute."

Before anyone could see, he zeroed the screen on his calculator and started all over again. Tap, tap, tap. "Sixteen, nine, twelve, fourteen, three ... "

Last page again. Henry hit "equals."

He looked. Same number. "Jeez," he said.

"Hey, c'mon," said Fantasia. She pushed Henry, who was hunkering very protectively over his calculator. "I wanna see, DAMMIT. I wanna know how many more DAMN signatures—"

Fantasia saw the number and shut up.

"Four sixty-one," said Henry.

"FOUR SIXTY-ONE?!" roared Moose Fulton.

"We're over the top!" crowed Ralph Haddock.

"We're done?" said Fantasia, in disbelief.

"We done, baby!" said Colonel Fate.

"We're not done. *They're* done!" said Ray McCloskey. "We've just made history."

"Gloriosky," said Dexter D. Lee.

"Henry," said Helen Haddock, grabbing her son and hugging all the breath right out of him, "did it!"

A moment later, everyone was dancing around the table, waving wrinkled and ink-blotched—but perfectly legal—petition pages over their heads. Lt. Col. Lafayette Fulton, in his stentorian baritone, began to sing "We Shall Overcome," and everybody joined in. But this seemed too solemn, so they switched to "We Shall Not Be Moved," which was better but sort of religious. They ended up with "Happy Days Are Here Again." Henry pointed out that it was the theme for Franklin Delano Roosevelt's 1932 presidential campaign, but nobody cared about that. They all sang it twelve times before tiring out and ordering pizza.

The celebration ran on for another three hours. The grown-ups had pizza, beer and wine. The kids had pizza and soda. Helen Haddock went out and got ice cream. Even Penelope, smelling pizza, came down and joined in—but sat quietly at one corner of the table. Once, her father said, "C'mon, Pen, cheer up."

Penelope replied, "This isn't over, you traitorfaces."

The next day, after school, Ray McCloskey drove Henry and Fantasia to City Hall, where they delivered the petitions to City Clerk Al Disney, who was also the Registrar of Voters. After Al Disney had studied the petitions for almost an hour, spot-checking them against the voter list, he tallied everything and, like Henry, reached a total of exactly 461.

"Henry, my boy," said Al Disney in a completely impartial tone of voice, "it looks like you're going to get your recall election."

At that, Al Disney placed a telephone call to Town Counsel Charlie Mulcahy, who arrived within ten minutes. He joined the City Clerk in verifying the petitions. Together, they certified a recall election for four School Board members on Tuesday, January 30.

"Wow," said Henry.

"Far out," said Ray McCloskey.

"Hot DAMN," said Fantasia.

"Congratulations, Henry," said Charlie Mulcahy, whose smile and handshake revealed nothing of what his true feelings might be.

The following night, the high-school library was jammed. Many teachers and students had come. There was a large delegation of Band Parents, which would have been larger except many members were still working their way back home from Fort Smith. The junior band, however, was out in force. The Fultons and Haddocks were present, except for Penelope—who stayed home in protest. Moose had rallied the basketball team and half the football team. Coach Finkel was there. Henry saw Peg Bradner, head librarian of the Blackhawk Public Library. Buzz Skelton was in attendance, of course, with a delegation from the teachers union. Darren Flack represented the *Weekly Argument*. Dexter D. Lee had brought along nine people whom no one had ever seen before. Dexter had alerted Melissa McFarland at Channel 8, who said she might attend.

So far, no TV crew.

Town Counsel Charlie Mulcahy and City Clerk Al Disney were seated at the table normally occupied by Superintendent Bob Ptaschnik and secretary Myrtle Arnold.

There was no sign of Paul Lamartine.

Henry, as usual, was in the front row with Fantasia. Unusually—every other front-row seat was filled. This throng had come to hear Chairman Farrell McDuff announce, as the law required, that four members of the Board, including Scooter himself, were required by law to stand for election or rejection as a result of Henry Haddock's successful recall petition.

At 7:30 p.m., exactly, looking sleek, pressed and unruffled, Scooter McDuff gaveled the School Board to order. "Hm," he said, "nice crowd we have tonight. I hope we can all behave."

Fantasia stuck out a lip. "Oh, we'll behave, blimpface," she said.

She and Scooter glared at each other, childishly, for a moment.

Finally, McDuff broke the spell by opening a manila folder. He shuffled a sheet of paper and said, "Before we get into the agenda, folks, I have a bit of business here."

Everybody thought they knew the "bit of business" Scooter was talking about. A few people inched forward in their seats.

"I have a letter here," said Scooter.

Everybody thought they knew what was in the letter. A few people actually held their breath.

"It's from the state capital," said the Chairman. "It's signed by Administrative Judge Howard G. Dolphy."

"Judge?" whispered Fantasia. "What judge?"

Just like that, a whole roomful of cocksure people had no idea what was up.

Scooter looked down at the letter. He said, "In here the judge says, among other things, that 'although the behavior of the Blackhawk School Board is worthy of censure, for its clear failure to uphold the letter of the Open Meeting Law, I can find no intent to evade the law.'"

Scooter paused and looked around. There was a smirk forming at the corner of his mouth. He read on: "... 'Nor do I find that the Board used these ill-advised executive sessions for unlawful or unethical purposes. As noted, the Blackhawk School Board merits a severe reprimand for these deviations from good government practices. But I find in their mere negligence no reason to deem the members of the Board unfit for office or subject to any subsequent action, either judicial or electoral ...'"

The Chairman paused. "The letter goes on," he said, "but there you have the nutshell, folks."

Fantasia grabbed Henry by the arm. "Wha'd he say?" she said. "What's that mean?"

Scooter McDuff leaned forward, smirking across the big table at Fantasia. "It means, young lady, that your little election is off. The judge has put the kibosh right on your little nose."

Fantasia tried to ask Henry if the Chairman was right. But Henry couldn't hear. The cheering of the Band Parents drowned out Fantasia's question. Scooter tolerated the pandemonium for a while before tapping the gavel and asking the crowd to settle down.

Henry sat limp in his chair, oblivious to everyone. He had not understood everything in Judge Dolphy's backbreaking letter, but he got the drift. The drift was that Scooter and Mrs. Gazelick, Lyle Lehnherr and Randy Zink had misbehaved a little, but not a lot. Nothing they'd done—in the open or in secret—was corrupt enough to get them kicked off the School Board. The judge, in a stroke of his pen, had erased 461 signatures and canceled Henry's recall.

Penelope, thought Henry humbly, was right. Two days before, she had said it wasn't over.

Now it was.

CHAPTER 14

31 DECEMBER

Just before the new year, the Haddock household experienced its three quietest days in history. For a while, after she came to understand the significance of Judge Dolphy's bombshell, Penelope went about strutting and gloating. But since this behavior was intended mainly to torment Henry, Helen Haddock quickly ordered Penelope to desist. Afterward, the great silence descended.

Henry was grateful that school was out for Christmas vacation. He didn't have to go to class and face kids who knew about his civic catastrophe. He didn't have to apologize—yet—to teachers who had courageously signed his petition. He was especially glad he didn't have to see Mr. McCloskey, who had risked his job for Henry, only to see Henry fail.

Henry's father, one night, tried to explain that politics was a sort of gamble. You bet on people to do the right thing, But then they might decide that you're wrong about the right thing. Henry retorted that it was not "the people" who decided to kill the recall petition. It was one person, one old fuddy-duddy judge who didn't even live in Blackhawk.

"Yes, Henry, but the judge is also part of the government. He's a politician, too."

"Well, it's not fair," Henry complained.

"Maybe so," said Ralph Haddock. "After all, you know what President Carter said."

"Yeah yeah," grumbled Henry. "Life isn't fair."

"So," said Henry's father, "what're you going to do about it?"

"Do about it?" said Henry. "What can I do now? It's over."

"Is it?" asked his father.

On New Year's Eve, Fantasia came over to Henry's house, to mope on the couch with him. Nobody else was home. As midnight in New York City neared, Henry and Fantasia ate cheese balls and swilled soda. Forlornly, they watched a lot of people dance and sing and whoop it up, celebrating the new year on television.

About 11:30 (Central Time), Penelope, who had been at the Band Parents' annual nonalcoholic New Year's party for teenagers, came home. She grunted at Henry and Fantasia, grabbed a handful of cheese balls and headed to her room. Halfway up the stairs, unable to restrain herself, she paused and said to Henry and Fantasia, "Ha ha HAH!"

Henry threw an empty soda bottle at her, but missed.

Next to show up, a few minutes before the new year, were Ray McCloskey and Dexter D. Lee. They were bearing pizza, which they placed on the coffee table in front of Henry and Fantasia. Having failed him, Henry felt a little uncomfortable with Mr. McCloskey. But Mr. McCloskey seemed as cheerful as ever. He and Dexter D. Lee actually seemed to be enjoying New Year's Eve. When the TV burst into music and showed pictures of joyful people in Chicago dancing, Mr. McCloskey and Dexter D. Lee began to dance together around the Haddock living room.

Henry felt a little funny about this.

"Henry, it's okay," said Fantasia, chucking her friend on the arm. "They're gay."

Hearing this, both Mr. McCloskey and Dexter D. Lee laughed. Then Mr. McCloskey swept Fantasia off the couch and began to dance with her. Dexter D. Lee did the same with Henry. They all danced around the Haddocks' cluttered living room 'til Henry banged into the coffee table, knocking over a glass of soda. Then, suddenly, everyone scrambled for paper towels to clean up the spill before Henry's mother got home—which she did before they were finished.

But she wasn't upset. She had brought more soda, and pizza.

This wasn't the last of the pizza. A half hour into the new year, Amy came home, along with Tiff Melrose and Moose Fulton, and pizza. Two minutes later, attracted by the sound of revelry and the ambience of pizza wafting through the neighborhood, Lt. Col. and Mrs. Fulton moseyed over.

With everybody together, eating and drinking, making jokes, celebrating the new year and talking about the success of Blackhawk High School basketball, Henry found it hard to remain miserable.

The party continued. The pizza diminished dramatically. Even Penelope came downstairs.

Finally, Dexter D. Lee, sitting on the rug by the coffee table, raised a glass of wine and said, "To Henry, who fought the good fight."

Everyone toasted Henry. He turned a little red but smiled. Then, in response, he said, "Big hairy deal. We lost."

"Just one round," said Ray McCloskey.

Henry thought this a strange remark. He knew, from reading the newspaper, that Judge Dolphy's decision was final. Any hope of recalling the School Board was dead. He looked curiously at Ray McCloskey.

Penelope scowled at him.

Mr. McCloskey just grinned. He said, "You wanted a special election, right, Henry? That's what your petition was all about."

Henry nodded.

"But the judge said you can't have a special election, right?"

Henry nodded. He didn't see what Mr. McCloskey was getting at.

But suddenly, Moose Fulton did. "Hey! Yeah, that's a great idea, Mr. McCloskey."

Ray McCloskey, who loved to ask questions, turned toward Moose and said, "What's a great idea, Darnell?"

"Ray's right!" said Ralph Haddock before Moose could answer. "We don't need no stinking special election."

"Because?" said Ray McCloskey, opening his arms.

"Because there's a regular election every year, my fine-feathered friend," said Colonel Fate.

Ray McCloskey bowed deeply.

Henry sat up straight. He realized how dumb he was. Why hadn't he thought of this?

"When?" said Fantasia.

"Every April," said Helen Haddock.

The sun rose anew in Henry's world. His father saw the light in his eyes. He said, "Henry, you forgot the first rule of politics. There's always another election just around the corner."

"Yesssss!" said Henry, standing on top of an ottoman and pumping his fists.

"Oh no," said Penelope.

Suddenly, Henry's brain was churning, as everybody started talking all at once. There was a local election in April. But which members of the School Board were up for reelection? No one remembered the date of the election. They had no idea who could run against the current Board members. Henry, who deserved the nomination more than anyone, was too young to run.

"Wait!" said Ray McCloskey. "It's New Year's Day and it's really early, and we're all tired. We don't know enough about this election to make any plans. Do we even know why we want to start this fight?"

Henry was ready for this one.

"Yeah!" he said.

"Henry, the floor is yours," said Ray McCloskey.

"Because it's not fair!"

"Is that so? What's not fair?"

"What's not fair? What's not *fair?*" said Henry. "Mr. McCloskey, it's right there in the school budget. Do you know how much the budget spends on the band?"

"No," said Ray McCloskey. "How much is it?"

"Hey!" Penelope broke in. "How come you're always picking on the band?"

Mr. McCloskey pounced on Penelope. "That's a good question, Penelope," he said. "Would you mind telling us how much money we spend on the band?"

Penelope shrank slightly. "Um," she said, "how much?"

"Yes, how much? Per annum."

"Per what?"

"Every year, Penelope."

"Oh. Every year?" said Penelope, "I don't know. But—"

"Henry?" said Mr. McCloskey, returning to the expert.

"Well, Mr. McCloskey, the total cost in this year's budget is $850,000 ... "

There was a gasp from everyone.

"But only half of that is covered by the school budget. The rest comes from contributions raised by the Band Parents. So, the schools' share is $425,000."

"Still," said Ralph Haddock, "whoo-ee!"

"Henry," asked Ray McCloskey. "Have you calculated how many teachers we could hire for, say, $425,000?"

"Sure," said Henry. "About seven or eight."

"So, instead of seven or eight teachers in, say, French, art, music, physical education, math, science, shop, we have this really big marching band that people in Blackhawk hardly ever see?"

"Hey!" said Penelope. "We play *here*."

"Twice a year, maybe," said Amy.

"That's 'cause we're the best band in the whole—"

"Henry?" said Ray McCloskey.

"Even if the band only had the money that's raised by the Band Parents," said Henry, "the band would still have lots of money. The band is rich."

"Filthy rich," added Fantasia, unnecessarily.

More McCloskey questions. "Henry, is there any other school program that costs that much?"

"No."

"Or even *half* that much?"

No."

"And is that why you believe the school budget isn't fair?"

"DAMN right that's why!" said Fantasia loudly.

"Yeah. That's why," said Henry, not quite as loudly.

"Well," said Ray McCloskey, "it sounds like you have a platform, Henry."

"A platform?"

"Henry, when you run for office, you put together a platform. Your platform is a list of promises to the voters. These are the things you're going to do after you win," said Ralph Haddock.

"The simpler the platform, Henry," added Mr. McCloskey, "the better your chances."

"And Henry, you've had the same platform for months. One word, " said Dexter D. Lee. "Unfairness."

"Unfair!" said Moose, remembering Henry's signs.

"Unfair!" said Amy and Tiff, in cheerleader unison.

"Hey, no fair!" said Penelope. "The band is the best thing in town. Who's gonna fight for the band?"

"Oh, don't worry, Pen," said Helen Haddock. "They're the Thundering Three Hundred. They've got the Band Parents, Wally Wilcox, Scooter McDuff and Paul Lamartine. I think they can fight for themselves."

“Boy, that sounds tough,” said Moose. “Henry, whoever you find to run against Mr. McDuff, they’re gonna be the underdog.”

Henry suddenly realized that his battle against the School Board wasn’t over after all. In politics, there’s always a second chance.

“Henry, I’m warnin’ you,” said Penelope, brandishing a pizza slice at her brother, “you better not do this.”

“Oh yeah?” said Henry, biting off the end of Penelope’s pizza slice. “Who’s gonna stop us, platformface?”

CHAPTER 15

4 JANUARY

"Okay, Henry, think of us as your brain trust."

Henry was seated in the Blackhawk High School library on a Tuesday night, in his personal chair, with his customary sketchbook and his usual sign, reading "UNFAIR!" But besides Fantasia, who sat demurely next to him, Henry was surrounded by helpful grown-ups—Mr. McCloskey, Dexter D. Lee and teachers union spy Buzz Skelton. Eavesdropping on the conversation among Henry's team, from the School Board's big table, was Annabella Moss.

No other Board members had yet arrived, so Henry's "brain trust" could talk openly about the overthrow of the School Board.

Thanks to a little research, Henry now knew that three seats would be up for election in April. The candidates for reelection would be Chairman McDuff and two of his strongest allies, Darlene Gazelick and Lyle Lehnherr.

"This is the perfect storm, kid," said Buzz Skelton. "All we need to do, to tip the balance on the Board, is win two outa three."

"That's right, Annie's already on our side," said Mr. McCloskey, winking at Mrs. Moss, who responded with an enigmatic smile.

"Course, Scooter's safe," said Mr. Skelton.

"He is?" asked Henry.

"Yeah, he's got the money. He's got organization. He's got the senior citizens' vote locked up, 'cause he gives all the geezers a free ride to the polls and lunch afterwards."

"He does?" asked Henry.

"But we still need three candidates," said Ray McCloskey.

"I'll run," said Dexter D. Lee.

"You can't run," said Mr. McCloskey.

"Why? Because I'm gay?"

"Yes."

"Well, that's unjust," said Dexter D. Lee. "I want a second opinion."

"Okay," said Henry, "you're ugly."

And everyone cracked up. Even Mrs. Moss laughed.

After things quieted again, Mr. Skelton said, "Look, fellas, it's early days. The deadline for filing candidates isn't 'til the 15th of February. Other than the three incumbents, we don't know about anyone planning to run for School Board."

"You mean, there are people we don't know who might run?" asked Henry.

"If they're on our side, it doesn't matter if we don't know them," said Mr. Skelton.

"I don't agree," said Mr. McCloskey.

"Well, you know me!" insisted Dexter D. Lee. "And I'm running!"

"D.D., quit kidding around," said Mr. McCloskey.

The argument continued, all around Henry, while Fantasia ducked. It stopped suddenly when Chairman Scooter McDuff arrived and took his seat.

The meeting commenced on time and moved quickly. Scooter introduced a "resolution" commending the band on its brilliant performance (with roughly 20 seconds' actual airtime) on national television in the Kaopectate Bowl. This passed unanimously. Also unanimous was another resolution congratulating the basketball Blackhawks for starting the season with nine straight victories. Scooter called it a "refreshing contrast after the sorry performance of our football team."

Henry, meanwhile, accomplished a very flattering sketch of Mrs. Moss, which he planned to give her after the meeting.

He couldn't do this, however. After about ninety minutes, Scooter rapped his gavel once and said, "That concludes the public part of our meeting."

He looked up. "Mr. McCloskey," said the Chairman. "I see that you're here."

"Yes," said Ray McCloskey. "But why ... "

"Good," said Scooter. He glanced at Superintendent of Schools Robert Ptaschnik, who sat quietly, but looking very solemn, between Myrtle Arnold and Town Counsel Charles Mulcahy. "We have a short executive session now. Mr. McCloskey, we'd like you to stay. Everyone else, please ... "

Henry got up to leave. As he started toward the exit, he looked inquiringly at Ray McCloskey, who shrugged and shook his head. He was as mystified as everyone else.

Henry was going to go home, but Dexter D. Lee stopped him and Fantasia. "I don't like the looks of this," he said. "Wait with me, kids."

For more than 45 minutes, Henry, Fantasia and Dexter D. Lee loitered in the corridor outside the library, unable to see or hear what was transpiring between Ray McCloskey and the School Board.

Finally, near ten o'clock, Charlie Mulcahy emerged. As the door swung open momentarily, Henry could hear raised voices in the library.

Charlie Mulcahy approached Dexter D. Lee. Solemnly he said, "Mr. Lee, they've dismissed Ray."

"What?" Dexter D. Lee paled with shock.

"It was against my advice," said Charlie Mulcahy.

"Because he's gay?" asked Dexter D. Lee.

Charlie Mulcahy cocked his head. "Technically, no. That wouldn't be legal," said Charlie. "They said he was parading his sexuality in front of impressionable young people."

"WHAT the HELL?" cried Fantasia.

Dexter D. Lee laughed, but there was no mirth in his laughter. "Parading?" he said. "Do you have any idea how many parades Ray has refused to go to?"

"I understand," said Charlie Mulcahy. "I warned them not to do this. But they said they were firing him on moral grounds."

Fantasia was furious. "Those, those, those ... CREEPS! DAMMIT, they can't *do* that!"

"Well, I'm afraid they did," said Mulcahy. "I'm sorry, Mr. Lee."

And with that, Charlie Mulcahy shuffled away, looking as though he was carrying a great weight.

"My God," said Dexter D. Lee.

"Those stinking, rotten, brain-dead, egg-sucking ... " Fantasia was so upset she ran out of words.

Henry was speechless, too, but mainly because this was another tragedy that he had caused. Moose had gotten kicked off the football team. Penelope and every band kid in school had become his mortal enemies. His grades were deteriorating. And now this—the worst of all unintended consequences.

A moment later, Ray McCloskey opened the library door and stepped into the corridor. For a moment, he looked pallid and shattered. But then Henry, tears in his eyes, approached him, saying, "Oh, I'm sorry. I'm sorry, Mr. McCloskey. I'm sorry, I'm sorry ... "

Confronted by so much guilt and penitence, Ray McCloskey couldn't suppress a smile. He crouched to Henry's level, grabbed the boy by the shoulders and said, "Henry, you're an egomaniac."

"What?"

"You really think you make everything happen in the world?"

"Huh? What? Me? Oh, no!"

"Well then, don't take credit for me getting fired," said Mr. McCloskey. He produced a handkerchief and handed it to Henry. "You think you're the only one in the world who irritates Darlene?"

"It was her idea?" said Fantasia.

"Well, her motion," said Ray McCloskey.

"That COW! That SOW!"

"It wasn't just Mrs. Gazelick," said Mr. McCloskey, taking Fantasia's hand, "it was a majority vote."

"Those RATS!" said Fantasia. "Those VERMIN!"

"Fantasia, excellent word," said Mr. McCloskey. He turned to Henry, "Here's the point, Henry: This was none of your doing. Darlene's been out to get me ever since she found out I'm gay. Plus, it was partly my fault. I could have kept a lower profile."

"Well, pshaw to that!" said Dexter D. Lee.

"Well, that's what I thought," said Ray McCloskey. "And look how I ended up."

"You haven't ended anything," said Dexter D. Lee.

Mr. McCloskey and Dexter D. Lee hugged for a long moment. When they were finished, Henry was still there, looking melancholy.

"I'm really sorry," he said.

"That's your last apology, young man."

"PIGfaces, that's what they are. Big fat prejudiced baconfaced pigs!" said Fantasia.

"Not all of them," said McCloskey. "The vote was three to two."

"Really?" asked Dexter D. Lee. "You got two votes?"

"Yes. Randy Zink voted to keep me."

"Ooh! You think he's gay?" asked Dexter D. Lee. Mr. McCloskey laughed.

"Hey!" said Fantasia. "Does this mean Mrs. Moss is gay?"

Even Henry laughed this time.

For some reason, it didn't seem strange to Henry that he and Fantasia and the two men were laughing their way out of the school on the night that Mr. McCloskey lost his job.

"Well, that clinches it," said Dexter D. Lee outside the school. It was a bitter cold January night and his words came out in great white puffs.

"Clinches what?" asked Mr. McCloskey.

"I'm definitely running for School Board!"

"Yay!" said Fantasia.

"Oh, dear God," said Ray McCloskey.

CHAPTER 16

7 JANUARY

The Blackhawks were walloping the Warriors from Wingra.

Darnell Fulton backed into a Wingra defender and floated a jump-hook into the basket, getting fouled in the process. The crowd erupted into the most popular cheer anyone could remember in Blackhawk.

"Mooooooooooooooooooooooooooooose!" they roared.

Then, when Moose hit the free throw to put Blackhawk ahead by fourteen points: "Mooooooooooooooooooooooooo oooose!"

From one side of the gym, the Haddocks and Fultons—when not paying heed to the game—were watching Dexter D. Lee as he worked the crowd, campaigning for School Board. It was a colorful sight. Resplendent in a lavender tam o'shanter and a maroon velvet blazer, Dexter waved his lavender scarf and cheered the Blackhawks. Then, he plopped down between two young women and flashed his nomination petition.

Observing Dexter D. Lee, Ralph Haddock smiled. This was a time of the year when a lot of recent Blackhawk High School graduates were home from college. Dexter D. Lee, probably the most charming person in the gym, was seeking them out for signatures on his petition.

"Hooray, Moose!" shouted Dexter. "You go, big boy!" Both girls signed his nomination.

Lt. Col. Lafayette Fulton leaned down from his perch in the bleachers and said, "So, Henry, my man. You've decided to put together a reform ticket for the School Board. And thus far, your only declared candidate is ... " He looked over at Dexter. " ... him?"

"Yeah," said Henry. "But he's doin' good. He's got almost all the signatures he needs."

"Well, he can't possibly win," said Lt. Col. Fulton.

"Why?" said Henry. "Because he's gay?"

"Unfortunately, yes."

"Yeah," said Henry forlornly. "I think you're right."

"Not fair," said Fantasia. "Dexter's really sweet. And funny. If people only got to know him."

"That's the problem, honey," said Delia Fulton. "If people find out someone's gay, they don't want to get to know him. They think he's ... contagious."

"Well, people are BUTTheads!"

"Not all of us," said Helen Haddock.

"Oh no, Mrs. H!" cried Fantasia. "Not you!"

"Oh, good. Glad I'm not a butthead."

Hearing Mrs. Haddock say that word made Fantasia turn a rosier shade of cocoa.

Helen Haddock started waving her own scarf—not at the game but at Dexter D. Lee. After a while, Dexter and Ray McCloskey got her message. They crossed the gym and joined the Haddock/Fulton cheering section.

Just before halftime, Amy Haddock, Tiff Melrose and the Blackhawk High School cheerleading squad dashed onto the basketball court and unfurled a banner that read, "Happy Birthday, MOOOOOOOOOOOOOSE!"

The crowd read the banner aloud, extending the third word

for at least 20 seconds. Then they sang "Happy Birthday."

Afterward, Helen Haddock turned to Delia Fulton. "It's Darnell's birthday?"

"Yes, well, tomorrow, actually. But the girls wanted to do that. I told them Moose would be embarrassed."

As she said this, Moose stepped out of the team huddle and raised both hands to the crowd.

"Embarrassed?" asked Helen Haddock.

Moose coaxed the crowd into a standing ovation.

"Well, now *I'm* embarrassed," said Delia Fulton.

"Mooooooooooooooooooooooooose!" wailed the crowd.

Moose's father stood, applauded and cheered. "Let the boy bask in his glory," he said, smiling. "You only turn eighteen once."

"He's eighteen?" said Ralph Haddock.

"Oh, yes. He was held back in second grade," said Colonel Fate. "He had what they called a developmental delay. I called it a matter of being a lazy goldbrick who couldn't read a lick. I'm glad they did it."

"He's fine now," added Delia Fulton. "His grades are very good."

"Eighteen?" said Fantasia.

"Yes, Fancy," said her mother. "You knew that."

"Eighteen," said Fantasia.

A moment later, Fantasia whispered to Henry, "Listen. I have an idea."

"What?"

She whispered it to Henry, and then said, "Don't tell anybody."

Henry immediately whispered Fantasia's idea to Mr. McCloskey, who passed it on to Dexter D. Lee, who said, "Who thought of that?"

Fantasia said, "I did."

Dexter D. Lee said, "Fantasia, you are fabulous!" He picked her up and swung her in a circle, kissing both her cheeks.

"I know I am," she replied, enjoying the ride and kissing Dexter smack on the mouth.

Dexter D. Lee tried out Fantasia's fabulous idea on a stranger beside him, who said, "Cool! Yeah. That'd be great!"

Of course, Fantasia's fabulous idea required agreement from one key party. He would not be available 'til the game was over.

This seemed to take forever. Wingra was no match for Moose, who scored 28 points and rested for the entire fourth quarter. By the time the buzzer blew, ending the game with a score of 83-61, Henry and Fantasia were on the court, poised to intercept Moose before he disappeared into the locker room.

Moose spotted his sister, lifted her up and set her on his shoulder.

"Put me down, ya big bully. Yecch! You're all sweaty. C'mon, I wanna ask you somethin'. This is IMPORTANT!"

Moose set Fantasia down.

"Okay, brat," he said. "What?"

Fantasia asked her question, whispering so that Henry couldn't hear. Henry watched Moose.

Moose's mouth formed a quizzical "O." His brow crinkled. He crouched down to face his sister. He said, "Ya think?"

"Absolutely, Spaldingface!"

"Okay. Well then. I guess that settles it!"

"Yay!" cried Fantasia, skipping around her big brother and slapping him on the sweaty butt.

Watching from the bleachers, Colonel Fate said, "Looks like he agreed."

"This better not affect his grades, Fate!" said Moose's mother.

Back down on the court, Moose said, "But first, I gotta shower."

"Yeah," said Fantasia. "Boy, you need it. Whew!"

This is how Moose Fulton, covered with perspiration, became a candidate for School Board.

"Far out," said Ray McCloskey.

By the time Moose had showered, dressed and emerged from the locker room, Amy and Tiff had composed a campaign slogan: "Choose Moose!" Later, when the crowds at Blackhawk basketball games uttered these two words, they came out sounding more like: "Choooooooooooooose Moooooooooooooooooose!"

Ralph Haddock summed up the strange new politics of Blackhawk this way: "Well, we have two candidates now. One is new in town and he happens to be gay. The other is a teenage basketball star who recently got arrested for whacking a cop. It might be a good idea for us to find a third candidate who might actually have a chance to win."

"Hey! I can win!" said Moose.

"Here, on the court, yes," said Henry's father, indicating the now almost-empty gymnasium. "Politics, Moose, is a whole different game played a whole different way."

"On the other hand," said Ray McCloskey, "Moose right now might be the most popular thing in town."

"Thing?" said Delia Fulton.

"The THING," said Fantasia, turning her hands into claws and approaching Henry, zombielike.

"Yes, but he's not exactly qualified," said Ralph Haddock.

"Or smart," said Tiff Melrose. She ducked as Moose pretended to take a swing at her.

"Qualified?" said Dexter D. Lee. "To sit on the local School Board? C'mon, Ralph. What's it take? Henry figured everything he needed to know about this job by attending one meeting. Didn't you, Henry?"

Henry said, "Well ... "

Dexter D. Lee said, "Is there anybody here who doesn't believe Henry could sit on the School Board right now, and make better judgments than the four idiots in the current majority?"

Henry felt self-conscious. Ray McCloskey said, "Dexter, my

man. You have a point."

"Yeah, Henry's the man. But Henry can't run," said Fantasia.

"I can," said Moose. "And Henry can be my coach. And Mrs. Moss, too. She always liked me."

"She did?" said Delia Fulton.

"Well, I guess that's settled," said Ralph Haddock. "How about we all go someplace for a burger?"

"Yes. We need to talk about Candidate Number Three," said Helen Haddock.

The whole gang trooped out of the gym and into the cold January night. Henry, who hadn't said much, followed behind, thinking about politics. He really liked Dexter D. Lee, but he knew a lot of people would be prejudiced against him. Moose would get a lot of votes because he was an athletic hero. But could he get enough to win?

Henry worried even more about who else was going to run for School Board, especially Candidate Number Three. Henry had an idea—a dream, really—about who that ought to be. He was the best possible candidate in the whole town. Henry wanted to go right up and ask him to run. But Henry knew he would say no. Besides, Henry respected him too much to bug him.

Henry was left with nothing to do but hope for a miracle.

He heard his father's voice across the high-school parking lot. "Henry! Hey, c'mon! It's cold out here!"

Henry shook off his anxieties and ran for the car.

CHAPTER 17

11 JANUARY

The atmosphere, for the second School Board meeting of the new year, was different. Something was in the air.

Henry Haddock, true to form, was seated right up front in the middle, armed with pens and sketchbook. On the chair beside him, as usual, was a sign that read, in large capital letters, "UNFAIR!" As always, Fantasia Fulton sat on Henry's right, glaring hatefully at Chairman Farrell McDuff every time he dared to look Fantasia in the eye.

But next to Fantasia, rather than an empty chair, there was a second sign. It proclaimed, in bold letters,

CHOOSE MOOSE!

Fantasia felt justified in displaying the sign because Darnell Fulton, the day before, had gone to City Hall and formally taken out his nomination petition for election to the School Board (and had already collected more than thirty of the one hundred signatures he needed to get on the ballot). After school that day, Curly the subversive janitor had (gladly) opened Ms. Webster's forbidden art room to Henry and Fantasia. Fantasia had been very careful handling the sign because the paint was still tacky.

Fantasia studied the three Board members up for reelection in April, Chairman McDuff, Darlene Gazelick and Lyle Lehnherr. She noted that they were all annoyed by the presence of the pro-Moose campaign sign. However, when Scooter asked Town Counsel Charlie Mulcahy if he could order the "Choose Moose!" sign removed, Charlie said no, this was a public building where public expression was entirely appropriate.

Fantasia grinned right up at Scooter McDuff.

Henry wondered why Charlie Mulcahy was there that night. Charlie only attended School Board meetings when needed to render a legal opinion. There were no legal matters on tonight's agenda.

Henry looked around. The audience was a little bigger than usual. Moose, being a candidate, was present—collecting signatures for his candidacy and praise for his 28 points against Wingra. Because Moose was there, so was Tiff, and so was Amy. The other declared "reform" candidate, Dexter D. Lee, was in the audience, along with Mr. McCloskey. In all, Henry counted fifteen people, including Darren Flack, editor of the *Weekly Argument*. Flack's appearance suggested even more strongly to Henry that something was brewing. He turned and peered into the depths of the library for the patrician presence of Paul Lamartine.

He was not there. Henry was beginning to think of Paul Lamartine as Macavity the Mystery Cat.

When Chairman McDuff whacked the table and called the meeting "to order," the audience quieted. The reading and approval of last week's minutes (not including the firing of Mr. McCloskey, which had been done in secret) went off languidly. The scene grew livelier when Scooter reached the "Correspondence" line in the agenda and said, "I have a copy of a letter from the Town Counsel to City Manager Harold Hannon."

Scooter paused. His face was as blank as the skin on a pudding.

Before he could speak, the library door burst open. In rushed Melissa McFarland of Channel 8 Eyewitness News. Her cameraman Bernie, sound woman Debbie and Speed, the light man, clattering and thumping beneath their equipment, followed noisily on her heels.

"Pardon me!" shouted Melissa McFarland. "Excuse me, Mr. Chairman!"

"Oh my God," said Lyle Lehnherr.

"TV!" Fantasia whispered joyously. "It's *her* again!"

"Something," said Dexter D. Lee just loudly enough for everyone to hear, "is *up!*"

In a matter of seconds, the skillful Channel 8 crew had established a beachhead between the third and fourth row of chairs. Speed's lights shone directly into Scooter McDuff's face. Debbie's microphone hung above his head, out of camera range. Melissa McFarland stood gazing at Chairman McDuff. Her arms were crossed, her eyes were alight with anticipation. Bernie the cameraman said a word: "Ready."

Scooter McDuff started to give Melissa McFarland a dirty look, but remembered he was on camera. He ended up looking like he had gas.

"May I?" he said to the newswoman.

Melissa McFarland nodded.

"Roll 'em," said Dexter D. Lee.

"As I was saying, I have a letter to the City Manager from Charlie Mulcahy," said Scooter. "It begins: 'Dear Harold, It is with deep regret that I am herewith submitting my resignation as Town Counsel, effectively immediately ... '"

The Chairman broke off and looked up at the audience. He said, "It goes on for another paragraph or so, but it's fairly personal. It's signed by Charles D. Mulcahy. I would move that the Board dispense with the reading of the full text."

"Second that," said Lyle Lehnherr, as though he had rehearsed.

"All in favor?" said Scooter.

Four Board members said, "Aye."

"Opposed?"

"NO!" said Annie Moss in the voice that had terrified several generations of Blackhawk schoolchildren. "Scooter, what on earth are you trying to get away with here?"

Scooter looked nervously at the Channel 8 camera, as Bernie made an adjustment and zoomed a close-up of Scooter's kisser.

Before Scooter could say anything or even gavel Annabella Moss to silence, Charlie Mulcahy rose to his feet from his place beside Superintendent Ptaschnik.

"Mr. Chairman," he said.

"Yes? Oh! Charlie," said Chairman McDuff, looking over his glasses at the Town Counsel.

"I'd like to speak, Mr. Chairman."

The camera swung toward Charlie.

Scooter's eyes seemed for a moment to lose their moorings, wandering around their sockets like gerbils on a treadmill. But he recovered and said, "Um, well, Charlie ... no! I can't allow that. Since you're no longer Town Counsel ... "

Bernie smoothly panned to Scooter, but returned to Charlie as he spoke again.

"No, Scooter," he said. "I am Town Counsel, 'til the Board of Aldermen meets tomorrow night and accepts my resignation."

"Oh," said the Chairman. "Right."

"As Town Counsel, Mr. Chairman, I insist on my privilege of addressing the Board."

Scooter McDuff slumped in his chair and shrugged. "Well,

okay, Charlie. G'head."

Charlie Mulcahy returned to his seat, put his elbows on the table and leaned forward. Channel 8 zoomed in. "Mr. Chairman, I have a copy of my letter to Mr. Hannon. Whether you read it or not, I intend to share its contents with the press after this meeting. And I'll read it aloud to anyone interested in hearing me. Besides, Scooter, it's part of the public record, whether or not you read it out tonight, the Board of Aldermen will do so tomorrow night."

Channel 8 took a quick look back at Scooter.

"Okay, okay, okay," said McDuff. "We'll read the darn letter." He looked to his left and shoved the letter into Annabella Moss' hands. "Here, Annie. You're the Board secretary. You read it."

"Very well, Mr. Chairman."

The Channel 8 camera had a new star. Mrs. Moss was wearing a charming little faux-fur hat, dyed dusty rose, with a cameo pin. Her earrings matched the pin and her cardigan matched the rose-colored hat.

The key passage of Charlie Mulcahy's letter, read with perfect diction by Annabella Moss and recorded word-for-word by Debbie, the sound woman, was as follows: "My resignation became necessary when the School Board, on 4 January, against my advice, chose by a three-to-two vote to dismiss Mr. Raymond McCloskey from his position as a teacher at the middle school. I warned the Board that their moral objection to Mr. McCloskey's so-called 'lifestyle' violates not only the contract between the school system and the Blackhawk Education Association, but also flouts state laws against employment discrimination based on race, religion, gender, disability or *sexual orientation*. In good conscience, I could not retain my position as Town Counsel, which would force me to defend this ill-conceived decision by the Board ... "

At this point, the reading was interrupted.

"Goodness me!" said Dexter D. Lee. "You go, Charlie!"

For a moment, the laughter in the library competed with the whanging of Scooter's gavel. Bernie widened his angle, capturing the whole scene for Channel 8's 10 o'clock news viewers.

While Mrs. Moss finished reading the letter, Darren Flack crept forward with his camera and took pictures of Charlie Mulcahy beside Superintendent Ptaschnik. He also snapped a shot of Scooter McDuff, looking flushed and waving his gavel threateningly. He even sneaked a photo of Melissa McFarland.

After that, the meeting resumed its customary tedium. Melissa McFarland took a seat. Debbie, Bernie and Speed withdrew to a distant library table.

Soon, Charlie Mulcahy stood, nodded toward the Board members, paused to shake Superintendent Ptaschnik's hand and proceeded quietly toward the exit. As he departed, he caught the eye of Darren Flack.

Charlie Mulcahy conferred with the *Argument* editor for about ten minutes in the recesses of the library. No one could hear them, but everybody knew they were talking. Melissa McFarland watched them like a cat stalking a dove.

People started to suspect that Flack and Charlie weren't just discussing Charlie's resignation.

Buzz Skelton turned to Ray McCloskey. "Something's up," he said.

"I toldja," whispered Dexter D. Lee.

The meeting droned on.

Charlie Mulcahy left the building, followed by Channel 8. Darren Flack returned hurriedly to his place at the back of the gallery. He shouldered his camera bag and turned to leave. Buzz Skelton stopped him and asked a question. But Darren Flack was a journalist with a deadline. He just smiled at Buzz and headed toward the exit.

With that, Buzz Skelton bolted from the library, beating Darren Flack to the exit and galloping toward the parking lot.

"Where's he going?" Dexter D. Lee asked Ray McCloskey.

"After Charlie," said Mr. McCloskey. He, too, headed toward the door.

Moose said to Tiff, "Well then, me, too!" And Moose split, followed by Tiff, followed by Amy.

All these departures caused a small commotion. Chairman McDuff pounded the table. "Could we have a little order here, people?" he shouted. He was greeted by the thunk of the library door as Amy rushed to catch up to Tiff, Moose, Mr. McCloskey, Buzz Skelton, Charlie Mulcahy and Channel 8.

The School Board meeting proceeded with all signs of normalcy. But suspense hung in the air. Ten minutes passed. Then eleven, twelve, thirteen.

At last, led by Ray McCloskey—all of them rubbing their arms and blowing into their hands after all that time in the frigid parking lot—everyone except Charlie Mulcahy and Channel 8 returned.

Something was *up*, and they all knew what it was.

As Dexter D. Lee, Myrtle Arnold, Superintendent Ptaschnik, the members of the School Board and the rest of the audience beheld the faces of Ray McCloskey, Buzz Skelton, Tiff, Moose and Amy, it was as though they were looking right into the smug whiskers of a klaven of cats who had just eaten a flock of doves.

"So? Whassup?" whispered Dexter D. Lee to Mr. McCloskey.

Ray McCloskey whispered an answer.

"Really?" exclaimed Dexter D. Lee, not whispering. "And he said it on TV?"

Mr. McCloskey nodded, his smile distinctly feline.

"Hallelujah!" said Dexter D. Lee.

Scooter's gavel banged in response.

In response to that, Dexter D. Lee, accompanied by Moose, Tiff, Amy and Buzz Skelton, whispered the news to everyone in the audience, who began to murmur, smile, clap and make just enough noise to raise the Chairman's hackles.

Since the news traveled from back row to front row, Fantasia and Henry were the last to hear. Henry's only reaction was to drop his pencil. Fantasia jumped from her chair, danced in a circle, pumped her fist and said, audibly, "Yesssss!"

This drew another gavel blow from Scooter and a curious glance from Annie Moss. Fantasia noticed.

As fast as she could, Fantasia found a piece of notebook paper in Henry's backpack, borrowed his pencil, and wrote a note. Then, her back as straight as a broomstick and her chin high, Fantasia Fulton strode across the gap between the gallery and the School Board. She paused to scowl once more at Chairman McDuff, then turned to Annie Moss. Fantasia's face softened and she smiled as she passed her note.

"Thank you, Fantasia," said Annabella Moss.

The Chairman stood up, mainly to scare Fantasia—which didn't work. "Mrs. Moss, this sort of fraternization with the audience is completely out of order," said Scooter.

"Oh, Scooter," said Annie Moose. "Don't be such a fathead. Sit back down."

Then, she read the note. "Oh," she said, "wonderful."

With that, Mrs. Moss returned the note to Fantasia, indicating wordlessly that Fantasia should deliver it to Myrtle Arnold and the superintendent. Fantasia did this.

So, by the time the meeting ended just after 10 p.m., the only people in the library unaware that Charlie Mulcahy had decided to run for School Board were School Board members McDuff, Gazelick, Lehnherr and Zink.

But Annie Moss told them immediately.

"Ooh!" said Darlene Gazelick. "That turncoat!"

CHAPTER 18

15 FEBRUARY

Henry Haddock looked around the Blackhawk High School gym in wonder.

"Looka this!" said Fantasia Fulton. "Hot DAMN!"

"Curb your tongue, young lady," said Lt. Col. Lafayette Fulton.

Much had transpired in the month since Charlie Mulcahy told Darren Flack and Channel 8 that he was joining Moose Fulton and Dexter D. Lee on the School Board reform ticket. For example, Lt. Col. Lafayette Fulton, in a burst of fatherly pride, had financed the professional printing of hundreds of "CHOOSE MOOSE!" lawn signs.

Then, a funny thing happened. No sooner did a Moose supporter plant a "CHOOSE MOOSE!" placard on the front lawn than it disappeared. Eventually, most of the stolen "CHOOSE MOOSE!" signs showed up at Blackhawk High basketball games, both at home and away. Colonel Fate ended up ordering a whole new batch to replace the stolen signs. Sure enough, most of the replacement signs were swiped. Nobody, however, was really upset at all this petty larceny.

"Everybody loves Moose," said his little sister, waving her own sign and blocking the view of the people behind her.

"That's nice," said Colonel Fate. "But I'm going broke printing campaign signs."

"Daddy, they're not campaign signs," said Fantasia. "They're Valentines!"

"This interpretation, child, does not console me."

Tonight, the gym, as usual, was a sea of "CHOOSE MOOSE!" placards. Mixed in were about twenty signs that read: "D.D. LEE!" In one corner of the gym, a small stubborn cluster of grim-looking fans was holding up signs that read: "Reelect SCOOTER."

Never before had a School Board election race migrated to the bleachers at Blackhawk High. And no one could decide whether mixing basketball with politics was a good idea.

Ralph Haddock's verdict: "Couldn't hurt."

The game tonight was against Blackhawk's mortal enemy, Wolf Creek. The Werewolves, who had lost only two league games, had defeated the Blackhawks two weeks before. So far, that was Blackhawk's only loss. With the season winding down, tonight's game amounted to the league championship. The gym was overflowing. Fans teetered on the brink of hysteria.

By leading the team to victory after victory, Moose had atoned for his expulsion from the football team. Tiff Melrose proudly proclaimed that Moose was "the most popular person in town—ever."

One Saturday night over pizza, Tiff proclaimed that Moose was the veritable apple of Blackhawk's eye. Moose cast his eyes downward in an "Aw shucks" sort of way, and Lt. Col. Lafayette Fulton rang a sobering note: "That may be true, young lady. But how much of that celebrity will translate into votes?"

Fantasia noticed that most of the people in the gym that

night holding up "CHOOSE MOOSE!" signs were students. None were old enough to vote.

"Oh, but grownups love Moose, too," was Tiff's usual defense.

"Maybe so," replied Colonel Fate, who enjoyed playing devil's advocate with idealistic young people. "But the incumbents are saying that Darnell is a dumb jock, too young to hold public office. If the boy doesn't make a good impression at the Candidates Forum next month, it won't matter how many points he scores tonight, or even if we beat Wolf Creek."

"Oh, you're just a stiff-necked old killjoy," Tiff said.

Colonel Fate couldn't help smiling at that and saying, "My enlisted men often say the same sort of thing. But not to my face."

The School Board battle was the only hotly contested race in Blackhawk's spring elections. But so far, the campaign had been low-key. This was partly because it was still early in the campaign. People in Blackhawk normally didn't start thinking about politics 'til March. Also, townspeople had been distracted by the best basketball team they ever had. Moose was averaging 25 points, leading the league in rebounds, blocking a half-dozen shots a game and making headlines all over the state.

There had been one political surprise. A mysterious candidate named Joyce Tweedy had filed School Board papers at the last minute. Nobody seemed to know anything about her. After she announced her candidacy, she started attending Board meetings, where Ray McCloskey sat down beside her and asked a few questions.

Mr. McCloskey told Henry later that Joyce Tweedy was "medieval." She had two children, ages eight and six, but didn't allow them in school. She thought public schools were "immoral." She said the whole School Board was "ultraliberal." She told the *Weekly Argument* that her goals were to replace evolution with creationism in the science curriculum, separate boys from girls in every class, dress all students in "modest school uniforms," purge the library of "vile and blasphemous books" and start every school day with a prayer, the Pledge of Allegiance, the Ten Commandments and everyone singing "God Bless America."

"So," said Henry. "She's a nut."

"Yes, but she's a good nut," said Ray McCloskey. "She won't get many votes, but all the votes she gets are votes that would normally go to Scooter, Darlene and Lyle. Especially Darlene."

"Really?"

"Judging from her beliefs, Mrs. Tweedy's appeal is to people who hate school and love church. She's calling out to purists."

"Purists?" asked Henry.

"Yes, people who are *pure*. They have absolute, unbreakable principles. They believe that any compromise is a betrayal of one's deepest convictions. For true believers, compromise is a sin," said McCloskey. "Now, Darlene and Lyle are also conservative. But they're not purists. They make deals. They play politics. They compromise."

"But Mrs. Tweedy doesn't compromise?"

"Well, that's what she seems to be saying."

"So, all the purists will vote for her," said Henry.

"If there are any, yes, they will," said Mr. McCloskey.

"Well, there must be some!" said Fantasia Fulton.

"Let's hope so," said Ray McCloskey.

"So," said Henry, "even though she's crazy, we like her?"

"We love her."

"Politics," said Henry, "is weird."

"You can say that again, kid."

"Politics is weird."

Tonight, besides being the big game, was a School Board night. Henry knew he should be at the meeting, but he couldn't resist Moose's grand showdown with Wolf Creek. Besides, he loved the sight of all those signs and the sound of a thousand people wailing, "Choooose Moooose!" every time the six-foot eight-inch candidate scored.

Five minutes before tip-off, Fantasia grabbed Henry by the arm, almost yanking it right off his shoulder, "Oh my GOD!" she said, "Looka THAT!"

Henry looked. What he saw was Band Director W.C. Wilcox, tall and bald in the blue-serge suit that he always seemed to wear. He led a contingent of about twenty band members into the gym. They quickly began to set up instruments and music stands on an open patch of floor beyond the far bleachers. After a few experimental tootles and blats from the musicians, Wally Wilcox raised his arms, swung them forward, tapped three times with his toe and launched the debut of his miniband (the Thundering Two Dozen?) with a rousing version of "Hey, Look Me Over!"

For a moment, the entire gymful of fans was thunderstruck. But soon they were swaying with the music. Afterward, they clapped wildly.

As Wally's new pep band shuffled hurriedly through sheet music for their next number, Helen Haddock tapped her son on the arm. "Henry," she said, "you did that."

"Did what?"

"You shamed that old fossil into playing for the basketball team," said Helen Haddock. "This is the first time we've had a pep band since ... well, I don't know when."

"Nah," scoffed Henry Haddock. "I didn't do that."

"You sure did, Henry," said Ralph Haddock.

"Indeed the boy did, but ... " said Colonel Fate.

"But what?" asked Fantasia.

"We might've gained a little entertainment at the game," said Colonel Fate. "But we've lost a campaign issue."

"Whaddya mean by that, old man?" asked Fantasia.

Henry broke in, "He's right, Fance. We made a big stink about how the band gets a lot of money and then they use it to leave town and play at football games in Texas. Right?"

"Oh," said Fantasia.

"Yeah, well," said Henry. "The band's not in Texas anymore."

Fantasia scowled. "Oooh, that's really sneaky."

With that, the pep band broke into a brassy arrangement of "Johnny B. Goode," including a solo by Eric Wallis (one of Moose's football buddies) playing an instrument no one had ever seen before among the Thundering Three Hundred—an electric guitar. Fans started to dance in the bleachers.

"I hate to admit it," said Ray McCloskey. "But they sound great."

Wally Wilcox, looking very pleased with himself, kept the pep band playing at every break in the game. He conducted a halftime concert featuring ABBA's greatest hits. The music seemed to inspire the home team, especially Moose.

Early in the game, Moose ran his offense straight at the Wolf Creek center, a bruiser named Diggs. Early in the second quarter, Diggs committed his third foul, forcing him to the bench. From then on, Moose was unstoppable. He ended up with forty points in an anticlimactic 84-67 win.

The racket, as people filed out of the gym, was deafening. Half the crowd (led by Amy and Tiff) continued to chant, "Choose Moose! Choose Moose! Choose Moose!" at the top of their lungs. The pep band fought back by blasting out "Old-Time Rock 'n' Roll" and "When the Saints Go Marchin' In."

From the gym to the high-school library—where the School Board was still in session—was not far to go. Henry was hoping to keep the Board from doing something crafty and underhanded behind his back. As he was about to barrel through the library door, he screeched to a halt because—just ahead—tall, elegant and unmistakable, stood none other than Lamartine the Mystery Cat.

"Uh oh," said Henry to himself.

"It's him," said Fantasia, catching up.

"Well, well," said Paul Lamartine, turning and looking all

the way down the length of his nose until his eyes lit on Henry and Fantasia. "You young people are late tonight."

"We were, um," mumbled Henry, "at the game."

"Of course," said Paul Lamartine, his voice far above. "Did we win?"

"Yeah. We kicked their hairy butts, Paul," said Fantasia. She crossed her arms and stared up fearlessly at the richest man in town.

Lamartine stepped back, opening the door. "Well, after you, young lady," he said. "And you, too, Mr. Haddock."

They went in. Seeing Paul Lamartine, Scooter McDuff smiled and said, "Oh, good. Hello, Paul. We're just coming around to new business."

He tapped the gavel.

"Lady and gentlemen of the Board," he said, "I'd like to welcome Mr. Paul Lamartine, to address us on a matter of importance."

Henry and Fantasia found seats beside Charlie Mulcahy. "What matter?" said Henry suspiciously.

"Hello, Fantasia, Henry," said Charlie.

Henry and Fantasia greeted the former Town Counsel, who said, "I don't know what's going on. But if it brought Lamartine out of hiding, it'll probably be a humdinger."

The Board voted unanimously to "suspend the rules," allowing Paul Lamartine to speak.

"Yeah, right," grumbled Henry. "They never suspended their stinkin' rules for me."

Paul Lamartine cleared his throat softly and began. "Much to my sorrow," he said, "the high-school band, our beloved Thundering Three Hundred, has lately become a subject of public controversy. I know everyone in town is proud of the band. But as you know well, Mr. Chairman, a marching band of such supreme excellence is a costly proposition."

"It certainly is, Paul," replied Scooter. "You're right about that."

"Aren't they cozy?" said Ray McCloskey, who had just arrived with Dexter D. Lee. They sat down behind Henry.

"Ya think they're gay?" said Dexter D. Lee.

Fantasia giggled. Charlie Mulcahy, smiling, said, "Ssh."

Paul Lamartine continued: "Yes, well, Mr. Chairman, frankly I agree with several of the School Board candidates who are demanding that the Board reduce its funding for the band."

"You do?" said Annabella Moss.

"He does?" whispered Dexter D. Lee.

"Yes, I do indeed," said Paul Lamartine.

"Check out Scooter," said Ray McCloskey. "Cool as the other side of the pillow. He knew this was coming."

"On the other hand, reducing the band budget by as much as 50 percent—which has been proposed by my bright young friend, Mr. Haddock—well, that's going too far. A cut that large would destroy the band as we've come to know and love it," said Paul Lamartine. "I mean, how would that sound: the Thundering One Hundred and Fifty?"

"How about the Dundering Dozen?" muttered Dexter D. Lee.

"Lamartine's got something up his sleeve," whispered Charlie.

Lamartine continued: "Reluctant though I am to intrude on public matters, I felt it was my civic duty to intervene, in hopes of solving this problem."

"Here it comes," said Ray McCloskey.

"So I met with Wally—rather, Walter C. Wilcox, the band director, truly one of Blackhawk's great men."

"Yes, he is," said Chairman McDuff.

"I think I'm gonna puke," said Fantasia.

"Hush," said Charlie.

Lamartine was still talking. "And I suggested to Wally that, considering its size, its budget and its extraordinary value to this community as an artistic institution, the Thundering

Three Hundred should be reorganized as a nonprofit corporation, with a board of directors composed of prominent local leaders."

"Huh?" Henry whispered.

"What's he saying?" said Dexter D. Lee.

"This is clever," said Charlie Mulcahy. "Pay attention."

Paul Lamartine said, "Mr. Chairman, as you know, right now, the school budget provides the band a certain annual stipend, and that amount—every year—is matched dollar-for-dollar by the heroic fundraising efforts of the Band Parents Association. My proposal is to simply continue that arrangement, but without any demands on the school budget. The Band Parents will continue to raise money with concerts and car washes, bake sales and raffles. And I will personally match every dollar they raise."

"What's that mean?" said Fantasia.

Charlie Mulcahy shook his head. "It means he's turning our high-school band into an arts charity, like the Boston Symphony or the Metropolitan Opera."

"Metropoliple what?" said Fantasia.

"Far out," said Ray McCloskey.

"Wait a minute," said Henry. "He's gonna pay for half the band budget?"

Charlie Mulcahy nodded.

"But that's $425,000!" whispered Henry. "He's *that rich?*"

"Apparently," whispered Mr. McCloskey, "he's that rich."

"Besides, Henry," added Charlie, "he'll be able to write off every nickel on his taxes. If the band is a nonprofit arts organization, whatever Paul pays is a great big, fat charitable contribution."

"Far out," said Henry and Ray McCloskey, in unison.

The School Board ended up talking back and forth for more than an hour with Paul Lamartine. Of course, the members were not prone to look a gift horse in the mouth. They promised to surrender the school system's control of the band and all its activities to the Band Parents Association, and to something that was going to be called the Thundering Three Hundred Music and Artistic Foundation.

"Artistic? ArTIStic?!" hissed Fantasia. "Artistic, my ASS!"

On the highway just outside of Blackhawk, there was a 24-hour pancake house, the All-State Truck Stop Diner. After the School Board meeting, which had gone on 'til almost midnight, Henry's reform campaign convened there, including all three candidates and Annabella Moss.

"This is well past my bedtime," said Annie Moss. "Do they have beer here?"

Everybody got pancakes. The grownups ordered beer and Mrs. Moss said, "Charlie, what's it all mean?"

"It means that we don't have the band to kick around any longer," said Charlie. "My guess is that Wally will be free to go on running the band just the way he always has. I'm sure the band will still be allowed to practice on the middle-school football field. And there will still be a band room at the high school. But financially, the band is no longer part of the school system."

"Can they do that?" said Henry.

"They're doing it," said Charlie.

"Wait a minute," said Henry. "Tonight, the band played at the game. I mean, part of the band was there."

"I heard about that," said Charlie. "Also a smart move."

"Yeah, but they only did it," said Henry, "'cause we kept sayin' that the band's our band, but *our* band never shows up at *our* school."

"Henry, if this scheme goes through," said Charlie Mulcahy, "our band won't be our band anymore. It will be a separate organization. It'll be Wally Wilcox's band and Paul Lamartine's band. And you'll be in no position to complain about where they go or what they do."

"Is that true?" said Fantasia.

"That's about the size of it," said Charlie.

"Far out," said Ray McCloskey.

"Stop saying that," said Dexter D. Lee.

"Okay, so, Paul Lamartine's gonna buy the band. And the town doesn't have to pay anything?" asked Henry.

"That's right," said Ray McCloskey. "The band's budget used to be our big campaign issue. But it just disappeared. Abracadabra!"

"Does that mean the band is going to disappear from games?" asked Moose.

"My guess? Wally's little miniband will probably keep playing 'til the end of the season, Moose," said Ray McCloskey. "It's good politics. By suddenly showing up at basketball games, Wilcox looks like he's doing the whole town a big favor."

"Everybody knows that Wally and Scooter have been friends all their lives," added Annie Moss. "People will make the connection: A vote for Scooter is a vote for more fun at the game."

"Boy," said Henry, adding a little maple syrup to his blueberry pancakes, "are we in trouble."

"So," said Fantasia, looking up at the grownups, "politics just comes down to who has the most money?"

The grownups looked around at one another. But none of them ventured an answer.

CHAPTER 19

19 FEBRUARY

For the second time in his political career, Henry Haddock was ready to give up. He had aimed his entire School Board reform campaign at the world's most wasteful and extravagant high-school band. He had argued, astutely, that by reducing the band's bloated budget, the school system could afford to hire back a bunch of teachers.

That was the plan. But thanks to the meddling of the richest man in town, the bloated band budget wasn't an election issue any longer. It wasn't even *there*.

It was gone.

Paul Lamartine had outflanked Henry, and Henry had no "Plan B." Henry's candidates, Moose Fulton, Dexter D. Lee and Charlie Mulcahy, were DOA.

Henry, worn out by the ups and downs of politics, was ready to give up and go back to baseball. But, apparently unaware of Henry's total defeat, lots of people were still (strangely) bursting with hope and enthusiasm about the dumb campaign. This mass delusion reared up before Henry on Friday night at, where else? Another basketball game.

Blackhawk was playing its last home game of the season. While the Blackhawks hammered the Walleyes from Castle Rock, the bleachers were a rippling sea of "CHOOSE MOOSE!" signs, highlighted by a "MOOOOOOOOSE" banner that ran the whole length of the basketball court. There were also many "D.D. LEE" signs and a few that read "Mulcahy for School Board."

Henry attended the game. He saw it all. But in the middle of this Moose-loving mosh pit, Henry Haddock could hear the terrible truth. Drowning out even the loudest cheers came the sound of Wally Wilcox's new pep band. The music was funded entirely by Paul Lamartine, the coldblooded tycoon who also happened to be financing the reelection of Scooter, Darlene and Lyle. The pep band might sound like they were playing "Born to Be Wild" and "Sweet Home Alabama," but to Henry, it was the Scooter McDuff Victory March.

On Saturday, Henry retired to his room, where he searched the internet for places to escape—Albania, Argentina, Aruba, sweet home Alabama. But then, inevitably, his mother barged in and flicked off the computer. She ordered him downstairs, to help get ready for the pizza party.

Party? What party? Henry thought cynically. More like a funeral. Maybe the Thundering Three Hundred should come over and play "Nearer My God to Thee" over the putrefying corpse of Henry Haddock's innocence.

Henry wished he could lock the house and cancel the party. He didn't want to face all those people and own up to his failure. He knew now that getting a lot of kids interested in a political campaign—kids who COULD NOT VOTE—might be fun, for a while. But it was also a surefire formula for defeat. Humiliation. Disgrace.

Of course, Henry obeyed his mother. He went downstairs to a still mostly empty house. Henry sat down at the dining-room table and buried his face in his hands. Penelope appeared.

Oh, great! thought Henry. She's come to gloat.

"Henry," said his sister.

Henry looked her in the eye, ready to be ridiculed. He deserved it.

"Truce," said Penelope.

Not the word Henry expected. "Huh?" he said.

"Mom said you gave up on your evil plan to wipe the band off the face of the earth."

"Well, I was never planning to—"

"I know that, Henry. But we were still on opposite sides. And I had to fight for my side. I'm in the band."

"Uh huh."

"Well, so we don't have to fight anymore, Henry. Mom said the band is safe. Things are gonna be the same as always."

"Yeah, I guess so," said Henry. He didn't tell Penelope that the band was only "safe" as long as its new "owner," Paul Lamartine, felt like paying the bills. Henry kept this to himself. He didn't want to pick a new fight with his sister.

"So," said Penelope, sticking out her hand. "Truce."

"Sure," said Henry. He shook.

"Good!" said Penelope. Having done her duty, she flounced away, humming the title tune to "Hello, Dolly," which was the Thundering Three Hundred's main theme in its upcoming performance at the state marching-band tournament. Since Penelope had been humming the very same song for the last month, Henry was grateful when she left the room. But the song turned into an earworm, lingering stubbornly in his head.

"... You're lookin' swell, Dolly

"I can tell, Dolly ... "

Suddenly, something about this preposterously happy tune started Henry thinking.

By the time Moose Fulton had arrived with Tiff and six of Tiff's BFFs, along with Dexter D. Lee and Ray McCloskey, followed by Fantasia with her parents and Sarge the dog and eight middle-school friends, and the dining room was packed and noisy and redolent of pepperoni (with a hint of anchovy), Henry was still thinking.

The pizza party raged all around Henry Haddock as he reached out to Sarge with a half-eaten slice of thin-crust sausage-and-mushrooms. The pizza disappeared into Sarge in a fraction of a second.

“Wait a minute,” Henry suddenly said to nobody.

“Yes?” Dexter D. Lee was the only person close enough to hear Henry.

“We’re not dead,” said Henry with more volume.

“Who said we were?” asked Ray McCloskey.

Henry didn’t answer because he was interrupted by the arrival of Charlie Mulcahy, the “guest of honor,” and his wife, Maribel. Charlie shook hands with all the grown-ups, except for Henry’s mother. Charlie kissed Helen Haddock on the cheek, as usual, because they had been friends all the way back to kindergarten.

Henry wondered if he would be friends with Fantasia as long as his mother and Charlie. He hoped so. But kissing her?

Twenty minutes later, Charlie Mulcahy brought a plateful of pizza and a bottle of beer, and sat down beside Henry. They said hello and then Dexter D. Lee, on the other side of Henry, spoke to Charlie.

“Henry was expressing the opinion that we’re not dead.”

Charlie looked severely at Henry. “Who said we were?”

“Well,” said Henry sheepishly, “I thought we were dead, for a while. Because I thought politics should be like school. But it’s not like school.”

“Like school? Whaddya mean, like school?” said Penelope Haddock. She was across the table, eavesdropping.

“Well, okay,” said Henry. “In school, you pass all your tests, and you do your homework and you write all your book reports and stuff, and then you get whatever grade you earned. I mean, if politics was school, I'd be getting an A and we'd be winning."

"Henry, what're you talking about?" said Penelope.

"I see what you mean, Henry," said Charlie Mulcahy.

"Well, I don't!" said Penelope.

"Look, tomatosauceface," said Henry, talking down to his elder sister. "In school, if you're the best student in your class, okay?, the teacher gives you an A and says you're the best, right? She puts your name up and sticks a gold star next to it. But in politics, being the best and the smartest and even the teacher's pet—that doesn't mean you get the gold star. Matter of fact, working your butt off to be an A student might be the worst thing you could do."

"Henry, I'm still not getting it," said Penelope.

"Wait for it," said Charlie Mulcahy, smiling.

Henry said, "Okay, if you had politics in school, here's what would happen. Let's say I'm having the best semester of my life and I'm at the top of the class. And it's the last day and the teacher's about to announce everybody's grades. And I'm sittin' there in the front row expecting my A-plus. But then—at the last minute—okay, there's this slob in the back row who's been absent half the semester, and even when he comes to school all he does is throw spitballs and make fart noises. He hasn't passed one quiz or answered one question. But suddenly, he stands up and says 'I'll give everybody a hundred bucks if you vote to give me an A-plus. Oh, and another thing: You also have to vote to give Henry an F. And everybody thinks about this for maybe two seconds and they all go, 'Hey, cool. For a hundred bucks? Sure!' And the teacher says, 'Well, this is America! I gotta go along with democracy,' and she says 'Henry, too bad. Everybody voted and you just flunked!'"

"Well, that's not fair," said Penelope.

"Yes, but it's politics," said Charlie Mulcahy.

"But Henry. Weren't you just saying that you've changed your mind, and you're done with all that?" said Ray McCloskey.

"Well, partly," said Henry. "I still think politics can really be unfair. But it doesn't have to be."

"That's also true," said Charlie Mulcahy. "Very good, Henry."

"So, we're not dead? You still think we can win?" said Mr. McCloskey.

"Yeah," said Henry, smiling like Satchmo and singing off-key. "We're still glowin', we're still growin', we're still goin' strong."

"Okay, Henry, let's be realistic. What are the odds. Do you really think we can beat Lamartine's money?" asked Ray McCloskey.

"I think we can win," said Henry, "*because* of Lamartine's money."

Ray McCloskey was smiling. He urged Henry along. "You're going to have to explain that, Henry."

"Well, Mr. Lamartine saved the School Board $425,000, right?"

"Yes."

"They were going to spend it all on the band," said Henry. "But now they don't have to. Right?"

"True," said Dexter D. Lee.

"All that money is still, like, in the bank, right?"

"Right."

"So," asked Henry, "what're they gonna do with it."

"Yeah," said Moose, joining the conversation. "What *are* they gonna do with a-a-all that money?"

"Ah, now here's a question I can answer," said Charlie Mulcahy.

Charlie, who had a knack for catching people's attention, had everyone's attention.

Charlie Mulcahy smiled. He said, "I took the trouble to buzz Lyle Lehnherr. (He and I are both deacons at Immaculate Heart.) And I asked him. 'Lyle,' I said, 'that's a big windfall you just got. Four hundred twenty-five grand. What on earth are you going to buy?' And you know what Lyle said?"

"I bet I know," said Henry.

"I don't. What did he say?" asked Lt. Col. Lafayette Fulton, who was hovering over Henry's left shoulder.

"Well," said Charlie, "Lyle said exactly what I expected him to say."

"Yeah, well, what was that?" Fantasia said with a note of impatience. "Wha'd he say?"

"Lyle said they weren't going to spend any of it."

"Not gonna spend it?" said Moose.

"Not a penny," said Charlie.

"I don't get it," said Moose.

"Well, I do," said Fantasia.

"I don't," said Fantasia's mother. "Charlie, please."

"It's simple," said Charlie. "Lyle's plan—which the rest of the Board apparently agrees to—"

"Except Annie Moss!" came a voice from the doorway.

Annabella Moss stepped into the dining room, removing her coat. Everyone greeted her effusively. She demanded a glass of dry red wine and received it immediately from Henry's mother. Then she spoke.

"Charlie, excuse me for busting in on you. Please, spit it out."

Charlie, who was one of Annabella Moss' many former pupils, said, "Yes, Mrs. Moss." Then he looked at Henry. "Lyle wants to save all that band money this year and apply it to next year's school budget. That will reduce the budget next year by $425,000 and everybody in town will get a little bit of a tax cut."

"How much of a tax cut do you get with $425,000?" demanded Ralph Haddock.

Charlie smiled. "When you spread it all around, it doesn't come to much," he said. "But that's not important. Everybody kind of loses their mind when you promise to cut their taxes."

"Oh, bosh!" said Annabella Moss. "While they're promising

to cut a few pennies in taxes, why don't they admit that they're cutting the heart out of the children's education."

Charlie smiled again. "Mrs. Moss, I wish they would."

"We can," said Henry. "Why don't we?"

Everyone stared at Henry Haddock.

"Why don't we tell them that the schools were crummy this year, and next year they're gonna be crummier."

They still stared.

"Okay, what's wrong with that?" asked Henry.

Annie Moss said, "Nothing, Henry. You're right. It's been a crummy year. We cut the budget. We fired good, gifted, wonderful teachers. We cut programs. We took away part of the curriculum. We cheated our children. Cheated them."

Now, people were staring at Annie Moss.

Moose, after a moment, broke the silence.

"I think we should go with Henry's plan."

"What plan?" asked Fantasia.

"Yeah," said Henry. "What plan?"

"We tell the truth," said Moose.

Everybody waited for more.

Moose said, "Okay. We tell the voters we cheated the kids—like Mrs. Moss said. And we tell 'em we need more money if we wanna stop cheating the kids. I mean, I'm running for School Board. So I should be telling everybody that if I'm elected, I'll raise the money. But ... "

Moose looked perplexed.

"But what, budgetface?" said Fantasia.

"Mr. Mulcahy," said Moose, "how do we do that? Where do we get the money?"

"It's always the same, Moose. Whether it's schools or public works or the public library. When the cost of everyday stuff—like paper clips and fire hoses—goes up, you raise taxes a little bit. For big stuff—like a new fire engine or new rain gutters all along Main Street—you borrow a lump sum. That's called a bond issue. Trouble is, the School Board or the Board of

Aldermen can't authorize a bond issue by themselves. The whole town has to vote for it."

"Or against it," said Colonel Fate.

"A referendum," said Penelope Haddock.

"A plebiscite," said Dexter D. Lee, grinning.

"That's fine. It's fair!" said Moose. "So we go out and tell the voters the truth. If they want good schools instead of crummy schools, if they want their kids to go to college and get good jobs, then we all gotta spend a little more money. Taxes. Referendums. Whatever."

"A daring platform," said Dexter D. Lee. "Truth and taxes."

"Sounds pretty bad," said Delia Fulton. "Like fear and loathing."

"Scylla and Charybdis," added Annie Moss.

"Well, it's Henry's idea," said Moose.

"Hey. Don't blame me," said Henry.

"Well, you thought of it, Henry," said Moose.

"Let me get this straight," said Colonel Fate. "Darnell, you say you want to go out in public and tell voters the truth? And then you're going to raise their taxes?"

"Not much," said Moose. "Just enough."

"Just enough," said Ralph Haddock, smiling. "Maybe that should be your campaign slogan."

"Son, you're out of your mind," Colonel Fate told Moose.

"Well now, Colonel, not so fast. I agree that this approach is crazy," said Charlie Mulcahy. "But it just might work."

"Charlie, you're out of your mind, too," said Moose's father.

"I think I just admitted that," said Charlie.

Over the next two hours, Henry and his candidates hammered out a four-point plan.

Point #1 was: Keep $425,000, formerly assigned to the band, in the school budget. Use it to bring back seven or eight teachers right away.

Point #2 was: Increase next year's school budget enough

to hire back all the fired teachers and restore all the lost programs.

Point #3 was: Pay for the budget increases with a bond issue that would be on the ballot in the fall election.

Point #4 was: Tell the truth. Tell everybody about Points #1-3, how much it will cost and how to pay for it.

Fantasia Fulton proposed a fifth point. "I want Mr. McCloskey to get his job back."

Charlie Mulcahy said, "Fantasia, I'm already working on that—in court. I went down to the capital and filed a complaint with the Education Commissioner. I'm also filing a complaint in federal court, because the School Board violated Mr. McCloskey's civil rights."

"You think you'll win?"

"We have a good case, Fantasia," said Charlie Mulcahy.

"Okay, good, I guess," said Fantasia. "But if you get Mr. McCloskey back but then we lose the election, then all we end up with is Mr. McCloskey, right? We don't get music, or shop class, or gym or—"

"Shut up, kid. We're gonna win," said Moose.

"Yeah, but Dad says no politician ever got elected telling the truth about taxes."

"Dad's a wet blanket," said Moose.

"Hey!" objected Colonel Fate.

"You are a wet blanket, sweetheart," said Delia Fulton. She kissed him, wetly.

"Colonel Fulton might be a wet blanket, but we should take his warning to heart," said Annabella Moss. "People understand that taxes are often necessary, but they hate them all the same. Taxes are like snakes and spiders."

"Yeah, but people only hate snakes and spiders 'cause they don't understand 'em. Snakes eat mice and rats," said Henry. "And spiders! They eat flies and mosquitos. And mice and rats and flies and mosquitos spread disease, and—"

"Henry, I wish I still had you in class," said Annie Moss. "Henry has just shown us how we can promise everyone higher taxes and still win the election."

"I did?" said Henry.

"Henry says we don't need to talk about how much people might lose in taxes. The other side will be yammering on about the poor, pitiful taxpayer's terrible tax burden 'til the cows come home—even though the increase only comes down to a few pennies a day," said Annie Moss.

"Instead," she went on, "we campaign on Henry's message. He says let's talk about how many mosquitos one hungry spider can eat. Henry says let's explain what those pennies are going to buy—teachers and books and art supplies, gym class and computers and more custodians to clean up the schools. Henry says let's talk about the future, for our kids. For our town."

"When did I say that?" said Henry.

"So, Henry's sayin' that if we want our teachers back," said Moose, "we have to teach people."

"Very good, Moose," said Annie Moss. "You get an A."

Charlie Mulcahy said, "As I recall, that was Thomas Jefferson's point when he wrote, 'Whenever the people are well-informed, they can be trusted with their own government; that, whenever things get so far wrong as to attract their notice, they may be relied on to set them right.'"

"That only goes to show," said Colonel Fate, "that Thomas Jefferson was out of his mind, too."

"Oh, Fate," said Delia Fulton. "You really are a wet blanket."

ROUND IV:

HENRY HITS THE HUSTINGS

CHAPTER 20

8 MARCH

Henry Haddock felt lonesome. Here he was again, parked in the front row waiting for the School Board to convene. He had his backpack, his sketchbook and a "CHOOSE MOOSE!" sign, but no Fantasia.

Henry turned in his seat to check the crowd. There was none. Buzz Skelton, who had to be there, nodded at Henry. Seated beside Mr. Skelton was Dexter D. Lee, wearing his favorite midnight-blue corduroy suit with a hibiscus shirt from Tommy Bahama, cowboy boots and a mahogany walking stick. He looked fabulous. He smiled at Henry and opened his arms, indicating the emptiness of the high-school library.

Only three School Board members—Annabella Moss, Darlene Gazelick and Lyle Lehnherr—were present. Like everyone else, Chairman McDuff, Randy Zink and Superintendent Bob Ptaschnik had gone to Mendota, where the Blackhawk basketball team was playing the Mendota Meteors in the Division III sectional finals. If the Blackhawks won, they would be going to the State Tournament, for the first time ever.

Henry wished he could be at the game, but he had his duty.

So did the Board. As Annie Moss started the meeting (without using the gavel), she apologized to Darlene, Lyle and Myrtle Arnold for not canceling the session, so they could all go to the game. She explained that the Board, tonight, was under a deadline. A majority of members had to approve annual contracts for all sorts of school services, like custodians, heating fuel, sanitation and so forth.

This would be boring work, she said, but necessary.

She was right. It was boring. Amidst all the dullness and in spite of drawing a pretty good three-headed sketch of the depleted School Board, Henry's mind wandered. He had been thinking for weeks about how Thomas Jefferson said that democracy requires a well-informed citizenry. Henry hit the Blackhawk Public Library and read more about Jefferson. He discovered that Jefferson had proposed an unsuccessful Constitutional amendment to establish public schools. Henry also read about other great Americans who believed education was the linchpin of American liberty.

That's why Henry was upset when the *Weekly Argument* printed a story about the three reform candidates, Moose, Dexter D. Lee and Charlie Mulcahy. The story, as Henry saw it, was all wrong. The headline read:

'REFORM' SLATE VOWS HEFTY TAX BOOST

Below the headline, Darren Flack had written that Charlie, Dexter and Moose were planning to "install a prep-school curriculum heavily concentrated in the arts, classical music and the so-called humanities, to be paid for with a steep increase in the local property-tax burden."

Flack also wrote that, "if the 'reformers' gain a School Board majority, they will seek to override state-required limits on local school spending. They plan to seek a massive increase in the school system's long-term debt."

The next time Henry saw Darren Flack, which happened to be Sunday morning at Maggie's Muffins, Henry walked right up to the *Argument* editor and demanded a retraction.

Darren Flack then pointed out that every word in his story was factual, including the "fact" that private prep-school curricula concentrate on the arts, humanities and classical music.

Henry argued back at Flack that his story had left out most of the reasons Mr. Lee, Mr. Mulcahy and Moose were trying to add money to the school budget. Darren Flack's answer to that was, simply, that he did not have "space" in the newspaper to include all those "niggling details."

Then Flack said, "You know, Henry, if you really want to get your story out, you should think about going on the radio."

Henry, of course, had thought of this. He knew radio was probably the best way to reach people in Blackhawk. Every day, for instance, his grandmother turned on the local station, WBHA, before 6 a.m. and listened all day while she did her chores. Henry's parents had the car radio on all the time. Just about everybody in Blackhawk listened, for at least a while every day, to WBHA. Plus, WBHA had a website that people everywhere could access on their laptop or tablet or mobile phone.

And so it came to pass, one morning just after 7 a.m., that Henry arrived at the WBHA studio, up above the First Bank of Blackhawk on Main Street, to be interviewed on the "Early Bird Show with Jack Sharkey."

Henry thought Charlie Mulcahy, or Dexter D. Lee, or Moose, should be interviewed. But on the phone, Jack Sharkey had said, "Hank, kid, you're the story. A youngster like you stirring up local politics! That's man bites dog, kiddo."

Sharkey assured Henry that he would eventually invite

all the actual candidates for interviews. But first, he wanted Henry. So Henry said okay.

A sleepy-looking receptionist led Henry into a glassed-in booth full of electronic equipment with switches, dials and tiny red lights. There were microphones sticking up, hanging down and mounted on the equipment console. Tape cassettes and disks were stacked and strewn here and there, among empty cardboard coffee cups, crushed soda cans, sandwich wrappers and pencils that someone had chewed. For two minutes, Henry sat by himself in the booth, on a stool, facing a large comfortable-looking chair on wheels.

Then, into the studio burst a short, wiry man in a backward baseball cap with streaky black and gray hair sticking out underneath. A skinny little mustache looked like a chocolate-milk streak above his lip. He wore wire-rimmed glasses and a bulky snowflake sweater with food stains on the front. He shook Henry's hand vigorously, plopped into the big chair and stretched a microphone close to his mouth. Then, in that familiar WBHA morning-radio voice, Jack Sharkey talked really fast for a while. He covered several subjects, the last of which was the School Board election and the "welcome arrival into the usual tedium of local elections of a wild-card game-changer! In the form of Henry Haddock, a sixth-grader with a glint in his eye and a chip on his shoulder."

Henry wasn't sure this was an accurate description, but he was powerless to object because Jack Sharkey was still talking, faster than anybody Henry had ever heard. Watching his mouth move was like bubbles in boiling water. And his mustache was like a worm squirming on the surface.

Suddenly he stopped, looked into Henry's eyes and said, "Hank, whatever possessed you to pull this sort of stunt? What do your parents think of what you're doing?"

In fact, Henry's mother had brought him to the WBHA studio. Henry could see her through the window in the booth. She seemed proud of Henry. But he said to Jack Sharkey, "It's not a stunt, Mr. Sharkey. And please call me Henry."

Jack Sharkey grinned and chuckled. "Very well, Henry, now why—"

"I'd like to thank you for having me on your show," said Henry, interrupting. Mr. McCloskey had counseled Henry that interrupting might be necessary—or he wouldn't get much chance to talk.

Jack Sharkey said, "Well, you're welcome, Hen—"

Henry interrupted again. "Because I don't think people understand what we want to do."

"Well, as I understand it, you want to raise taxes."

"Well, jeez, Mr. Sharkey, that's not really right."

"You're saying, son, that you don't want to raise taxes? I'm a little surprised at that, young man, because the rhetoric I keep hearing from the group of so-called 'reform' candidates for the School Board here in Blackhawk … "

And on, and on.

Ray McCloskey had also warned Henry that the radio host might try to either trap him in a corner "or just talk you to death." So Henry settled back for a moment. He watched Jack Sharkey's mouth. As soon as he saw Sharkey pause to take a breath, Henry spoke.

"Mr. Sharkey," said Henry, changing the subject. "I've been reading a lot about taxes, at the library."

"Oh?"

"Do you know what Justice Oliver Wendell Holmes said about taxes?"

"Oliver Wendell what?" asked Jack Sharkey. He looked a little nonplussed.

Henry, who had brought notes on index cards, read from one. "Justice Holmes said, 'Taxes are the price we pay for civilization.'"

"Really," said Jack Sharkey. "What do you suppose he meant by that, Hank?"

"It's Henry."

"Oh, Henry. Right."

"Well, if we're talking about school," Henry began, turning to a fresh index card. But he got no further.

"Yes, Henry, let's talk about schools. Schools here in Blackhawk. Henry, do you know what a homosexual is?"

Henry switched cards again. He was prepared for this question. He looked up, caught Jack Sharkey's eye, and said, "Yes, I do."

"Well, good, Henry. Now there are three so-called reform candidates. And I understand that you've encouraged each of them to run for School Board. Is that right?"

"Yeah, I guess so."

"And do you know, Henry, that one of your reform candidates is a homosexual?"

"Well, now that you mention it," said Henry, "I sort of wondered about Mr. Mulcahy?"

"Mulcahy?" said Jack Sharkey.

"He doesn't look gay, does he?"

"Son, what are you—"

"Jeez, I wonder if his wife knows?" said Henry.

"No, no," insisted Jack Sharkey. "It's not Mulcahy. Of course it's not—"

"So, it's Moose?" said Henry. "Wow. Moose Fulton is gay?"

"Moose Fulton is not gay!"

"Well, if Moose isn't gay, why would you say he's gay, Mr. Sharkey?"

"I didn't say that. Did I say that?"

Henry did it again. He paused, waiting. He looked Jack Sharkey straight in the eye. He was amazed how well this interrupting trick worked. He would have to thank Mr. McCloskey.

"Henry, I think we need to get to the bottom of this homosexual issue."

"No," said Henry.

"No?"

"No, Mr. Sharkey. I'm only eleven and I don't know very much about that. I came here to talk about teachers, about how they got fired even though they were doing a good job."

Jack Sharkey did what Henry had done. He paused, looking hard at Henry. Henry could almost feel the radio host's eyes, like hot spots on his skin. Finally, Sharkey said, "Okay, Henry. Let's get down to brass taxes. You want those teachers back. You want them back so bad that you were out to decimate the Thundering Three Hundred, the town's pride and joy. You want your teachers back so bad that you're now trying to raise taxes on everyone in town and float a bond issue that will bury our children under a mountain of debt in the not-too-distant future."

"Fifteen years," said Henry quickly.

"Fifteen years?" said Sharkey.

"Yes, but it wasn't my idea. It was Charlie's. Charlie Mulcahy, I mean. He was the Town Counsel. Now he's running for School Board."

"Well, of course, Henry. I know who—"

"Well, Mr. Mulcahy said we should ask the voters for a bond issue that matures in fifteen years. You know why, Mr. Sharkey?"

"No, Henry, please."

"Okay, first of all, right now, interest rates are really low, so the payback won't be that expensive. If there's any inflation at all, we could end up paying back less than we borrowed."

"Really?"

"Yeah, and as for burying our children in debt? You just said that, right?"

"Yes."

"Well, I'm one of those children, and I'll be, like, 26 years old when the bond issue is all paid off. And besides, it isn't like I'll be paying it back all by myself. That's 'cause everybody pays a little bit. Charlie—I mean, Mr. Mulcahy—he says it'll prob'ly come to about sixty cents a week on everybody's taxes, which won't even get you a cup of coffee, right, Mr. Sharkey? Besides, it's like a car, isn't it?"

"A car?" asked Jack Sharkey.

"Sure, if you need a car, you need it right now—not fifteen years from now, right?"

"Well, I already have a car."

"Jeez, you're lucky, Mr. Sharkey. I'm too young to drive. But my dad has a car, and he has car payments every month. Don't you?"

"Well, yes."

"Well, there!" said Henry. "Teachers are like your car. We need our teachers right now, not fifteen years from now, when we're too old for school."

"Henry, I'm not sure ... "

"It's simple. We buy the teacher now, just like your car. And then we make payments, just like your car payments. Only they're teacher payments."

"Teacher payments."

"Right. 'Cause you gotta remember."

"Remember what, Henry?"

"Teacher payments are money for education, which is civilization, which is democracy. Like Oliver Wendell Holmes said."

"That's sounds nice, Henry, but—"

"And just think!" said Henry, sneaking a peek at one of his index cards. "You can get all the teachers we need for less money than buying a cup of coffee once a week!"

Jack Sharkey opened his mouth to reply. Henry interrupted.

"Can I ask you a question, Mr. Sharkey?"

"Well, yes, Henry," said Jack Sharkey, who—to his radio listeners—was sounding slightly exasperated. "Of course."

"Did you go to school in Blackhawk?"

"Oh, no, I didn't," said Jack Sharkey. "I'm actually from Syracuse."

"Syracuse? Really? Cool," said Henry.

"Syracuse is cool?" asked Jack Sharkey.

"Isn't it?" asked Henry.

"Well, I don't know. I guess so. I hadn't thought—" Jack Sharkey realized his mind was wandering. "Henry, what's your question?"

"Oh, okay," said Henry. "At your high school in Syracuse, did they have art classes."

"Art? Well, sure."

"And music, and individual music lessons for some kids?"

"Yes, I think they did."

"And shop classes. And lots of janitors. And gym class. Did they have gym class?"

"Well, yes, of course they—"

"Okay then," said Henry. "So you're a grownup, who had all that stuff in school. Oh, how about French?"

"Well, I didn't take French in high—"

"But you could have, right?"

"—school. Yes."

"Did you take any foreign language?"

"I had *tres años de Español*," said Jack Sharkey.

"Cool," Henry replied. "What about German, Italian, Latin? Did they have those at your school?"

"Henry, I see what you're getting at."

"No, wait. You see, here's the thing, Mr. Sharkey," Henry said. "My mom and dad, they went to school here in Blackhawk and they had all those subjects and teachers and activities. And you had all those things in Syracuse. And you know what? I've been talking to other grownups who grew up in other places, and they all had that stuff in school, too—even if they didn't want it."

"Well, Henry, that's true as far as it goes."

"So, why can't I have that? If you can have Spanish and gym, and my parents can have Spanish and gym, why can't I? Why can't Moose and my two sisters and all my friends have that? What's wrong with us? Why do you think it's okay to take all that education away from us? Nobody tried to take Spanish and gym and all those other subjects away from you, did they? Why can't we be as civilized as you guys are?"

"Well, Henry," said Jack Sharkey. He paused and thought for a moment. "People don't want to pay for it any longer."

"Why?"

"Because they don't have the money, Henry."

"Oh, c'mon. That's dumb," said Henry. "It's only sixty cents a week! You know what the real problem is, Mr. Sharkey?"

Jack Sharkey's voice was a little weary when he said. "All right, Henry, what's the real problem?"

"The real problem is: Nobody wants to buy something they don't understand. Would you buy a car without looking at it, Mr. Sharkey?"

"Well, no, that would be—"

"Okay, but nobody's letting the voters look at the school budget. Nobody bothers to explain to people what their taxes are paying for."

"Well, Henry, I don't think—"

"So, they don't know what a good deal they're getting!"

"Henry, I don't—"

"Are you?"

"Am I what?"

"Explaining! Have you ever told people what's in the school budget?"

"Me?"

"Well, jeez, Mr. Sharkey, everybody in town listens t'you. And you're on the radio for, like, *hours* every morning. I think if you explained to people how important those teachers are, to us kids. And if you told people how a little bit of money from everybody can bring those teachers back, well, then they'd understand. And if they understood, they'd say, okay, what the heck? It's only sixty cents a week."

"That's an interesting theory, Henry."

"That's why I came on your show, Mr. Sharkey. To explain."

"Well, Henry, there's one more problem."

"What?"

"We're out of time, Henry."

Henry stared.

Jack Sharkey said, "Henry, you're a sharp kid. You've been a great guest. I wish you luck. Now, ladies and gentlemen, are you driving around on bald tires? Do you worry every time you hit the open road ... "

And Henry found himself being ushered out of the both by the same sleepy receptionist. Helen Haddock met Henry in the corridor. She told him he'd been "great."

Henry disagreed. He had hardly said a thing. He hadn't explained anything. Nobody wanted to sit still long enough to understand. He *ran out of time!*

At school that day, lots of students and teachers—teachers, especially—congratulated Henry on his radio appearance and said he'd done a "great" job. But Henry knew better. He still had a tons of unspoken information stuck on those dumb old index cards.

Henry was still pondering what he had left unsaid on the radio as he watched substitute chairperson Annie Moss run the School Board through its paces. She hurried Darlene and Lyle through a daunting pile of contracts, getting each one approved by the necessary three-to-zero vote. But it still took a long time. Henry was just finishing his portrait of all three Board members when the library doors burst open. In charged Amy and Tiff, Mr. McCloskey and others, all fresh and exuberant.

From people's faces, Henry could tell that the Blackhawks had won. Annabella Moss momentarily suspended the boring business of the Board. She caught Ray McCloskey's eye and said, "Is it good news?"

"Yes," said Mr. McCloskey. "We won, 71-68. We're going to State."

"Wonderful," said Annie Moss. "And how did Moose do?"

"Oh, he killed 'em," said Mr. McCloskey.

"Attaboy," said Annie Moss.

Fantasia, bouncing joyously into the library and taking her place in the front row, attempted to start a "Choose Moose" chant, but was silenced with one look from Mrs. Moss.

The one person in the library who didn't seem pleased by the success of Moose and the Blackhawks was Darlene Gazelick. Moose was her opponent in the election. The longer Moose kept winning basketball games, the worse things looked for Darlene's reelection.

At least this was what Ralph Haddock told Henry.

"That's dumb," said Henry.

"Dumb, why?"

"Because basketball," said Henry, "has nothing to do with politics. People shouldn't vote for you just because you're a good basketball player!"

"Oh yeah?" said Ralph Haddock. "Tell that to Bill Bradley."

Henry had no idea who Bill Bradley was. He was going to have to look him up. Sometimes Henry thought he spent half his life looking stuff up.

Henry slipped out of his chair and went to the high-school library computers. Fantasia Fulton tagged along.

It turned out Bill Bradley was an All-American basketball star at Princeton University who went on to play for the New York Knicks. He went straight from basketball to the United States Senate, where he served for eighteen years—and even ran for President.

"Whooee!" said Henry softly. "Wait 'til Moose hears about Bill Bradley."

"President Moose? Hah!" Fantasia's laugh was loud enough to draw a dirty look from Annie Moss.

CHAPTER 21

26 MARCH

Because of Moose, the annual School Board Candidates Forum had to be postponed for a week. It had been scheduled on a Wednesday in March, but that turned out to be the day before the Blackhawks made their first appearance in the state basketball tournament. Basketball was the only thing on everybody's mind—which was fine with Henry. If people were thinking hoops, they couldn't help thinking about Moose.

By leading the Blackhawks to greater glory than they had ever known (while scoring almost thirty points a game, along with more than a dozen rebounds), Moose was just about the biggest local hero in the history of Blackhawk. As long as the basketball team kept winning games—they were now 24-1—Moose couldn't do much campaigning for School Board. But he didn't need to. At every game, the Blackhawk bleachers were a sea of "Choose Moose!" signs, all of them waving, flapping and twirling every time Moose scored a basket.

The signs were everywhere because Lt. Col. Lafayette Fulton kept ordering more of them. The latest version read:

CHOOSE MOOSE!
GO, BLACKHAWKS!

Lots of these signs showed up at games, but they also started popping up on front lawns all over town.

Lt. Col. Fulton said to Henry, "Maybe somebody's not going to vote for Moose. But everybody supports the team. So, everybody's gotta have the sign."

On the fourth printing, after Blackhawk beat Mendota, Colonel Fate added a new message. Now, the signs—hundreds of signs, everywhere in town, on lawns, in store windows, on people's roofs, taped to cars and trucks, hanging from flagpoles and plastered on fences, blank walls and utility poles—all said:

CHOOSE MOOSE!
WIN STATE!

Henry thought it was a weird sort of political campaign. He said to Dexter D. Lee one day, "It's all just cheering and signs and basketball. Nobody is talking about, you know, issues."

Dexter D. Lee just laughed and said, "Kid, the last thing you want to do in a political campaign is talk about the issues."

Jack Sharkey had told Henry pretty much the same thing. Maybe he was right.

So, Henry just shrugged and smiled. Whenever anyone passing him on the street shouted "Go, Blackhawks," Henry hollered back "Choose Moose!"

Henry's particular "Choose Moose!" was about the election, not basketball. But he didn't know if anybody took it that way.

Once, in the hallway at school, Henry was passing a boy he didn't know and the boy said, "Choose Moose!"

Henry turned and said, "For what? State? Or School Board?"

And the boy replied, "Yeah!"

Almost every night, Henry joined Charlie and Dexter D. Lee as they visited with little groups of voters in living rooms. They talked, drank coffee, tried to discuss "issues" and—everywhere they went—agreed that the fighting basketball Blackhawks were terrific. Henry estimated that, if there were another thousand days in the campaign, they could talk to just about everybody in town.

On the first day of the State Tournament, Moose scored 31 points and the Blackhawks beat the previously undefeated Ospreys of Olin High. The next day, they made it to the Division III state finals with a breathtaking 63-62 victory over Vilas Catholic. Blackhawk only won because Moose rebounded a missed shot and scored the putback as the final buzzer sounded. Afterward, Moose encountered the basketball coach of Fredericksburg University. After a few minutes of friendly conversation, Moose discovered that the coach was offering him a basketball scholarship.

"Me?" said Moose.

"Yes," said the Fredericksburg coach.

"But I was kicked off the football team."

"I know," replied the coach. "I talked to a few people about that. And they didn't think it was fair. Did you?"

"Yeah, it was," said Moose. "I lost my temper and got into a stupid fight. I got arrested. I embarrassed my team."

"That's the answer I was hoping to hear, son."

At first, Moose wasn't sure he should accept the scholarship. He pictured himself flunking out of Fredericksburg, which was the best college in the state. He said, "But Coach, what about my grades?"

"Darnell, you're a leader in your school and community. You've been on the Honor Roll since tenth grade. And you're probably going to be the first School Board member I've ever coached," said the coach. "I think you're smart enough."

"Boy, I sure hope so," said Moose uneasily.

The town was only slightly disappointed when Blackhawk lost the championship game to mighty Carnegie Prep. Thousands of people, from all over the county, lined the streets to cheer the returning heroes. On the Wednesday after the State Tournament, a "Thank You, Blackhawks Rally" took place at the high-school gym. That's when Moose made the announcement about his scholarship to Fredericksburg University. For five minutes, a thousand people chanted, "Moose! Moose! Moose!," until Moose was so embarrassed he had to escape to the locker room.

Amy Haddock and Tiff Melrose, in their cheerleader outfits, were standing on the sideline of the basketball court, holding their pompons and listening in wonderment to the roar of Moose's fans. Amy turned to look for Henry. He was just behind her.

"Listen to that! They love Moose! We're gonna win," Amy Haddock shouted to Henry.

To protect herself against Election Day disappointment, Fantasia Fulton had decided to adopt her father's pessimism. She broke in. "Don't count your chickens, pompomface! Politics ain't basketball."

Amy laughed and replied, "Fantasia! You're a party pooper!"

Fantasia stuck out her tongue and yanked on Amy's cheerleader skirt. Amy and Tiff retaliated with a pompon attack that ended with Fantasia on the floor, giggling and spitting out strings of crepe paper.

That Wednesday was supposed to be the night of the Candidates Forum. But the Board of Aldermen postponed again. Moose's candidacy had generated an uncommon wave of public interest in the spring election. So, the Aldermen rescheduled the School Board debate for Saturday night and shifted it from the high-school library to the auditorium.

This turned out to be a good idea.

Henry arrived early, as usual, and took a seat in the front

row, with Fantasia beside him. He didn't have a sign, because "campaigning" wasn't allowed (also a good idea). With twenty minutes to go before the whole thing started, he stood and tried to count the audience in the auditorium. At 200, he lost count. People kept coming in.

"Well," he said to Fantasia. "There's a lot!"

"Yeah," said Fantasia, looking worriedly at the audience. "But whose side are they on?"

The stage was dressed up for the Blackhawk High School Drama Club's upcoming production of *South Pacific*. Already in place were Luther Billis' Bath Club and Bloody Mary's "Native Treasures" shop, all surrounded by bamboo branches and fake palm trees. Painted on a scrim at stage left was the island of Bali Hai, wreathed in pink and purple clouds and surrounded by a turquoise ocean.

As the candidates for School Board arrived, they were led to seven bare folding chairs on the forward edge of the stage. A member of the Blackhawk High School Audiovisual Club outfitted each candidate with a wireless clip-on microphone and warned them not to cover the mike. At stage right, just forward of Luther Billis' Bath Club, was a podium with a microphone.

At 7:30 sharp, Vance Cotterill, Chairman of the Board of Aldermen, emerged from between two fake palm trees and approached the rostrum. He paused to make sure all seven School Board candidates were present. They had been arranged in alphabetical order from stage right:

Moose Fulton (all splay-legged and gangly in a new blue suit that seemed a little too roomy up top and two inches short at the inseams) was a like a huge nervous cat, scratching his head, licking his lips, bouncing his knees and peering into the audience.

Darlene Gazelick (dressed as usual in a black pantsuit, ruffled white blouse and sensible shoes) kept looking uneasily—and distastefully—to the candidate on her left.

The candidate to Darlene's left was Dexter D. Lee (retro from head to toe in a tan double-breasted suit with black pinstripes, matching tan shoes with pink shoelaces and argyle socks in pink and black, black silk shirt and a very understated gray tie decorated with tiny Pink Panthers). Dexter D. Lee crossed his legs urbanely and reached to his right to shake Darlene Gazelick's hand. She recoiled. He smiled, bowed and withdrew his hand.

Lyle Lehnherr (in a gray suit, white shirt, regimental tie, brown wingtip shoes) sat rigidly upright with legs together, hands between his thighs, staring blankly outward.

Farrell "Scooter" McDuff (in a tailored navy-blue suit, soft blue shirt, dark-blue striped tie, tassled black loafers and patternless dark socks that disappeared far up his pant legs) projected an air of majesty, as his eyes searched the auditorium for familiar faces. He nodded, smiled and waved subtly when he found one.

Charlie Mulcahy (in a light-brown vested suit, with white shirt, plain dark tie and scuffed brown Oxford shoes, looking for all the world like Atticus Finch) appeared relaxed as he flipped through the pages of a small spiral notebook.

The mystery candidate, Joyce Tweedy, had arrived moments before. As she paused timidly in the wings, Charlie Mulcahy went to her and shook her hand. Then he led her across the stage to her seat. She nodded nervously and sat. Henry studied her. She reminded him of a sandhill crane, long-legged in a straight black skirt. She was slightly bent over, with a nose like a beak and her dull brown hair in a bun. She wore a black jacket buttoned to the throat with a little fringe of white lace showing above her collar. She was dressed "old" but didn't look any older than Henry's mother.

Alderman Cotterill tapped the mike and quieted the crowd, which had swollen to some 500 people, the biggest School Board "debate" in history (thanks to Moose's fame). Alderman Cotterill explained that each candidate was allowed a five-minute speech. The order of speeches had been decided by lottery, with Dexter D. Lee going first, Moose next-to-last and Scooter McDuff at the end.

Then, said the alderman, the floor would be thrown open to questions. But anyone who rose to ask a question had to wait 'til an usher—either Esther Hayes the high-school vice principal, or Fred Quilici, who ran the deli counter at the Piggly Wiggly—came around with a microphone.

Vance Cotterill said the candidates were welcome to challenge one another's statements. But he added that he would intervene if any disagreement became heated or "personal."

"I hope that's clear," said the head alderman.

"Crystal!" shouted Lt. Col. Lafayette Fulton.

With that, Alderman Cotterill—hesitantly—introduced Dexter D. Lee, who approached the rostrum with a dimpled smile and a spring in his step.

One by one, the candidates made their speeches. They all affirmed their devotion to the children of Blackhawk and assured voters of their qualifications for membership on the School Board. The incumbents emphasized their lengthy and invaluable experience on the Board. The challengers stressed the importance of bringing in new blood and a fresh perspective. Charlie Mulcahy talked about how he offered both fresh blood *and* experience.

Dexter D. Lee amused the crowd by talking about Ray McCloskey, who would come home from school every day, "all cranky and out of sorts, complaining about what a godawful mess" the school system was. "Every day he complained—until he got fired. Now all he wants in the world is to get back into that godawful mess."

Joyce Tweedy introduced Jesus Christ as an election issue, which was a new enough wrinkle that it got a buzz out of the audience.

Darlene Gazelick also mentioned Jesus. She offered the

darkest vision among all the candidates. She said "moral decay" was eating the souls of the younger generation. If the voters elected even one of the reform candidates, it would be the same as "packing our children onto an express train to the gas chamber."

"Ew," said Fantasia.

Moose got a standing ovation just for walking to the podium. He didn't brag about his basketball success or his college scholarship. He said he'd work as hard on the School Board as he worked on his sports and his grades. This got a murmur of approval from the audience.

"Yeah, good old hoop-star Moose," said Fantasia. "But I bet they don't vote for him."

"Why wouldn't they?" said Henry.

"Too young, too dumb, too black," said Fantasia gloomily.

Henry shook his head. "We'll see."

Scooter McDuff, speaking last, talked about how the town's economy was mired in uncertainty. "The only thing we're really sure of right now is that we have the best basketball team we'll probably ever see in Blackhawk!" With this, Scooter led the crowd in applauding the Blackhawk hoop team. He even coaxed Moose into standing up for an awkward bow.

But then, even before Moose could sit back down, Scooter continued by pointing out that an outstanding athlete is not by any means a sure thing as a School Board member, civic leader and "guardian of the community's purse strings." Chairman McDuff went on to emphasize "experience and stability." Scooter and his fellow incumbents, Darlene and Lyle, embodied these qualities. His last words: "We love ya, Moose. But you're pretty wet behind the ears."

Almost everyone laughed. Moose didn't. Nor did Henry—who was busy preventing Fantasia from charging up onstage and tackling Scooter.

Meanwhile, Alderman Cotterill returned to the podium. He tapped the mike, cleared his throat and said, "Thank you, candidates all. That was very enlightening. And allow me to echo Scooter's sentiments about our State Tournament basketball team. We're just as proud as can be of you boys."

More applause.

"Now, it's my duty to open the floor to questions. Again, I ask people to raise their hands and wait 'til the microphone arrives. And then, please, state your name before asking your question.

"So, who'll be first? Ah, I see a hand right up front here."

Henry had a hand up, but Alderman Cotterill was pointing at a spot about ten seats to his left. Henry slid forward and looked to see who got the first question.

"Uh oh," said Henry.

"I smell a rat," added Ray McCloskey.

Indeed, chosen by the town's top alderman to begin the Q&A, standing majestically in what would be the orchestra pit of the high-school auditorium if Blackhawk High School had an orchestra, was Paul Lamartine.

He accepted a wireless microphone from Fred Quilici. A spotlight, steered by a member of the high school's Audiovisual Club, shone on him. He seemed larger than life in his circle of light. Paul Lamartine began to speak, deliberately and sonorously.

"First of all, I want to say how proud I am of this town, for putting forward such an excellent group of people on the School Board ballot. I know we can only elect three of these outstanding citizens, but I honestly think that if we just went eeny-meeny-miny-mo, we'd do just fine. Every one of these folks is worthy of the job. Don't you agree?"

This was such a charming start that no one in the crowd seemed able to resist. The auditorium was swept again by applause.

"But, folks," Lamartine continued folksily, "I notice that the overwhelming emphasis among all our candidates was money. The budget is everyone's biggest worry. Some people believe the spending reductions voted by the Board were necessary. Some of us think we're shortchanging our kids by cutting some of the subjects and activities that they love. It's gotten bad enough that we've heard talk about shutting down our wonderful marching band."

A lusty round of boos followed, but Paul Lamartine raised an immaculate hand for silence. The crowd obeyed.

Smiling modestly, Lamartine said, "Luckily, I was able to help out a little on that score."

This remark forced a long pause. A majority of the assembly rose to their feet, cheering Paul Lamartine's generosity.

Henry, Fantasia and Ray McCloskey stood with the crowd but talked among themselves.

"I wonder what he's up to," said Mr. McCloskey.

"He's gonna do somethin'," said Henry.

"What I oughta do," said Fantasia, "is go over there and whack him one, right in the chops, and then shove that microphone down his throat."

"Right," said Henry. "That would sure help us win the election."

Ray McCloskey just laughed.

When the crowd finally settled back down, Paul Lamartine said, "We've heard these candidates offer solutions to the budget crunch. Some say we should just accept the cuts, but this harms our kids right now. Some are talking about tax increases and a bond issue that will reduce our options as we move toward the future, dumping our debts onto our kids and grandkids."

"So, for Pete's sake," said Fantasia in a stage whisper that covered a lot of ground, "when's the big windbag gonna ask a *question?*"

If Paul Lamartine heard Fantasia, he showed no sign. He just kept talking. "Well, folks, I've looked into my heart."

"A heart? The Tin Man has a heart?" whispered Ray McCloskey. Henry grinned.

Lamartine said, "And I think I've found a solution that will satisfy both sides of the argument, at least for a while—until our town gets back on its feet."

Lamartine paused to appreciate the silent anticipation that now gripped the immense room.

He said, "I'd like to offer the Blackhawk School District a two-year reprieve. I'm prepared to establish a trust fund, available to the schools. This fund will provide enough money to restore—next year and the year after—the financial resources, and I mean all the teachers and the programs, that were eliminated this year. There will be no repayment. I will charge no interest."

A gasp spread throughout the auditorium. Before the crowd could further react, Lamartine went on. "This will require that the Board of Aldermen override several provisions in the town's budget regulations. But I've been assured that the Board is willing to do so. And then, of course, the School Board would have to vote to accept this ... assistance."

As Lamartine paused again, a smattering of applause began. It spread across the auditorium, growing into an ovation and building into a roar. Amid the noise, Fantasia shouted, "What's he doing? What's it mean?"

"I think it means they win," said Delia Fulton, placing a hand on Fantasia's shoulder.

"They win? How? Why? How can he ... "

"Your mother's right. It looks as though we're dead, sweetie," said Annabella Moss, who was sitting just behind Fantasia.

"Dead? Why?"

"He just took away our issue," said Ray McCloskey.

"More like he bought it," said Ralph Haddock. "Lock, stock and chuckwagon."

"Wow," said Henry.

The applause died down eventually, leaving Paul Lamartine still under the glow of the spotlight, with a very small, very benevolent smile on his smooth-shaven, well-nourished face. School Board Chairman McDuff rose from his seat and, without benefit of a microphone, called out across the auditorium, "Ladies and gentlemen, we have just witnessed the greatest act of generosity in the history of Blackhawk. We have just seen one great and honorable citizen, singlehandedly, save our schools."

More applause.

Scooter went on. "And I pledge, right here and right now, that if you reelect me to the School Board, my first order of business will be to accept this offer and begin the process of restoring the programs that were previously cut, according to Mr. Lamartine's wishes."

Another standing ovation followed, during which Scooter McDuff applauded wildly, urging Paul Lamartine onto the stage. Lamartine, a paragon of patrician modesty, simply returned the microphone to Fred Quilici and took his seat.

Henry studied the stage. Everyone but Joyce Tweedy was standing and, for a moment, they all seemed to be clapping enthusiastically, especially Scooter and Alderman Cotterill, Darlene Gazelick and Lyle Lehnherr. But Moose and Dexter D. Lee clapped weakly. Most of the candidates seemed confused, looking toward each other quizzically.

Charlie Mulcahy and Joyce Tweedy were the exceptions. Joyce Tweedy remained in her seat, arms crossed, eyes downcast, apparently praying. Charlie had not joined in the applause. He simply stood, arms at his side, gazing thoughtfully down at Paul Lamartine.

Moose caught Charlie's eye. Henry saw this. He saw them nod to each other.

Finally, after all the hubbub settled, the crowd and the candidates all sat down again. Alderman Cotterill returned to the podium. He had a big smile on this face. He said, "Well, now! How about that?!"

Moose stood up.

Moose said, "I'd like to say something, please."

CHAPTER 22

Henry Haddock was incensed all over again.

He felt like screaming.

This isn't democracy, he wanted to shout. This is like a kingdom in a fairy tale, where some handsome white knight in shining armor rides into the village on a palomino stallion. He holds up his golden shield and proclaims that he has come, just in time, to save the villagers. Except, everything is fine. There's nothing to save the villagers from. No black knight has enslaved them. They're not being devoured by dragons or terrorized by trolls.

The real problem is that the people in the village *disagree*. Half the village is upset with the opinions of the other half of the village. So, they're calling each other nasty names. They're throwing eggs at one another, building spite fences, trampling each other's strawberry patches.

This is no place for a white knight to come along and get egg stains on his doublet!

Nevertheless, suddenly, here comes Sir Buttinsky, horning in for his own glory. And the villagers don't object. Why would they? His saddlebags are loaded with gold. He hands every villager a big shiny golden guinea. And for a while, as long as it takes for each villager to spend the golden guinea, peace and harmony return. Prosperity and goodwill prevail.

But the good times only roll 'til the guineas run out, thought Henry.

Moose Fulton was standing there, in front of his chair on the stage at Blackhawk High School, waiting for permission to speak

"By all means, Mr. Fulton," said Alderman Cotterill to Moose. "You have the floor."

With that, Moose walked—a little unsteadily—to the podium. He raised the microphone. He spoke.

"Mr. Lamartine," said Moose, looking down at the first row. "You're really a generous man."

Again, applause rippled across the auditorium before Moose could continue.

"But you're wrong."

A gasp.

"Ladies and gentlemen," said Moose, directing his gaze outward, "taking this money from Mr. Lamartine—boy! It's really tempting, huh? But it would be a big mistake."

A few people called out "No!"

Moose ignored the voices. He said, "You all remember me getting kicked off the football team, right? Boy, talk about stupid. I got into a fight. With a policeman. Billy Karkle, remember? Hey, Billy, if you're out there, I'm sorry, man."

And from somewhere in the back, a voice replied, "Forget it already, Moose."

There was a gentle wave of laughter.

"Well, I lost my football scholarship. I deserved to," Moose went on. "And we started losin' games. And pretty soon, there was this uproar. A lot of people in town wanted to bring me back on the team and fire Coach Grammus. But, jeez Louise! It wasn't Coach Grammus' fault that I got into a fight with Officer Karkle. Coach had rules and the rule was that any kid who gets in trouble with the police is off the team. Forever!

And that's a good rule, don't you think?"

Moose waited, and heard a weak murmur of agreement from the audience.

"Anyway, I was off the team, and the team was losing and a lot of people got mad at Coach," said Moose. "It got so bad that one day my dad—that's Lt. Col. Lafayette Fulton, U.S. Army—my dad came to me. He said a big group of football supporters were asking him to use his influence to get Coach fired. Well, that was sort of a surprise to me, 'cause I didn't know my dad had any influence with anybody. I mean, outside the Army."

Moose took a deep breath.

"But my dad said to me, Darnell, I could probably cause a lot of grief for Coach Grammus if I decided to cooperate with these people. And then he asked me what I thought. He said, 'What would you do, Moose?'

"Well, that was an easy question. I said right back to my dad, Jeez, Dad, you're talkin' about the *team*. A team is s'posed to do everything together. When I slugged Billy Karkle, that wasn't team. It was just me, bein' selfish. I hurt the team. But afterwards, those guys were still my team, all of 'em, especially Coach Grammus. It didn't matter if I could play or not. I said to my dad that if I got back on the team 'cause Coach got fired, what's the point? There wouldn't be a team.

"And you all saw what happened, didn't you? That team stuck together. Andy Wojczyk went out there and played quarterback in my place, and he got better every week, and we won a couple of games at the end."

Moose paused for a second, squinting a little under the stage lights.

"Well, I think the town of Blackhawk is like that," Moose went on. "We do things together. I mean, people have been goin' to school here for, like, a hundred years. And all that time, we always had enough money to pay for all the subjects kids need, and all the sports, and we all get a nice healthy lunch every day ... and all that.

"But then Mr. McDuff and the School Board cut the budget. I guess they had to, because of the new state law. Well, that was like me getting kicked off the football team. For a while, the town didn't know quite what to do—just like the football team when Andy Wojczyk was learning how to play quarterback.

"But that's all over. The team—I mean the town—it's comin' back together, and I'm ready to play. I haven't been kicked off this one yet."

Moose opened his mouth to say more, but had to wait for the laughter to subside.

"And we have a plan," said Moose. "Thanks to Henry Haddock. Henry's my neighbor. But he's also my friend, and one of the smartest people I know. Henry should be running for School Board, but he's not allowed, 'cause he's only eleven."

Suddenly, several voices in the audience—one of which sounded suspiciously like his sister Amy—shouted Henry's name, triggering a ripple of applause. Henry figured the people clapping were mostly just those who supported the reform candidates, but they were still pretty loud. This being the first time people had ever applauded for him, Henry shriveled up in his seat and blushed so hard his face burned.

Finally, to Henry's relief, Moose continued. "We have a team, which is the whole town. We have a plan to raise the money, to bring back our teachers, by ourselves. We don't need Mr. Lamartine's money."

Moose paused again, waiting for the audience to response, He was met with silence.

So Moose talked. "Hey, listen, we just lost in the state championship game. But you know who beat us. Carnegie Prep, which—maybe everybody doesn't know this—it's a private school. Their players come from all over the state and all over the country. They even had a kid from Brazil who was almost seven feet tall. But we almost beat those guys—you know why? Because we were a team. Those guys from Carnegie, they weren't a *team*. They were more like a corporation or something. They weren't friends or neighbors. They didn't grow up together and hang out with each other after school. They're not going to grow up and graduate and live down the block from each other and stay in touch for the rest of their lives. But us! We're gonna do all those things. We're gonna be friends all our lives, because we're a team. This town is the same way.

"The funny thing is, right now, we're arguing about money. My parents do that too, sometimes."

Moose tried to keep talking but laughter stopped him.

Smiling, Moose said, "Well, my point was, Mom and Dad argue about money sometimes, but we're not poor. I think my family has enough money to make out okay. Right, Mom?"

Moose peered into the audience, looking for his mother.

Softly, Delia Fulton's voice responded. "Yes, dear. We're fine."

"Okay," said Moose. "Well, this town is like my family. We're not poor. We're not starvin' or anything. But lately, our big problem is that we're cheap! We're all being selfish, like I was when I lost my head and took a shot at Billy Karkle.

"So, I think we've been selfish long enough. We're still all friends and neighbors. We're a better team when we all help each other out. Our basketball team might've beat Carnegie if we'd been able to bring in some big basketball star from Brazil or someplace. But if we did that, we wouldn't be as good a team. We'd all be less sure of ourselves and less sure of our friends. We wouldn't believe in ourselves the same way. I don't think we'd care as much, y'know?

"So, I don't think we should take Mr. Lamartine's money. He's like the tall kid from Brazil. We should say thank you and let him keep his money. Instead, we should believe in ourselves and we should take care of one another."

After a moment of heavy silence, the crowd applauded. Gradually, a "Choose Moose!" chant broke out, shaking the rafters until Alderman Cotterill rushed to the podium and started pounding on the microphone.

Scooter McDuff took charge of the mike as soon as order returned.

"Moose—I mean, Darnell Fulton! What a wonderful young man! Let's hear it for him."

More applause. More chanting. Scooter waited it out. Then he said, "Yes, a wonderful young man. He makes this town proud. But, of course, as he just proved in his little speech, Moose is ill-qualified for a seat on the School Board. He has no grasp of the realities of our economic situation here. After all, he admits it. He's running on a platform written by Henry Haddock, an eleven-year-old!"

"HEY!"

Before anyone could grab her, Fantasia Fulton was out of her seat and standing in the "orchestra pit," shaking a fist at Scooter McDuff.

"You big FAT tub of GUTS!"

Henry acted fast. He had a grip on Fantasia, with his hand over her mouth, before she could scream anything else.

There was more applause. Henry had no idea whether the clapping was for Fantasia, or for him shutting Fantasia up.

Chairman McDuff pretended that nothing had interrupted him. He simply said, "We are grateful to Darnell for his input. But now it's time for our young hero to go back to the playing fields while the grownups get down to the business of running our schools, properly and thriftily."

Moose stood, prepared to respond, but Charlie Mulcahy stood and touched Moose's arm. "Let me try," he said.

Moose nodded. Charlie Mulcahy went to the podium, nodding cordially as Scooter McDuff passed him.

"The name John Dewey is mostly forgotten, which is a shame," said Charlie Mulcahy as he leaned over the podium. "Dewey was one of America's great philosophers. To describe the American school system, he used the word 'genius.'"

Charlie Mulcahy stopped his speech. He left the podium and walked downstage, eventually sitting down on the edge of the stage, peering through the lights into the auditorium.

"This feels better," he said.

"I was talking about John Dewey. He grew up in an era when education went almost exclusively to the powerful, the privileged and the gifted," Charlie went on. "Ordinary folks were expected to remain blissfully ignorant and unlettered. At best, we were allowed a few years of reading and arithmetic in a one-room schoolhouse before being tossed into the workforce. It was visionaries like Horace Mann and John Dewey who believed that education is a human right, a uniquely American human right.

"In America, we attend public schools. That's a wonderful word: public. It means 'everybody.' The genius of American education, according to John Dewey, was the conviction that everybody could be—and should be—a learned individual. Until America tried it, no one on earth believed an entire nation could be educated.

"America proved the world wrong. Everybody went to school and everybody chipped in to pay for the public schools. Of course, we still haven't figured out how to pay for all schools equally, and we have lots of people who don't think they should pay for the education of other people's kids."

Charlie smiled. "I was talking to Vince Granger just a while back. Vince is in his seventies now. He says he shouldn't pay school taxes because he doesn't have any kids in school and—being a lifelong bachelor—he never did. But Vince also studied agriculture at the state university, which is a public school. That came after he graduated from Blackhawk High. He didn't pay a penny for high school and he sure didn't pay much for his university education. He learned to read and write and make a good, prosperous living for himself in his own house, driving his own paid-for car. Vince could live respectably because everybody chipped in for his public education when he was a little kid. The taxes he doesn't want to pay now are the dues he owes to the people, the public, who got him educated. They're his debt to everybody. The taxes Vince pays are his fair share.

"The money that Paul Lamartine is offering to the Blackhawk schools is not his fair share. Now, I admit it—wow. Mr. Lamartine's offer is astounding. It's an act of extraordinary generosity. He's volunteering to cover not just his fair share, but also the fair share of about 5,000 other taxpaying citizens like Vince Granger. And he's saying he'll do that twice over—next year and the year after that.

"But it ain't fair.

"As Moose says, it's wrong.

"All of us have one share in this town's job of educating our kids. If we take this deal, each of us will still just have one share. But Paul Lamartine, all by himself, he'll control 10,000 shares. In Wall Street terms, that's called a controlling interest. If we let one man buy a controlling interest in our school system, do we still have public schools?"

Charlie Mulcahy, like a lawyer (which he was) making his summation, waited a moment, letting the jury ponder the question. He rose from his spot on the lip of the stage and stood facing the audience.

"Or is this a private-school system, paid for and operated by Paul Lamartine?" he suddenly asked sharply. "Now, I have no idea of Mr. Lamartine's motives. But let's just imagine there's a teacher here in the middle school who just gave Paul's daughter a C even though the girl believes she earned an A. Or, what if there's a book in the high-school library that Mr. Lamartine doesn't approve of? What if there's a course he doesn't think is very important, or a sport he doesn't like? What if he calls up the school and one of the office ladies puts him on hold? Can he order Bob Ptaschnik to fire that woman? And would Bob have the authority to say no to him?"

Charlie continued, "I was just remembering, when I was in high school, I just couldn't get algebra. It was hell for me. If I could've wiped algebra out of the schools, I would've done it, and I would've driven my algebra teacher out of town with a whip. But I couldn't do that then and I can't now—because I only have one share. I have one little drop in the big tax bucket. But Paul Lamartine is about to buy the bucket. He's the only one in town who can afford to buy the whole kit and kaboodle. And if he gets his way, he'll be the only one in town entitled to do away with algebra, French, chemistry or any teacher his daughter doesn't like. And if he doesn't like the football team? No football team.

"He might not do that. He probably won't. But think about it. If you gave away that much money, wouldn't you expect to get a few privileges in return?"

Charlie Mulcahy let that question sink in as he rose from the edge of the stage and walked back to the podium. Then he spoke into the microphone. "Moose had it right," said Charlie. "This is our team. Blackhawk is our community.

"If we take Paul's money instead of buckling down and fixing the problem ourselves, well, it'll be his team. We won't be a community any longer."

Charlie left the podium. Dexter D. Lee stood up and shouted: "Yeah! What he said!"

In the first row, Fantasia jumped up and started clapping. Many joined in, but the applause was brief. Scooter McDuff cut it off.

He said, "Okay, folks. There you have it. This election comes down to whether you want to solve this budget battle right now. Or whether you want to raise your own taxes to line the pockets of a lot of ungrateful unionized schoolteachers."

Fantasia started to boo. Her mother threw a coat over Fantasia's head, and Scooter's last words boomed across the auditorium: "And don't forget the big rally, Monday night, the fourth of April, 8 o'clock! City Hall!"

This marked a disorderly end to the Candidates Forum, as the audience began to filter toward the exits. Henry watched people leave. Ray McCloskey was beside him.

"Whaddya think, Mr. McCloskey?"

"I really don't know, Henry. Charlie and Moose were pretty good. But Lamartine's money—that's a pretty big gift horse."

Henry wasn't sure what Mr. McCloskey meant by that.

"We're gonna kick their butts," said Dexter D. Lee, joining a group that included the Haddock and Fulton families.

But Dexter D. Lee didn't sound entirely convinced of his own words.

Meanwhile, Penelope, with entirely different priorities, offered the last word. "C'mon! Let's get home. It's pizza night!"

CHAPTER 23

4 APRIL

"Aren't you a little young to be drinking coffee?" asked the nice lady.

"Oh, I don't drink very much," said Henry Haddock.

"Well, you know, they say it'll stunt your growth."

The nice lady was Mrs. Celeste Benson, who was the hostess of the very last "candidate coffee" of the School Board campaign. Mrs. Benson was one of the "older voters" who "leaned" toward the incumbents, Scooter McDuff, Darlene Gazelick and Lyle Lehnherr. But her first choice was Charlie Mulcahy, because he had handled the Last Will and Testament of Mrs. Benson's late husband, Steve.

Henry sat in Mrs. Benson's parlor, on a sofa, in between Moose Fulton and Dexter D. Lee. Charlie Mulcahy had a chair to himself. There were about fifteen "older voters" surrounding them. They stared at each candidate—plus Henry—while Mrs. Benson and her sister Deanna poured coffee and encouraged them all to "have a brownie."

There were lots of brownies. Fantasia, who was standing next to a rubber plant in the corner, was eating one. She had a spare brownie in her other hand.

Henry never ate anything at candidate coffees, because he had to be ready to talk. If you had a mouthful of brownie, it could take as long as minute to chew and swallow before you could answer a question. Meanwhile, everyone would just sit there, watching you chew. Pure agony.

Henry, in fact, could barely stand coffee. But he knew it was rude to ask for something else. And he knew that coffee was his only hope to win the election.

Weeks before, Charlie Mulcahy had said, "The only way we can campaign, without any money, is to get into people's houses and talk to them."

That meant "candidate coffees."

Of course, Henry was not a candidate. But, as Fantasia told him pointedly, many times, "You're the one who started this whole thing, Starbucksface. Everybody wants to see ya."

So, Henry learned how to drink coffee, discovering soon that if he dumped enough sugar and cream into it, he didn't have to make a face every time he took a sip.

Still, he was really glad tonight was—he hoped—the last campaign coffee of his life.

Holding a flowered ceramic coffeepot, Celeste Benson looked around the parlor. She saw that everybody had their cups filled and also noticed that Henry was putting about six teaspoons of sugar into his coffee, which was already almost white from an overdose of cream.

Mrs. Benson said, "My stars, Henry, that's a lot of sugar."

Henry blushed, "Oh, not so much."

"You'll get fat, you know."

Henry patted his midsection. "Well, I guess I could use a few pounds."

This got a laugh from several people, which was good—although Henry was embarrassed—because it relieved the tension.

Mrs. Benson got down to business, introducing Charlie

Mulcahy by saying that Charlie needed no introduction. This was true. Over the years, Charlie had been the personal attorney for probably half the people in Blackhawk. His familiarity—which in politics, Henry learned, is called a "Q factor"—was better than any of the candidates, except for Scooter McDuff. Even better, people who knew both Charlie and Scooter liked Charlie better.

Likability was the "reform" candidates' only advantage. Charlie, Moose and Dexter D. Lee had almost no money, while Scooter, Darlene and Lyle were being supported by most of the businesses in town. The incumbents had endorsements from the Chamber of Commerce, the Rotary, the Kiwanis, the Knights of Columbus and the Masons. Charlie, Dexter and Moose did have the support of the Lions Club, but this was only because Rod Heimlich, the Lions Club president, hated the Rotary Club and tried to do everything opposite.

The Lions hadn't provided any money. Meanwhile, Scooter, Darlene and Lyle had carpeted the town with lawn signs. They had put up several billboards, with their big grinning faces six feet across (except for Scooter, whose face took up more like seven feet). The billboard said:

EXPERIENCE

under Darlene's face,

INTEGRITY

under Scooter's face, and

PRUDENCE

under Lyle.

This, of course, led Henry and Fantasia—and lots of other people—to wonder whether the right word was under the right face. For the last two weeks of the School Board campaign, people were rearranging EXPERIENCE,

INTEGRITY and PRUDENCE in ways they thought better fit the candidates. The one thing on which they all agreed was that Darlene should get PRUDENCE because it contained the word "prude."

And then there was the radio.

After trying to ambush Henry, WBHA morning host Jack Sharkey dutifully interviewed every School Board candidate. He was nice to Scooter, Darlene and Lyle, and not so nice to Charlie, Dexter and Moose—especially Moose. He treated Moose like a dope, asking him questions like who was his favorite sports hero and what flavor ice cream he likes best. (Moose's answers were Bill Russell and Cherry Garcia.)

The three incumbent candidates bought a lot of radio ads and even a few on local TV. Charlie, along with Henry and Moose's parents, and Dexter D. Lee (who had quite a bit of money), could only afford about six radio ads every day. Altogether, they were out-advertised by about 20-to-1. And they had no billboards.

Henry took some comfort in the fact that the "CHOOSE MOOSE!" lawn signs were cooler than anybody else's. But he had lost confidence in Moose's potential. Since basketball season, Moose's public profile had shrunk. His image had shifted, pretty suddenly, from swaggering hero to neophyte office seeker, and people were hinting he might be too young to be on the School Board.

Moose's age was, in fact, one of the five questions that had to be addressed during every candidates coffee. To Henry's great dismay, none of these five red herrings had much to do with the "issues."

After Moose's youth, the other four nagging questions came pretty much in the same order every time.

Next, somebody would sort of softly ask if it was really true that one of the candidates was "you know ... *that way*."

And Dexter D. Lee, in a big cheerful voice would always jump right in and say, "You mean, *gay?*"

After the questioner would nod or whisper "yes," Dexter would explain that he was a grown-up in an exclusive relationship with another grown-up, paying a mortgage, commuting to work and fighting crabgrass—just like all the married people in the room. He said that, normally, he preferred not to talk about "s-e-x," but he might feel less shy if a few other people opened up and spoke frankly about their own private sexual experiences. "Okay, who wants to go first?"

After a moment of awkward silence, Dexter D. Lee then said, "Good. Now, let's talk about *schools!*"

The "gay question" bugged Henry but even worse was the "homework question." This always came to Henry from some kindly-looking lady who wanted to know if all this extracurricular politics was affecting Henry's grades.

Henry's answer was always. "Well, the School Board cut so many subjects that I've got extra study halls. So, usually, I get all my homework done before school gets out."

Question number four was about Charlie's resignation as Town Counsel. Many people thought his resignation was a "power grab" that freed him to run for the School Board. Charlie's short answer was that the Town Counsel has a lot more power than anyone on the School Board.

His serious answer was: "The School Board fired a teacher, in secret, without sufficient grounds. They broke the law twice and expected me to back them up. I told them I wouldn't do it. When they refused to reconsider, I had no ethical alternative. I had to resign."

Question five went back to Moose's arrest. Moose always said he was wrong, but his only excuse was that he was trying to protect his little sister, Fantasia. Here, Charlie Mulcahy would intervene, explaining that Moose and Officer Billy Karkle had settled their differences and that Officer Karkle had endorsed Moose's candidacy.

By the time all these useless questions were answered, there was usually not much time left for the candidates to state their case. This night was even worse.

After about twenty minutes, Celeste Benson said, "I'm afraid we only have a few minutes left. I know many of us are planning to attend the big rally at City Hall."

The "big rally" was for the enemy.

Charlie, as usual, was ready with a very concise "summation." He said, "We don't need much time, Celeste, because the choice here is very simple. This all began when our wise young friend Henry learned that the School Board had fired Ms. Webster, his favorite teacher, and eliminated art, his best subject. Henry knew that wasn't fair—not to Ms. Webster and not to the students in the Blackhawk schools, because we have always had art, and music, and gym, and foreign languages, and plenty of vocational options here in Blackhawk. Until this year, our curriculum was comprehensive, and our schools were the equal of any school system in the United States.

"Henry went to the School Board. He wanted to ask them to bring back Ms. Webster and to simply keep the schools the way they had always been.

"He didn't want anything new or fancy or expensive. He just wanted the same education his parents—and their parents—had received right here in Blackhawk.

"Well, Henry went to the School Board, but they wouldn't let him talk. Not even one question. So he kept coming back. And when they finally let Henry ask his question, well, you know what the answer was.

"They said, 'No.' They said you can't have what your mother and father had. You're going to have to take less, less education, fewer subjects, fewer teachers, lower standards, less opportunity.

"And so Henry said, 'No!' He figured out a way, pretty simply, to bring back Ms. Webster—and everything Ms. Webster stands for—by getting everyone in town to pitch in just a little bit, pay a little bit more.

"Remember, we've always done it before. We've always said

'Yes' to our children's education.

"All we're asking is: Say 'Yes,' again."

Henry loved this little speech. It always got a lot of applause and Henry was sure it got most of the votes of the people who came for coffee. But Henry knew that after drinking all that coffee, Charlie, Dexter, Moose and he had talked to only about 300 people. That wasn't enough votes. They could only hope that their 300 would go out and convince hundreds more to join them.

But who knew if they did?

The coffee broke up at 7:30 sharp, and people took off fast. Charlie held back long enough to give Mrs. Benson a hug and thank her. Henry and Moose thanked her without the hug. Dexter, who was a habitual hugger, hugged her hard enough to lift her right off her feet—and she giggled.

Dexter whispered to Henry on the way to the car, "That was her first gay hug."

"Oh," said Henry, wondering if there were differences in hugs.

Henry Haddock expected the scene at City Hall to be pretty elaborate. Despite preparing himself, he was overwhelmed.

"Holy CRAP!" said Fantasia.

"My sentiments precisely," said Dexter D. Lee. They were standing on the small rise called Badger Hill that overlooked City Hall and City Hall Square.

Henry thought it's only the fourth of April—a chilly evening in early spring—but it looked more like the Fourth of July.

"This must've cost a *lot*," said Fantasia.

"Not to worry, dear child," said Dexter D. Lee. "Our nemesis, Lord Lamartine, *has* a lot."

Blackhawk's City Hall was built in the Greek style, with a wide staircase leading up to a portico complete with pediment, supported by six great columns twenty feet tall.

Scooter McDuff's supporters had built a speaking platform, adorned with patriotic bunting, all the way across the portico. Above this platform, stretched across four columns, was a white banner bigger than a dozen flags that read, in stark black capital letters:

BRUISE MOOSE!

For a moment, neither Henry nor anyone else saw anything but that banner. They just stared.

But then Henry heard laughter, from Moose Fulton.

"That's pretty good," said Moose, grinning. "Bruise Moose. It rhymes. I like that."

And so, they all laughed. Then Dexter D. Lee said, "I wonder if they tried out any other rhymes, like ... 'Refuse Moose.'"

"That's good, too," said Moose.

"Lose Moose!" said Fantasia.

"Abuse Moose!" said Henry.

This got everyone laughing again, which got worse when Fantasia shouted, "Goose Moose!" For good measure, she goosed her big brother, who goosed her back.

So, it was in a good mood, tossing around silly rhymes, that Henry and the candidates, with Fantasia, descended Badger Hill and joined the festivities of their political foes.

"Defuse Moose," said Charlie Mulcahy, waving to friends.

"Set Moose Loose!" said Dexter D. Lee as he spotted Ray McCloskey in the crowd.

The crowd was huge. This was not just the biggest School Board election rally ever. It was the biggest rally anyone in Blackhawk had ever seen. Henry looked around in awe. Besides the larger-than-life red-white-and-blue speakers platform, Henry noticed that half of the Thundering Three Hundred were setting up music stands on the City Hall steps. There was Wally Wilcox ordering kids around. Henry looked for his sister Penelope but couldn't spot her.

But he knew she'd be there. She had just been promoted to third clarinet.

Around the edges of City Hall Square, there were food booths selling hot dogs, corndogs, bratwurst, burgers, cotton candy, deep-fried Oreos, ice cream cones, soda, coffee, hot chocolate and all sorts of other stuff. Henry saw that Boyd Olson, who raised horses just outside town, was giving pony rides for five dollars and hansom-cab rides for ten. The Women's Catholic Foresters from Immaculate Heart were doing a bake sale. At another booth, the Rotary Club was selling chances on a raffle for a used car from Honest Mike Ottinger's Ford dealership. The Blackhawk Public Library had a whole table full of used books with prices from a dime to a dollar.

Henry couldn't resist this. He found an almost-new copy of *Animal Farm* for only a quarter, which he figured would come in handy later—to read during the speeches by Scooter, Darlene and Lyle.

There were vendors giving away balloons bearing portraits of the candidates. Henry grabbed one and decided that Scooter's big round face, on a balloon, only looked bigger and rounder. There were three or four clowns handing out "Bruise Moose!" t-shirts, and a juggler on a unicycle, an antique calliope, a flame-swallower, a barbershop quarter dressed all in green called the Four Leaf Clovers singing songs like "Shine On, Harvest Moon" and "Genevieve, My Genevieve," an Uncle Sam walking on stilts and an organ grinder with a live monkey. Also, there were about six pretty girls who didn't have enough clothes on (considering the weather) handing out buttons also with the faces of Scooter, Darlene and Lyle Lehnherr.

But the biggest spectacle of all—and Henry didn't know how Scooter (or, probably, Paul Lamartine) pulled it off—was a huge flag-colored hot-air balloon, like the one in *Around the*

World in Eighty Days, and they were giving away free rides. The man operating the balloon would fill up the basket with people, turn on the gas jets and the balloon would shoot up three hundred feet or more 'til it reached the end of a rope tethered to a truck whose outer panel advertised the proprietor as "Montgolfier & Co."

"Wow," said Henry, watching the balloon ascend as about twenty people in the basket whooped, screamed, laughed and waved.

Henry wanted a ride.

Fantasia sidled up to Henry, staring up. "Henry," she said. "We're toast."

Just then, the Thundering Three Hundred struck up its first tune: "I Heard It Through the Grapevine." The crowd cheered.

Henry sighed, looking at all the attractions, the smiling crowd, people eating hot dogs and taffy apples, terrified little kids running away from clowns, the hot-air balloons, the monkey, the pony rides ...

"Yeah, you're probably right," he said.

Charlie Mulcahy appeared above Fantasia, seemingly out of nowhere. Shouting against the blast of the Thundering Three Hundred (actually, about Sixty), he said, "Henry, the Romans had a term for this."

"Really?"

"Yes," said Charlie. "Bread and circus! The idea was to appease the restless masses and distract them from their hardships."

"Okay," said Henry, "did it work?"

"Often," said Charlie. "Often."

"Great," said Henry.

"But not always, Henry." And Charlie moved on.

Around the beginning of the band's second number, which sounded a lot like "You Light Up My Life," Henry bumped into his mother, accompanied by Penelope. He said to his sister,

"Hey, why aren't you up there, playing your clarinet?"

"They won't let me," said Penelope, her eyes filling with tears.

"Why?"

"Mr. Wilcox said I wasn't loyal. He said I was supporting the other side—against the band."

"That old FARTface!" said Fantasia.

"Are you?" Henry asked Penelope. "On our side?"

"Well, I am now!" said Penelope. "Wilcox is an old fartface!"

"That's what I said," said Fantasia.

Henry smiled at Penelope and Fantasia, who were doing high-fives and low-fives and some sort of dopey girl-fives and he thought, well, I might lose this election, but at least I've got my sister back.

"My daughter," said Helen Haddock, "the political martyr."

Eventually that night, after the queue at Montgolfier & Co. had gotten shorter and the band had begun to show signs of exhaustion, the master of ceremonies, none other than Jack Sharkey of WBHA, introduced Scooter McDuff, calling him a "pillar of the community" and a "courageous leader."

At roughly the moment that the speeches commenced, the Channel 8 news van arrived. It barreled as close as possible to the crowd and parked illegally. Out of it popped Melissa McFarland, followed by Bernie the cameraman, Debbie the sound woman and Speed on lights. They shouldered their way through the crowd and established a klieg-blazing observation post in the heart of City Hall Square. Henry noticed that, while Bernie aimed his camera at the speaking platform, Melissa McFarland was scanning the crowd, looking for "human interest."

Scooter began his speech, as usual, by trumpeting his experience on the School Board and the hundreds of sacrifices he had made on behalf of the schoolchildren of Blackhawk. After about three minutes listening to Scooter and staring at the "BRUISE MOOSE" banner (which was an aspersion against her brother), Fantasia turned to Henry.

"Henry, you got that Swiss Army knife?"

Fantasia knew that Henry never went anywhere without his backpack, which always contained a Swiss Army knife equipped with 12 different tools.

"Sure," said Henry, who was listening intently to Scooter's speech but was also interested in Melissa McFarland.

"I need to borrow it," said Fantasia.

Normally, because he knew Fantasia all too well, Henry would reply, "What do you want it for?" But tonight he was preoccupied with politics and media. So he just said, "Go ahead."

In seconds, Fantasia had found Henry's knife and disappeared. Henry felt a fleeting concern that Fantasia might be planning to stab Scooter McDuff. But he dismissed the idea as extreme (even for Fantasia).

Meanwhile, Fantasia worked her way forward. She climbed the City Hall steps and reached one of the building's great Greek pillars. She looked up and saw that there were ropes, wrapped high around the pillar, securing the end of the "BRUISE MOOSE!" banner. Fantasia also saw, leaning against the pillar, a ladder. It had been left there by the workmen who had put up the banner.

Everybody listening to Scooter was in front of the pillar.

Fantasia was behind the pillar, alone and unseen.

She had a ladder.

Fantasia started to climb. An excellent tree climber, Fantasia reached the top in seconds. There, she studied the two nylon ropes that held the corners of "BRUISE MOOSE!" in place. Whoever had hung the banner had wrapped the pillar about six times with each rope. Fantasia's mission was to bring down "BRUISE MOOSE!" She unfolded Henry's Swiss Army knife.

To cut the two strands that connected "BRUISE MOOSE!" to the pillar, Fantasia had to actually climb onto the pillar, using the rings of rope as hand and footholds. Fantasia had climbed at least a million trees without a single tumble. "No sweat," she whispered to herself.

Nimble as a squirrel, Fantasia leapt from ladder to pillar. Staying behind the pillar and out of public view, she inched within reach of the strands holding the banner. Down below, Scooter McDuff was talking about the "naiveté of a young man who, after showing his respect for law and order by striking an officer of our police department, thinks he is entitled—entitled, ladies and gentlemen—to make judgments affecting our children for years and years to come."

Hearing these slurs against her brother, Fantasia moved a little faster. "Loudmouth," she muttered. "You tub-of-lard breadandcircusface!"

Fantasia had to let go with one hand to cut the rope on the lower corner of "BRUISE MOOSE!" But this was no problem. She kept a death grip on the upper ring of ropes. If anyone saw her hanging onto the pillar like a high-wire act, they were watching in silent fascination. No one cried out as Fantasia neatly sliced the bottom rope.

Her hope was that after she cut the top corner, "BRUISE MOOSE!" would float down from its severed moorings and land right on top of Scooter McDuff, shutting up his big mouth in midspeech while the Channel 8 camera rolled.

Fantasia's plan might have worked. She still had a firm hold on the upper ropes with her left hand. Her sneakers provided a toehold below. But, as she sawed through the last threads holding up the derogatory banner, a stiff breeze rose up from the west. Suddenly, "BRUISE MOOSE!" flapped violently, snapping at Fantasia's face and breaking her concentration.

Fantasia's hand lost hold and her sneakers slipped. All at once, Fantasia felt herself suspended in midair—like Wile E. Coyote spinning his legs over the canyon. She did the only thing she could do. She dropped Henry's Swiss Army knife and grabbed the vast, flopping streamer as, once more, it whacked her in the kisser.

And then it fell, magnificently, away from the pillar.

As Fantasia Fulton held on for dear life, the banner swung a pendulum's arc, taking a collision course toward the speaker's platform. The crowd sucked in its breath. Bernie, Channel 8 cameraman, sensed the banner's movement. He panned upward.

"Oh, beautiful," he said.

Fantasia saw, rushing toward her, a row of figures. First was a state policeman, standing guard on the School Board candidates. Beyond him were Chairman McDuff, orating to the crowd, then Jack Sharkey of WBHA, then Darlene Gazelick and her husband, Garth. By inches, Fantasia missed flying smack-dab into the state trooper.

Scooter McDuff fared not so well.

Scooter, only for a split-second, noticed the eyes of the crowd shifting from him to something happening on his left. He'd only begun to turn his head to see what might be encroaching upon him when—foomp!—Fantasia Fulton trapezed bottom-first at fifty miles an hour, into his face. Although Scooter outweighed Fantasia by a ratio of perhaps six-to-one, her momentum was sufficient to send him tumbling into Jack Sharkey, who was helpless to prevent himself crashing into Darlene Gazelick, who threw up her hands, screamed and slammed her husband amidships. Then, like dominos tipped off-balance, Scooter, Jack Sharkey, Darlene and Garth Gazelick all tumbled together off the platform. They began rolling down the City Hall steps, grunting and griping as they did so.

Bernie's camera followed the action artfully.

Lyle Lehnherr, who had been cowering at the rear of the speakers platform, went unscathed. He remained frozen in place, gaping in helpless horror.

Fantasia had come to a jarring stop. She looked around, slightly dazed, and realized that she had landed, without a scratch, on the speakers platform. Inches from her face was a microphone. She said, “Er.”

Immediately, from an array of giant speakers all around City Hall Square, Fantasia heard, amplified a hundredfold, her very own, “ER!”

Fantasia, who was among the sharper pupils in the sixth grade at Blackhawk Middle School, instantly appreciated the possibilities of her perch. Still stuck on the podium like a bug on a windshield, Fantasia leaned into the mike and, quite modestly, said, “Choose Moose.”

In her voice, “CHOOSE MOOSE!” roared from every speaker.

Another voice, later identified as that of Amy Haddock, cried out, “You go, girl!”

Fantasia needed no encouragement. While Scooter found himself battered, woozy and tangled up in Darlene Gazelick’s legs at the bottom of the City Hall steps, Fantasia had command of Scooter McDuff’s platform. She said, again, louder, “CHOOSE MOOSE!” Then she repeated herself.

Again and again.

Louder and louder.

And pretty soon, it became evident that all the people who’d come to the big rally for Scooter, Darlene and Lyle Lehnherr were not entirely supportive of Scooter, Darlene and Lyle. A few spectators—including, of course, Henry and Penelope, their parents, Moose Fulton and Tiff Melrose—took up Fantasia’s chant. In a moment, it became contagious. Steadily, across City Hall Square, the refrain grew.

“Choose Moose! Choose Moose! Choose MOOSE! CHOOSE MOOSE! CHOOSE **MOOSE! CHOOSE MOOSE!** … ”

This might have gone on indefinitely if not for Band Director Wally Wilcox, whose jowls grew redder and redder as, with every repetition, his eyes shrank to angry slits. Waving his arms and shouting at his musicians, he ordered his obedient Thundering Sixty to play. Loud.

They broke into "The Stars and Stripes Forever," which, momentarily, could barely be heard above the rhythmic tide of "CHOOSE MOOSE! CHOOSE MOOSE! ... "

"Louder!" cried Wally Wilcox. "Play louder, you miserable brats!"

The band gained strength and made headway. But they didn't win out until Wally Wilcox had an inspiration. He broke off John Philip Sousa abruptly and—smashing his baton on a music stand—swung the band into Francis Scott Key.

With the sound of "The Star-Spangled Banner" sweeping across the square, the pro-Moose chant petered away. One by one, the gathered citizens removed their hats, covered their hearts and observed the silence that patriotism requires.

Wally Wilcox played the national anthem four times through, with mounting gusto, singing every thrilling word.

"*... And the ROCKets red GLARE, the bombs BURSTING in AIR ...*"

Meanwhile, the state trooper on the speakers platform awoke to his duty and pried Fantasia Fulton off the podium, just in time to hand the girl to her distraught mother.

Bernie, the cameraman, caught this scene. It was a good shot. He already had shots of Scooter and Darlene tangled together on the City Hall steps.

"Did you see me, Mom?" asked Fantasia.

"See you? *See* you?"

"Yeah. Up there!"

Delia Fulton's face radiated a rage that made the state trooper back away in naked fear.

"Sweetheart, I won't kill you," said Delia Fulton far too calmly. "Your father has reserved the privilege."

Garth Gazelick, who had suffered the least from Fantasia's mishap, scurried down the City Hall steps to extricate his wife from Scooter McDuff. He found her disoriented and disheveled, her glasses broken. But she was fully conscious and prepared to assist in Lt. Col. Lafayette Fulton's dispatch of his daughter. Freed from Darlene, Scooter McDuff staggered to his feet, tripped over Darlene's handbag and fell down again. He decided to stay on the ground until someone came along and lifted him.

Jack Sharkey was missing. After a brief search, an emergency medical technician from the Fire Department ambulance found him beneath the fallen "BRUISE MOOSE!" banner. Jack Sharkey had a bump on his head. He was rendering a medley of rock 'n' roll golden oldies apparently recalled from his youthful days as a Top Forty disc jockey on AM radio.

"Tutti-frutti," he sang woozily, *"all rutti. Tutti-frutti all rutti ... "*

Sometime during Wally Wilcox's third rendition of "The Star-Spangled Banner," the crowd seemed to understand that any further speechifying was unlikely. The Fire Department's paramedics had pounced on Jack Sharkey and the fallen politicians and were bundling them off to the emergency room at Memorial Hospital. Melissa McFarland, tugging on Bernie, chased the stretcher carrying Scooter McDuff. Debbie and Speed trailed behind.

People began to disperse. This included Fantasia, who had been hugged thankfully, then threatened with death, by her father. Unfazed by both hug and threat, she was skipping and bouncing toward the family car, along with her parents, Moose, Tiff and Henry Haddock.

"Didja hear 'em?" she was saying excitedly to Henry. "I got everybody over to Moose's side. Choooooooose Moose!"

"Maybe," said Henry, who had scant faith in the loyalty of the mob.

"Not all of 'em," said Moose, who agreed with Henry.

"Yeah, well, poop on both of ya," said Fantasia. She had been, 'til this moment, the soul of pessimism. Now she said, "I'm thinkin' we just might have a chance to win this sucker."

Fantasia's father squeezed his daughter's hand.

"Well, Fantasia. You know what Yogi Berra said."

Henry and Fantasia looked up to Fantasia's dad inquiringly.

"It ain't over," said Colonel Fate, "'til it's over."

CHAPTER 24

5 APRIL

On Election Day, at just about 7:30 am, Henry Haddock stood on the sidewalk on Pearl Street, in front of his house. Henry had been awake since about 4 a.m.

Since getting up, he had done everything possible to kill time. He had taken a very thorough shower, washing his hair twice in the process. He had brushed his teeth 'til his gums hurt. He had flossed. He had trimmed his nails—fingers and toes. He had spent extra time deciding what to wear. All this activity had gotten the time up to 4:45 am.

At 5 am, Henry had sat down in the living room to watch the early-bird news on TV. While doing that, he'd reviewed his homework and reorganized everything in his book bag. He reminded himself that he needed a new Swiss Army knife. He got a little relief at about 6:10, when the newspaper bounced off the front door. Henry rushed to get the paper. Standing on the doorstep, he opened to Page 3 and read all nine inches of information about today's election in Blackhawk. The story dwelt on the campaign for School Board (mentioning Henry's name once), because the other local races—for Alderman,

Zoning Board and Board of Assessors—were not heavily contested.

The news told Henry nothing he didn't already know. Except for Charlie Mulcahy, the paper said the "reform" candidates were "major underdogs" because Darnell "Moose" Fulton and "dark horse" Dexter D. Lee had refused to "take the pledge" not to raise taxes.

In frustration, Henry tossed the broadsheet aside. A moment later, he picked it up again to read the sports section. Then he refolded the whole newspaper in perfect order, because Ralph Haddock demanded a neat paper with his morning coffee.

At 6:30, Henry couldn't stand the house any longer and he went outside. He was dressed and ready for school, his book bag strapped to his back. It was still dark outside, and chilly. Henry took a walk around the block, arriving back in front of his house at 6:45. He did another lap around the block.

By 7 am, as Henry started another lap, a weak sunrise illuminated the neighborhood. He tried to appreciate his solitude in the still of early morning. He tried to absorb his surroundings. He listened for birds, but it was apparently too early for birds. This was a nice block, thought Henry, orderly and landscaped, but not green yet. It was too early for grass. Mostly the neighborhood's vegetation was wilted, leafless and brown. The only "growth" visible from the frosty ground was in the form of campaign signs. On Henry's block, because of the loyalty of the Fultons' neighbors, there was a concentration of "CHOOSE MOOSE!" signs, accompanied by signs urging a vote also for Charlie Mulcahy and Dexter D. Lee.

However, as Henry ventured off Pearl and down Ann Street, he saw more signs favoring Scooter McDuff, Lyle Lehnherr and even Darlene. By the time he got to Jackson Street, the balance tipped in favor of the incumbents. It didn't start to even out again 'til he was halfway up May Street, almost back to Pearl.

Figuring the odds just from his own neighborhood, Henry was worried.

At about 7:40, right on time, Fantasia Fulton burst from her front door. She was dragged across her lawn toward Henry by Sarge—a pet Lt. Col. Lafayette Fulton once described as "a cross between a Labrador retriever and a camel." Sarge planted both giant feet on Henry's shoulders, as usual, and licked Henry's face thoroughly, while Fantasia stood idly by and said, groggily, "Mornin', Henry."

"Mornin', Sarge. Hi, Fance."

And Sarge was off, galumphing down the block to "do his business," Fantasia tethered helplessly behind.

While Henry waited for Fantasia to get Sarge back inside and grab her school stuff, Henry thought about that day's newspaper. Coverage of the School Board election in Blackhawk was brief because, outside of Blackhawk, it wasn't very important. Political huffing and puffing was rampant, on a grander scale, all over the world. There were struggles over public policy—full of bizarre characters, extraordinary events and horrible violence—in places like Zimbabwe and Belgium, China and Denmark, Libya and Bolivia.

"Hey, Henry!" said Fantasia, bouncing up beside him.

Henry had been thinking so hard he didn't see Fantasia as she hauled Sarge back inside and galloped back outdoors. She was ready now to walk with Henry to the Blackhawk Middle School.

"Hey, Fance," said Henry. "I was jus' thinkin'."

"About what?" Fantasia cradled her books and relaxed. She was in no hurry to get to school, especially if Henry had an idea. She always paid attention to Henry's ideas.

"Well," said Henry. "You know, when somethin' really big happens in sports, like—you know—say, the Yankees lose the World Series?"

"Yeah, well, good. I hate the Yankees."

"Everybody hates the Yankees, Fance. That's not my point."

"Okay, then. The point?"

"Well, the next day, after the World Series, what's different?"

"Huh?"

"Nothin', right? The biggest sports team in just about the whole world loses the biggest game of the year, right?"

"Yeah?"

"And the next day, so what? Nothing's changed. Everything goes on, exactly like it was before. But!"

"But?"

"With politics, it's totally different."

"Huh?" said Fantasia.

"Okay," said Henry. "Let's say some little, rinky-dink country, like Latvia, has a revolution. They overthrow the king, or prime minister—or whatever—and they put him in jail. Everybody's rioting in the streets and looting. Okay, now this is just Latvia, by itself. No other country's having a revolution. But, then, wait a few weeks and you know what happens?

"What?" said Fantasia. She was mystified.

"The whole world is different. Everywhere."

"It is?"

"Yeah. Just from that one rinky-dink revolution in Latvia."

"Okay, if you say so. But why?"

"I dunno. It just is. Somehow, the whole world is connected to Latvia, or Ethiopia or anyplace. And if Latvia has a revolution, things start to happen in other countries nearby, and then farther away. And pretty soon, the whole world is changing. It's weird."

"It sure is." said Fantasia. "I don't like it."

Henry and Fantasia walked on slowly toward school. Henry was still thinking.

"Okay, Fance, what do you know about, say, the Yankees?"

"I know I hate 'em."

"Okay, what do you know about, well, Latvia?"

"Latvia? What's the deal with you and Latvia?"

"Nothing, Fance. It's an example, okay?"

"Okay, it's an example, like Cap'n Blood. I get that. So, what about Latvia?" said Fantasia.

"I was just asking *you*. What do you know about Latvia?"

"Me? Latvia? Nothin'!"

"You don't even know if you *like* Latvia, right?"

"No."

"So you know more about the New York Yankees than you know about Latvia, right?"

"Yeah, that's about it, Henry."

"Okay!" said Henry. "So, you're the same as everybody else! Almost everybody pays more attention to sports than politics."

"I guess," said Fantasia, cautiously. "Is there somethin' wrong with that?"

"No, it's just normal. But I can't help thinkin'."

Henry plunged back into thought, which resulted in silence, which annoyed Fantasia. "Hey!" she said. "Thinkin' about *what?*"

"Well, for one thing," said Henry. "I keep hearing grownups say that sports are like politics. An election is like a horse race or the Super Bowl, y'know?"

Fantasia nodded.

Henry continued. "But that's dumb. If you just think about a little place like Latvia, you can see that isn't so—because the biggest event in sports lasts a day and doesn't change anything. A week after the Super Bowl, hardly anybody remembers who won. But one little political earthquake, in some tiny country that nobody's ever heard of, that political earthquake could turn out to be bigger than a million Super Bowls. It could start a war that lasts twenty years and kills a million people."

Fantasia pondered this. Henry, out of habit, started walking toward school. Fantasia followed.

"That's how World War I got started," Henry said, mostly to himself.

"Really?" said Fantasia.

"Yeah," said Henry. "Mr. Kussow said so."

"Well, Mr. Kussow knows everything."

"Yeah."

They walked a little further. Henry started up again.

"People understand sports. They spend hours and hours watching it, and then more hours and hours talking about it. But they don't spend hours and hours on politics."

"Henry, I don't spend hours and hours on either."

"Well, that's 'cause you're a dope."

"I am not, Latviaface!"

With this, they began to noogie each other, harmlessly, for about a half-block. But as they turned on Hollister Avenue toward school, Henry said, "I guess my point is that if people *understood* what we're tryin' to tell them in this election, we'd win. But they don't. They don't want to pay attention. They don't understand how important politics is, even in little places nobody's ever heard of, like Blackhawk and Latvia. When Moose stopped playin' basketball and switched to politics, people stopped listenin' to Moose."

"Henry," said Fantasia, with an anxious look, "what are you saying? Are you givin' up?"

"Jeez, I dunno," said Henry, disconsolately.

"You can't give up, Henry. You know what Charlie Mulcahy keeps tellin' us," said Fantasia.

"Yeah, I know," said Henry Haddock irresolutely.

"Charlie says, sometimes when people don't seem to be listening, they are."

"I know, I know."

"You gotta keep faith in people," said Fantasia.

To Henry's amazement, Fantasia sounded like she truly believed this hogwash.

"Jeez, Fance, I guess you're back to being an optimist," said Henry.

"Yeah, I guess so."

Just before Henry and Fantasia arrived at school, Fantasia

mentioned that Moose had been "excused" from class that day. Moose, along with Charlie Mulcahy and Dexter D. Lee, were doing one more last-minute round of candidate coffee slurping.

"A lot of good that'll do," said Henry cynically.

If there was any similarity between sports and politics, he thought, it was the fact that—in either one—you could work your tail off, sweating and fretting 'til the very last second, and you could still end up getting walloped.

That day, Henry discovered that his campaign had been a big success at the Blackhawk Middle School. Just about every blackboard in school carried a variation of "CHOOSE MOOSE!" written in all sorts of colors and graffiti styles. Kids who saw Henry or Fantasia in the halls would slap hands with them, break out in cheers and charge toward their next class chanting, "Choose Moose, Choose Moose ... "

When Henry bumped into Ray McCloskey after fourth period, Mr. McCloskey was excited. This was Mr. McCloskey's first visit to the middle school since his dismissal. "Henry, I've never seen enthusiasm like this. You've gotten the whole school fired up. About politics, Henry! Politics. It's unheard of."

Henry peered up into Mr. McCloskey's face, surprised at the teacher's naiveté. "Yeah, but jeez, Mr. McCloskey," he said, "you know as well as me that all this excitement is pointless. These kids can't vote."

"Henry, Henry," said Ray McCloskey, shaking his head and ruffling Henry's hair. "Kids get excited. They go home full of energy and they share all their excitement with their parents. This kind of enthusiasm—it can be contagious."

Henry shrugged. He refused to be seduced by false hopes. "Yeah, we'll see," he said. He left Mr. McCloskey in the corridor, scratching his head.

Late in the day, Henry stuck his nose into the school gym, which had been taken over by the election. Election workers were under one of the basketball hoops at a table, checking in voters and handing out ballots. There were lots of voters. Henry couldn't remember what Charlie had said about a "heavy turnout," whether it was good or bad.

Probably bad, thought Henry.

The voting booths were really just portable tables on spindly legs with shields on three sides. Twenty were lined along the wall on the far side of the gym. Every booth had a voter, each voter hunched over the ballot, reading choices, making marks.

Suddenly, a small ruckus broke out. A little old lady in a baggy sweater and a dress that seemed to be one size too big for her, with her overcoat on one arm, was waving a ballot with the other arm.

"He's not HERE!" she was shouting. "They took him off the ballot! This is FRAUD!"

Three election workers, one man and two women, all about the same age as the little old lady, rushed toward her.

She shouted, "They took Moose away! Where's MOOSE!"

The election workers reached the madwoman. Everyone else in the gym, including the voters, stopped what they were doing and turned to stare.

Election workers surrounded the madwoman. She was so small that now she was invisible. But her voice was like a screech owl in a silent forest. "I wanted to vote for Moose! But he's not here! This is a crime! This is FRAUD!"

More people began to rush toward the madwoman, some of them saying, "No, no! He's there! Show her! Help her!" And so forth.

While Henry watched, it took at least seven election workers and another dozen bystanders ten minutes to explain to the woman that Moose, on the ballot, appeared by his legal name, "Darnell L. Fulton."

Henry thought someone should go into the voting booth to help the little old lady fill in her ballot. But this wasn't allowed. She would have to ferret out "Darnell L. Fulton" all by herself. Henry was sure she would fail. It occurred to Henry that his cute rhyming slogan and all those brilliant "CHOOSE MOOSE!" signs all over town—none of which mentioned Moose's legal name—had probably lost the election. Hundreds of people, looking for "Moose" and not finding "Moose," would go right past "Darnell L. Fulton" and vote for someone they recognized. Like Darlene.

Henry left school that day with his homework finished and a backpack full of blues.

He wasn't feeling much better that evening when he joined Fantasia for another walk, to City Hall.

When they arrived, there was a big crowd in the building's rotunda, just inside the grand columned entrance. Off to either side, city offices and meeting rooms branched off. Facing the entrance was the big meeting room where the Aldermen met every Wednesday. At eight o'clock sharp, its doors were pulled shut and the vote counters got to work.

By 8:30, all the ballots from the town's polling places had been delivered to the big meeting room. As election officials scurried in and out, Henry sneaked an occasional peek at the counting scene. The long Aldermen's table was lined with city employees. Each had a stack of ballots, and each was tallying results on a separate sheet of paper and then repeating the process on a computer. Two people stood behind each vote counter, verifying the count. Each vote counter had a second vote counter, doing the same thing all over again, with a tally sheet, a computer and two people leaning over his or her shoulder, making remarks, asking questions, pointing at things.

By nine o'clock, every candidate for every office was in the rotunda. The League of Women Voters had set up a table with cookies and coffee. By 9:10, the cookies had been reduced to crumbs and by 9:40, the coffee was gone.

Henry noticed that, after all the arguments in the campaign, the candidates seemed to be cured of all their hard feelings. Next to a pillar, Charlie Mulcahy was talking in the friendliest way with Darlene Gazelick. After a few minutes, Charlie summoned Dexter D. Lee to join them and Mrs. Gazelick. She shook Dexter's hand uncertainly but, after two minutes, laughed at something he said and seemed to relax.

Dexter was like that, thought Henry. Give him a chance and he'd crack anybody's shell.

Elsewhere, Henry noticed Scooter McDuff with his hand on Annabella Moss' arm, talking to her warmly and earnestly. Moose was circulating comfortably all through the crowd, acting like a veteran politician. Henry couldn't help wondering if he might have created a monster. The only candidate who didn't seem to be joining in the spirit of reconciliation was Lyle Lehnherr. He stood aside, staring out toward City Hall Square, clutching a half-empty cup of cold coffee.

Henry, who had stocked up on cookies, took the last one out of his jacket pocket around 10 pm, just when the big announcement came. All the ballots had been counted. However, to be absolutely sure, because it was such a tightly contested election, Registrar of Voters Al Disney had ordered the School Board ballots to be re-tallied.

A groan rose from the crowd.

"How long?" shouted Moose Fulton.

The person making the announcement was Teri Jefferson, the assistant city clerk, a large Black lady with an impressive bosom but the voice of a canary. Her manner was nervous. "Well," she chirped, "It should take about an hour ... I hope. I know it's getting late, everybody ... I'm really sorry."

"Aw, it's okay," said Moose, who felt bad for upsetting Teri.

Teri Jefferson smiled nervously and disappeared into the counting room.

So, another hour elapsed.

"Why are they recounting?" Henry wondered.

"My guess? Because it's close," said Ray McCloskey.

"Is that good?"

"Well, I guess so. It means that if we lost," said Mr. McCloskey, "at least we didn't get clobbered."

"We did not lose," said Lt. Col. Lafayette Fulton, who had just arrived.

"Daddy! Hi!" said Fantasia. "You made it."

Lt. Col. Fulton greeted Ray McCloskey and Henry. He said hello to Henry's parents, hugged his wife and also hugged Moose. "I had to stay late at the base. I thought I'd miss the results. Why is it so late?"

Just then, Teri Jefferson emerged again and said the School Board votes were still being recounted. But she had results in the other races. In a voice both sweet and shaky, Teri Jefferson provided the expected results.

In the race for the Board of Aldermen, two incumbents, Tony Vollmer and Mary Eagan, had easily outpolled their only challenger, Karl Weisbrodt. Every Zoning Board member had been reelected without opposition. And in the only contested seat on the Board of Assessors, incumbent Pete Saunders had swamped Erv Morgan, 2,486 to 391. This was Erv's sixth defeat, but it was his highest vote total ever. Near Henry in the rotunda, Pete Saunders was shaking Erv Morgan's hand vigorously and congratulating him on his performance.

"Another ten years and I've got ya!" said Erv.

"I can feel you breathing down my neck," said Pete, laughing.

Henry couldn't help smiling. Maybe politics isn't such a dark art after all, he thought.

Finally, just before 11 pm, Teri Jefferson swung open the doors of the Aldermen's meeting room. Behind her, most of the vote counters were still seated, weary looking, at the big table, behind stacks of ballots. The election observers were emerging from the big room. Tight-lipped and poker-faced, they filtered in amongst the hundred or so people in the rotunda. They knew the outcome, but were under severe orders to reveal nothing.

City Clerk Al Disney slipped into the doorway next to Teri. He nudged her and whispered, "You go ahead, Teri. Read 'em the results."

Teri nodded. She looked out at the crowd.

"Ladies, um," she began. "Ladies and, um ... well, then. Here are the results of the election for the Board of the Blackhawk School District."

A deathly silence settled over the rotunda. Teri was trembling ever so slightly, a condition that primarily affected her bosom.

But her voice trembled, too, as she continued. "Um, as you know—gee, I hope you know—the three candidates with the highest vote totals are elected to the Board."

A murmur of assent followed.

"Okay, good," said Teri Jefferson. She shuffled the top sheet off a handful of papers that she was gripping damply with both hands. She stared at the papers.

"In first place, with 2,209 votes," Teri Jefferson read, "elected to the Board ... Charles Mulcahy."

The roar of surprise and exultation that rocked the building almost scared Teri back into the meeting room. She stood wide-eyed and shaky while Charlie raised one fist in victory, then pushed through the crowd, hugged Fantasia and lifted Henry up by the armpits, showing him off to the crowd like a prize piglet.

"Hey!' bellowed Al Disney. "Quiet down! We're not finished! Dammit! Settle down!"

"He's right," said Henry to Charlie. "That's only one seat. We could still lose."

"Henry, you're a killjoy after my own heart," said Charlie.

But Teri Jefferson had mustered her courage. She was reading from the next sheet on her stack. "In second place, with 1,857 votes, elected to the Board ... Farrell Xavier McDuff."

Of course, this threw Scooter's supporters into a celebration. It was not as raucous as Charlie's outburst, however, partly because this was the first time Scooter had ever failed to "top the ballot."

Al Disney got the crowd under control and nodded to Teri Jefferson, whose voice seemed steadier. "Okay, now, this is the third one, the last available seat," she said. "In third place, with 1,672 votes, elected to the Board ... Lyle—"

A gasp went up. Somewhere in the back of the room, a voice, recognizably that of Lyle Lehnherr, cried out, "Yes!"

"Wait!" wailed Teri Jefferson.

"What?" yelled Fantasia.

"Oh, for God's sake!" shouted Al Disney, "Hold everything!"

Al Disney took Teri Jefferson by the shoulder and turned her away from the crowd. They whispered together for a moment, shuffling Teri's papers as they did so.

Finally, Teri Jefferson, wiping a tear from the corner of her eye, turned back. "I'm very sorry," she warbled softly. "I got some pages mixed up. But now it's okay."

"What the HELL—" This was Lyle Lehnherr's voice again.

"Everything's in order now," said Al Disney.

"Well, it's too late now," said Fantasia Fulton. "I already wet my pants."

This, of course, caused a fresh uproar. Al Disney regained order again. Teri Jefferson read the results.

"In third place, with 1,684 votes, elected to the Board ... Darnell L. Fulton."

The celebration this time went on for ten minutes. Al Disney made no effort to stop it. Eventually, Teri Jefferson joined the snake dance around the rotunda, which was led by Dexter D. Lee, who was not disappointed that he finished "out of the money."

"Are you kidding?" Dexter said later to Henry. "I was scared to death I might win. I don't know how to act like a grownup!"

While Dexter and the winners celebrated, Lyle Lehnherr and Darlene Gazelick departed the building quietly. Scooter stayed, watching the festivities and smiling enigmatically. He did not see Lyle and Darlene to the door.

"That's politics," said Ray McCloskey, observing the behavior of the three incumbents. "Once you've lost the election, you might as well be dead."

Then he had a second thought.

"Unless, of course, you're Dexter."

Eventually, Teri Jefferson got back around to the also-rans. It turned out that Lyle Lehnherr was a close fourth place, with 1,672 votes, followed by Dexter D. Lee with 1,511. Darlene Gazelick ended up with 984 votes. Joyce Tweedy, the mystery Christian, came in last, with 179 votes that would have otherwise gone to Lyle or Darlene.

It was about midnight, under a clear and starry sky, when Henry Haddock— with Fantasia on one side and Ray McCloskey on the other—stepped out of City Hall into a Blackhawk that was completely changed, as if Latvia had been overthrown by elves and hobbits.

Mr. McCloskey summed up Henry's feelings.

"Far out," he said.

CHAPTER 25

9 APRIL

When Charlie Mulcahy arrived at the Haddock family pizza party on Saturday night, with his wife, Maribel, he got a "Charlie, Charlie, he's our man" cheer from Amy Haddock and Tiff Melrose. Then there was a standing ovation. By then, the best political minds in town had concluded that the election finally boiled down to who really—Charlie Mulcahy or Paul Lamartine—was the most respected man in town.

Charlie settled down at the dining-room table. He accepted a slice of pizza and a glass of champagne. Then he made an announcement.

"I have it on good authority—"

"Who?" asked Fantasia. "Name your authority!"

Charlie laughed. "Good question, Fantasia," he said. "Scooter McDuff is my source. He called to tell me that Paul Lamartine has officially withdrawn his offer to turn our school system into a wholly owned subsidiary of the Lamartine Development Corporation."

"So what?" said Moose. "We would've voted against taking

his money, anyway."

The pizza party, which included all Haddocks, all Fultons, Ray McCloskey and Dexter D. Lee, plus Tiff Melrose and a dozen of the campaign's most devoted workers, whooped it up.

When the whooping subsided, Charlie said, "This isn't over. We've barely started. If we want our teachers and our curriculum back, we're going to have to raise the money we need, without Paul Lamartine's largesse. We're going to have to propose, float and approve that bond issue we've been talking about."

"Which means another election," said Ray McCloskey.

"We'll win," said Henry.

"Henry, this bond issue," said Charlie. "We're talking about at least two million dollars. Maybe more."

"We'll win," said Henry.

"Faith in the people, Henry?" said Ray McCloskey.

Henry grinned.

"What about the band?" asked Penelope.

"The band?" asked Amy. "What about the band?"

"Why should you care about the band?" Tiff said to Penelope. "I thought they kicked you out?"

"No, that was just temporary—for the rally at City Hall. They couldn't keep me out forever. After all, I'm the Benny Goodman of Blackhawk, " said Penelope.

"Benny who?" said Tiff.

"So," said Amy, pressing her point, "there's still gonna be a band?"

"Sure! We all love the band," said Charlie.

"C'mon. Who's Benny Goodman?" said Moose.

"Yeah, but the new band's gonna be smaller," said Henry. "No more parades in New York. Or football games in Texas."

"Well, that's okay," said Penelope. "I guess."

"But you'll be playin' at every Blackhawk game, Penelope—football, basketball, wrestling," said Moose.

"Wrestling?" said Penelope. "Ick!"

Charlie lifted his glass. "I'd like to propose a toast to a great campaigner who took fifteen hundred votes away from Lyle and Darlene—fifteen hundred votes that got our man, Moose, elected. A toast! To Dexter D. Lee!"

Everyone cheered and toasted and slapped Dexter D. Lee on the back. Dexter D. Lee bowed extravagantly, made faces and danced in a silly circle, but there was a tear in his eye. And then, in both eyes, when Ray McCloskey gave him a hug that lasted quite a while.

Four nights later, the same crowd—give or take a few bodies, overflowed the gallery in the high-school library for the first meeting of the new School Board. Superintendent Ptaschnik and Myrtle Arnold were at the usual table, along with the new Town Counsel, Russell Farrington (who happened to be Charlie Mulcahy's law partner). In the audience, Buzz Skelton looked happier than he had for years. Darren Flack was present to represent the media and get a group photo of the new Board.

Scooter McDuff, in his customary seat, looked out benevolently and tapped his gavel.

"I call this meeting of the School Board to order for the purpose of electing officers. Do I have a nomination for Chairman?"

From his new seat on the Board, Moose Fulton spoke unhesitantly. "I nominate the best teacher I ever had, Mrs. Annabella Moss."

Annie Moss turned to Moose and said, "Young man, you are a flattering prevaricator. You hated every minute in my class."

Scooter broke in, "I'd like to set the gavel aside, if I may," he said, "and second the nomination, as well as Moose's compliment. I'm still learning from this woman."

Turning back, Mrs. Moss said, "Scooter, you're a blowhard."

"Yes, I am," said Scooter. "Are there any objections?

Good, hearing none, I declare this matter settled. Madame Chairwoman, let's you and me switch seats. And here's your gavel."

"Oh, I don't want that infernal thing. You take it home and pound walnuts."

There was some applause for the new Chairwoman. Then the Board selected Randy Zink as secretary.

"Y'see that?" whispered Dexter D. Lee to Fantasia. "If I'd won, they would've stuck me with that job."

"So," said Fantasia, "secretary is a gay job?"

"Very," said Dexter.

"So, Randy Zink? Is he?"

"We'll ask him afterwards."

Dexter and Fantasia giggled together, drawing a reproachful look from Annie Moss.

Scooter was speaking. "Madame Chairwoman, I'd like to take up one matter out of order."

"What would that be, Scooter?"

"Well, I'd like to correct an injustice for which this Board is responsible," said Scooter. "A while ago, on very weak grounds, we dismissed one of our best teachers. At this point, I would like to move that the Board reinstate, with restitution of lost salary and benefits, our middle-school history and social-studies teacher, Ray McCloskey."

"I second that motion," said Charlie Mulcahy.

"If there is no objection?" said Annie Moss.

If there was an objection, the applause drowned it out.

After the meeting, Scooter McDuff approached Henry. "You've had a good night, young man."

"I guess so," said Henry.

Then, McDuff reached out and shook Henry's hand. As he did so, he said, "Henry, I'd like to ask you a favor."

"What?" said Henry, a little suspiciously.

“Henry, I’d just like you to promise me something. When you get old enough and decide to run against me, you’ll give me a chance to retire first.”

Henry felt his father’s arm on his shoulder and he looked up. Ralph Haddock and Mr. McDuff were both smiling at him.

“Okay,” said Henry. “Scout’s honor.”

A moment later, as they were leaving the building, Scooter McDuff said to Ralph Haddock, “Wait a minute. I didn’t know Henry was in the Scouts.”

“He’s not,” said Henry’s father.

“I was afraid of that,” said Scooter.

STUDY GUIDE

CHAPTER 1

Henry's conflict is with his town's School Board. In some towns, this municipal council is called the School Committee, and in other locales, the county government manages schools. What is your community's "school board" called? How many members are there? What are its powers and responsibilities? Is it elected or appointed? When do they meet? Have you ever attended a meeting?

Henry is "incensed" at the cancellation of the art curriculum at Blackhawk Middle School. What is a curriculum? What are all the parts of the curriculum in your school? And in your school system?

The rule at the Haddock house is no phones at mealtime. Is this a good rule? Defend your answer.

Part of the problem for the Blackhawk schools is a statewide referendum limiting the school budget. How are schools funded in your community? In recent years, what statewide referenda in your state have been passed? What effect have they had?

Henry is incensed because the Blackhawk School Board has made serious budget cuts. Has your local school board also made cuts? If so, how has this affected schools in your community? How has the community reacted?

Clarence Darrow was involved in one of the most famous courtroom trials in U.S. history. What trial was it? What were the issues in the trial? Who was Darrow's opponent?That trial was made into a stage play and a famous movie, *Inherit the Wind*, in which Spencer Tracy played Clarence Darrow. Have you seen the film?

What is socialism? What role has it played in U.S. history? And in world history?

Socialism is often described as a rival to capitalism as a governing principle for nations. What are the major differences between the two?

What is a bond issue? Has your community recently passed, or defeated, a bond issue? What was the purpose of this bond issue?

What does Henry mean when he says he'll "beard the lion in his den"?

VOCABULARY

abolition
beard the lion
catastrophe
histrionic
incense (v.)
incense (n.)
mandate
profane
protégé

rabblerouser
referendum
socialism
socialization
vindictiveness

PEOPLE TO LOOK UP

Mark Twain
Eugene V. Debs
Clarence Darrow
Henry Wallace
Bernie Sanders
Simon Winchester
Daniel Boorstin
Mother Jones
Samuel Gompers
John L. Lewis

CHAPTER 2

In the previous chapter, Mrs. Haddock restricted her children's cell-phone use. In this chapter, Fantasia's parents place limits on her videogaming. Do your parents have rules for your use of electronic devices? If so, what are they? Do you think kids should have these sorts of rules? Defend your answer.

Henry is a heavy user of his public library. Do you have a local library? Do you use it often? Can you look up old newspaper articles there? If so, what are the available media for reading these articles?

Buzz Skelton monitors the School Board for the Blackhawk teachers' union. Do your teachers belong to a union? If so, what's the union's name and what national union does it belong to? What are the most common arguments in favor, and against, teachers belonging to unions? Do you think teachers should be organized into unions? Defend your answer.

On the broader topic of labor unions, do you know anyone who belongs to a union? If so, why did they join? What sort of different "shops" exist in a unionized workplace? Can you name three major national labor organizations? Can you name three national business organizations opposed to organized labor?

The "most important" board in Blackhawk is the Board of Aldermen. In other towns, this leading deliberative body is called the Town Council, City Council, Board of Selectmen, etc. What is this group called in your community? How large is it? What are its powers? Is it elective or appointive? When does it meet?

The Blackhawk School Board has five members. What is the importance of this number?

Among Darlene Gazelick's favorite issues are some of the biggest controversies in American public education. Discuss each of these:

Prayer in schools
Bible study
"Abstinence"
Censorship of texts and library books

Henry learns that the School Board's meetings do not allow discussion by members of "the public." This is true for many municipal boards and committees. What are the rules for boards and committees in your town? How can a member of "the public" get onto the agenda?

What is *Robert's Rules of Order*?

The manager of the Blackhawk schools is a "superintendent," Robert Ptaschnik. What is the title of this person in your school system? What are his or her powers and responsibilities? What other officials govern your local schools, and what do they do?

VOCABULARY

abstinence
alacrity
arteries
majestiferous
moniker
Paleolithic
phalanx
shmooze
stringer

CHAPTER 3

Henry encounters extreme crowding in his American History class. Class size is a big issue in American education. What is the average class size in your school? In your school system? Do you think this class size is helpful or harmful to students' ability to learn? If you could determine class size in your school, what would you do? Defend your answer.

A big issue for the Blackhawk School Board is its decision to fire some teachers. This is done for budgetary reasons, but such firings also occur for other reasons. What are some of these reasons? What are some protections teachers have against being fired? How would you judge teachers' performance if you had the power to hire and fire them?

VOCABULARY

anarchy
barbarian
decimate
dilettante
moral support
solidarity
vehement

PEOPLE TO LOOK UP

Lech Walesa
Joan of Arc
Attila the Hun

CHAPTER 4

Darlene Gazelick thinks of Scooter McDuff as a "militant Christian." What does the term mean?

Mrs. Gazelick is a believer in "creation science," which is one of the most controversial subjects in education. What is it? What is the scientific theory opposed by "creationists"? Has creation science been discussed in your school system? If so, what was the outcome? Explain your own opinion on this subject.

Randy Zink is often asked by senior citizens: "Why must I continue to pay for schools when neither I nor my children have been to school for 25 years?" What's your answer to that question?

Lyle Lehnherr's philosophy of public education is that there shouldn't be any. Do you agree or disagree? Defend your answer.

Amy thinks Henry's battle against the School Board is "windmill tilting." This is a reference to a famous character in literature. Who "tilted at windmills"?

In what story does the Cheshire cat appear? What is the significance of his smile?

VOCABULARY

certitude
creationism
crusade
fiefdom
havoc
lion's den
militant
panache
pathology
quixotic
sardonic
sobriquet
status quo
stoic
subvert
surreptitious
tilting at windmills

PEOPLE TO LOOK UP

Bullwinkle J. Moose
President Richard M. Nixon
The Cheshire Cat
President Jimmy Carter

CHAPTER 5

This chapter revolves around the state "Open Meeting Law," which requires municipal boards to conduct almost all their business in public. Why do you think American government places so much importance in holding "open meetings"? What are some problems caused by the insistence on open meetings? What are some dangers in closing meetings to public scrutiny?

Henry is described as a "thorn in the paw" of Scooter McDuff. This is a reference to a famous fable. What's the title of the story, and what happens in it?

Darlene Gazelick calls Henry a "bad seed." What's the origin of this term and what does it mean?"

Birmingham and Selma, Alabama, mentioned here, were two of the most historic sites in the U.S. civil-rights movement. Describe at least one event in each place that changed the course of history.

Moose is cut from the football team after the fight at the School Board. Do you think this is fair?

VOCABULARY

arraign
bad seed
cahoots
can of worms
cause celebre
dexterous
donnybrook
in cahoots
incubus
Nazi
volatile

CHAPTER 6

Henry learns the importance of the "minutes" of the School Board's meetings. What are "minutes"? See if you can get copies of the minutes from public meetings in your town.

The "minutes" of the United States government are published daily in *The Congressional Record*. Take a look.

VOCABULARY

banishment
crestfallen
dearth
ennui
equanimity
illiberal
Je ne sais quoi
quandary
repudiate
Third World

PEOPLE TO LOOK UP

Che Guevara

CHAPTER 7

Henry's research focuses on secret sessions of the School Board. This poses the issue of "transparency" in government. Why is transparency such an important issue? Can you cite examples of transparency, and lack of transparency, in local, state and national government?

VOCABULARY

baleful
chastened
implication
inquisitive

hightail it
maven
taboo
transparency

CHAPTER 8

Henry has written to his state's Attorney General. Attorney General is one of the so-called "constitutional offices" that are subject to popular election. Name the constitutional offices in your state. Who are the current holders of these offices?

What is the Attorney General's job?

Most states also have elected legislatures consisting of two "houses." What are these houses called? How many members are elected to each? How long do they serve between elections? How often does the legislature meet and for how long? Which party holds a majority in each house, and how great is this majority?

One state has a single-house or "unicameral" legislature. Which state?

French, Gabrielle O'Connor's favorite subject, is usually included among subjects called the Humanities. These include foreign languages, music and art. What Humanities courses does your school offer? Has your school system cut any Humanities courses?

Often, when budget cuts occur, the first targets are the Humanities. Why is this so? Do you agree? Defend your answer. Can you name any federal programs involved in promoting the Humanities?

In this chapter, Henry asks question after question. Inside politics and government, who usually asks most of the questions? Who's expected to have the answers? Outside of government, what group is expected to ask the questions? Explain why.

What's the origin of "the $64,000 question"?

What is the Philosopher's Stone?

VOCABULARY

alma mater
cranium
deceitfulness
jot and tittle
posse
postscript
$64,000 question
skimmer
stadia
subterfuge
surmise

CHAPTER 9

In this chapter, Henry thinks of thirteen famous pirates, both real and fictional. Identify each of these pirates. If they're fictional characters, identify their sources and authors.

Among the real pirates on this list, which do you think was the most important historical figure? Defend your answer.

Where is Far Tortuga?

What are differences between an analogy, a metaphor and an allegory? How do terms such as "simile" and "fable" fit into this discussion?

VOCABULARY

allegory
analogy
candor
carouse
chaperone
divvy
existential
hypothetical
metaphor
mutiny
rhetorical
running amok
sacred cow
whistleblower

PEOPLE TO LOOK UP

Captain Kidd
Long John Silver
Henry Morgan
Jean LaFitte
Sir Francis Drake
The Dread Pirate Roberts
Captain Hook
Sinbad
Jack Sparrow
Davy Jones
Edward Teach
Captain Blood
Jake and Elwood Blues

CHAPTER 10

Let's figure out the real-life characters in Henry's pirate "analogy." Who are Cap'n Blood and Cap'n Bluebeard? What is the riverboat?

Mr. McCloskey mentions "the great protests of the past." Can you find ten examples of great popular protests in American history? Are there any current examples of the American protest tradition?

Possibly the greatest "philosopher" of political protest was Mohandas Gandhi. Where did he lead his protests and what was the outcome? What was Gandhi's guiding principle? Which great American adopted Gandhi's tactics, and what was the result of his movement?

What is a Bolshevik? Why does Darlene Gazelick call Henry a Bolshevik? Is this accurate?

Melissa McFarland, the TV newswoman, says the protesting students are "expressing their First Amendment rights." What is the First Amendment? Of what document is the First Amendment a part? What right or rights in the First Amendment are the students expressing? Are the protesters using or abusing the First Amendment? What right or rights in the First Amendment is Channel 8 expressing?

What is a "sound bite"? Why are "sound bites" so important in modern American politics? Are they too important? Defend your answer.

VOCABULARY

Bolshevik
dissent
dog-eared

fedora
flamboyant
flummoxed
gauntlet
inquisitor
mellifluous
misfeasance
motley
plutocrat
precocious
protagonist
rejoinder

CHAPTER 11

Henry wants to recall four members of the School Board, which is a very drastic measure. Recall rules vary from town to town and state to state. What are the recall rules in your town and state? Do you think Henry is justified in taking this step? Defend your answer.

Several times in history, Congress has tried to "recall" a president. When this happens, what is it called? What presidents were subjected to this process? What were the results? In each case, was it fair? Defend your answer.

VOCABULARY

acquiesce
collusion
cattle prod
heavy (n.)
impeachment
insurrection
picket line
proofreading
prudence

recall
transparency
unindicted coconspirator

PEOPLE TO LOOK UP
President Ronald Reagan

CHAPTER 12

Henry's petition quickly gets attention in two of the three branches of state government. One branch is represented by the Attorney General and Education Commissioner; another by a state judge. What's the third branch? What does each branch do? Why does state government have three separate branches? Are they equally powerful? How does this compare with the federal government?

What is the job of the District Attorney? How does this job differ from the Attorney General's job?

Wagner, the dog, is named for a famous 19th-century German composer. What's the composer's full name? What sort of music did he write? Name one of his most famous works. Long after his death, Wagner, the composer, was associated with a 20th-century political movement. What was it? Who was its leader? Was it appropriate to associate these two men from two different centuries?

VOCABULARY
alleged
antagonist
bellicose
catapult
eminence
encore
derision

flotsam and jetsam
genial
Grecian
illiterate
irate
kibitz
malevolent
metaphorical
oratory
pagan
sabotage
stiff upper lip

PEOPLE TO LOOK UP

Wilhelm Richard Wagner

CHAPTER 13

Mr. Kussow offers Henry a lesson in politics. What's his point? Do you agree?

To count the petition signatures, Henry acquires the list of voters from the City Clerk. Does your town have a similar list? Is it available for anyone to see, and copy? What information appears on such a list?

VOCABULARY

canvass
censure
gimlet eye
guerrilla
kibosh
maestro
moribund
off-register

pagan
prestigious
stentorian

PEOPLE TO LOOK UP

Alfred E. Newman
Rufus T. Firefly
Franklin Delano Roosevelt

CHAPTER 14

Henry realizes that, although he has lost his recall effort, he has another chance to take on the School Board in the town's regular election, in April. When does your town hold regular elections? What local offices and boards are elected at these times? What are the qualifications for someone to run for office in your town?

Henry has a political "platform" in his effort to defeat the School Board. Every four years, in presidential elections, the major parties, Democratic and Republican, also write official platforms. In the last election, what did these platforms promise? How many of those promises have been kept by the winning party?

VOCABULARY

ambience
nomination
per annum
platform

CHAPTER 15

Henry finds himself surrounded by a "brain trust," a term associated with the administration of President Franklin D. Roosevelt. What is a "brain trust?" Who were the members of President Roosevelt's "brain trust?" What was their role and how well did they succeed? Does the current president have a brain trust? If so, who are they?

Buzz Skelton tells Henry that Scooter has the senior citizen vote "locked up," because he drives older people to the polls and gives them a free lunch. This is part of an election strategy known as getting out the vote, or GOTV. What other GOTV tactics are common in local and national elections? Do you see such tactics as fair? Defend your answer.

Dexter D. Lee's "threat" to run for School Board highlights controversies that have emerged over "gay issues" in elections for many years in the United States. Describe at least three of these electoral controversies. Explain your opinions on each.

Ray McCloskey's firing is another "gay issue," the question of whether LGBT people should be allowed to teach in public schools. What is the position of your school system on this issue? How do you feel about this issue? Defend your answer.

VOCABULARY

brain trust
demure
eavesdrop
egomaniac
enigmatic
geezer
incumbent
LGBT
penitence

perfect storm
unintended consequences
vermin

CHAPTER 16

Moose, at 18, is old enough to run for School Board. What is the minimum age to run for office in your town? What is the minimum age to run for statewide office in your state and for state legislative positions? What are the age minimums for U.S. Congress, U.S. Senate and President?

The 26th Amendment to the U.S. Constitution, passed in 1971, changed the voting age in the United States from 21 to 18. This occurred during the war in Vietnam. What did the war have to do with the 26th Amendment? Do you agree that 18 is "old enough to vote"? Defend your answer.

VOCABULARY

goldbrick

CHAPTER 17

Macavity the Mystery Cat occurs in both a book and a musical play. Can you name them? Who wrote the book?

Blackhawk has a city manager, but no mayor. What is the city manager form of government and how does it differ from a mayoral system?

Charlie Mulcahy resigns over an issue of discrimination. Two historic racial anti-discrimination laws were passed in the 1960s. What were they? What important Supreme Court decision in the 1950s foreshadowed these two civil-rights laws? What were the effects of these two laws? What other groups and minorities later benefited from anti-discrimination laws?

Some critics say that anti-discrimination laws have "gone too far." Do you agree? Defend your answer.

VOCABULARY
beachhead
deadline
faux
feline
fraternization
hackles
languid
patrician
subversive
turncoat

CHAPTER 18

Joyce Tweedy, who thinks public schools are "immoral," is running for School Board. Should she? She home-schools her kids. What reasons do people give for choosing to home-school their kids? What rules govern home-schooling? How do you feel about home-schooling?

We know the Boston Symphony is in Boston. But where is the Metropolitan Opera?

Charlie Mulcahy says, "We don't have the band to kick around any longer." What famous American politician said, "You won't have me to kick around anymore," and what was the occasion?

VOCABULARY
anticlimactic
atone
blasphemous
devil's advocate

gift horse
hysteria
medieval
migrate
purist
ultraliberal

CHAPTER 19

Who's Satchmo?

Why does Henry smile like Satchmo?

Who were Scylla and Charybdis?

Who was Thomas Jefferson? Jefferson wrote the most important document in American history. What was it? Who was co-author, with Jefferson, of *The Federalist Papers*? What was the purpose of *The Federalist Papers*?

Charlie is filing suit in federal court, arguing that the firing of Ray McCloskey violated his civil rights. Can you make the argument in Mr. McCloskey's favor? Can you make an argument against Mr. McCloskey?

VOCABULARY

DOA
delusion
dry red wine
earworm
effusive
plebiscite
preposterous
redolent
teacher's pet
tycoon

PEOPLE TO LOOK UP

"Satchmo"
Scylla and Charybdis
Thomas Jefferson

CHAPTER 20

The School Board is "under a deadline" to approve contracts. What is a deadline? What profession is most associated with a "deadline"? What is the origin of the term "deadline"?

Thomas Jefferson's Constitutional amendment to establish public schools was a failure. When were the first public schools eventually started in America? Who was the leader of the public-school movement? When did public education become mandatory for all American children? Lately, there has been pressure to replace public education with a number of "free market" alternatives. What are some of the options? Do you think public schools should be replaced with another system? Defend your answer.

What state did Bill Bradley serve in the U.S. Senate? Can you name three other successful athletes who served in Congress?

VOCABULARY

decimate
hibiscus
hustings
mahogany
man bites dog
niggling
linchpin
nonplussed

PEOPLE TO LOOK UP

Tommy Bahama
Oliver Wendell Holmes
Bill Bradley

CHAPTER 21

Henry has problems stirring interest in the election because of Blackhawk's interest in basketball. Getting people out to vote in America is vital to democracy, yet hard to do. Why do you think this is so? Getting young people out to vote is even harder. Why do you think this is so?

Dexter D. Lee says, "The last thing you want to do in a political campaign is talk about the issues." Why does he say this? Do you think he's right?

The focus of this chapter is the School Board Candidates Forum. Do you have similar debates in your town? Have you ever attended any sort of campaign debate? Have you watched debates on TV? What is the intended purpose of such candidate debates? In your view, are they usually successful? Defend your answer.

Paul Lamartine offers his own money to cover the school budget shortage. Do you think this is a good solution? Defend your answer.

VOCABULARY

argyle
immaculate
paragon
patrician
regimental tie
scrim

slough
sonorous
trust fund

PEOPLE TO LOOK UP
Atticus Finch

CHAPTER 22

Moose and Charlie make two strong arguments for public education. Do you agree? Defend your answer.

Scooter ends the debate by calling teachers "ungrateful." What is his implication in this statement? Is he being fair? Defend your answer.

VOCABULARY
doublet
spite fence
visionary
unionized
Wall Street

PEOPLE TO LOOK UP
John Dewey
Horace Mann

CHAPTER 23

Henry is frustrated because the first five questions people ask when they meet School Board candidates have little to do with School Board issues. In general, in politics, personal issues tend to get more attention than policy issues. Is this bad? Who do you think is responsible for this emphasis on the personal? Should something be done to change this emphasis? If so, what?

Charlie Mulcahy mentions the Roman custom of "bread and circus." What are some examples of bread and circus in modern American politics?

This chapter highlights the imbalance in campaign spending between the incumbents and the challengers. Campaign spending has been the subject of much legislation in the U.S. Congress. What laws apply to campaign spending now and how do they work?

Campaign spending was also the subject of the U.S. Supreme Court case called "Citizens United." What did that case decide? What was its effect? Do you agree with the decision? Defend your answer. How would you solve the problem of inequality in campaign spending?

VOCABULARY

ambush
bread and circus
bunting
derogatory
ethical
incumbent
klieg
martyr
naiveté
nemesis
neophyte
Q factor
queue
pediment
portico
red herring

PEOPLE (AND BOOKS) TO LOOK UP

Bill Russell
Animal Farm
Around the World in Eighty Days
The Montgolfier brothers
Wile E. Coyote
John Philip Sousa
Francis Scott Key
Yogi Berra

CHAPTER 24

Henry has begun to study politics by reading newspapers—which were once called "the rough draft of history." What is your closest local newspaper, and how often does it appear? How often do you read a newspaper—either in "hard copy" or online? Is anyone in your family a regular newspaper reader? If you don't read a newspaper regularly, how do you get your news?

News nowadays comes through many sources. What are they? Which of these do you regard as most thorough? As most reliable? As least reliable? Defend your answers.

How would you respond to Henry's comparison of sports and politics?

Why do you think the Blackhawk School Board election came out the way it did?

VOCABULARY

cynical
dark arts
dark horse
disconsolate
ferret

galumphing
irresolute
largesse
optimism
poker face
prevaricator
rampant
rotunda

CHAPTER 25

To get Henry's budget plan through, what still needs to be done?

VOCABULARY

prevaricate

PEOPLE TO LOOK UP

Benny Goodman

JACKIE'S EXTRA QUESTIONS

The copy editor for this story is a smart woman named Jackie, who asked the author a few really good questions about Henry and his parents. Besides answering Jackie personally, the author decided to pose her questions to readers. Here they are.

Henry's parents never seem to drive him to any of his meetings or activities. How does he get around? Is it normal for a boy or girl Henry's age to move around so independently? How do you get to where you want to go?

Henry usually stays 'til the end of the School Board meeting, which can run past midnight. Obviously, Henry has no curfew, nor do his sisters and Fantasia Fulton. Why do you think Henry has no curfew? Are his parents—and Fantasia's parents—irresponsible? Do you have a curfew?

At what age can kids be trusted to go out on their own and come home on time, without parental supervision?

Are parents today too protective? Explain your answer.

HISTORIC FIGURES

All of the historic people listed below are mentioned somewhere in this book. Locate each one in time. Who were they? What did they accomplish? How were they viewed in their time, and how are they seen today?

Stephen Ambrose
Louis Armstrong
Attila the Hun
Daniel Boorstin
Andrew Carnegie
Jimmy Carter
Clarence Darrow
Eugene V. Debs
John Dewey
Sir Francis Drake
Samuel Gompers
Benny Goodman
Che Guevara
Thomas Jefferson
Joan of Arc
Mother Jones
Captain Kidd
Rev. Martin Luther King, Jr.
Jean LaFitte
John L. Lewis
Joseph-Michel and Jacques-Étienne Montgolfier

Bullwinkle J. Moose
Henry Morgan
Richard M. Nixon
Ronald Reagan
Franklin Delano Roosevelt
Bill Russell
Bernie Sanders
Edward Teach
Mark Twain
Wilhelm Richard Wagner
Lech Walesa
Henry Wallace

ABOUT THE AUTHOR

David Benjamin is a lifelong storyteller, dating back to Mrs. Poss' second-grade class at St. Mary's School in Tomah, Wis. His loosely told memoir, *The Life and Times of the Last Kid Picked,* was originally published by Random House and has been reprinted in a revised version by Last Kid Books. His Last Kid Books include a collection of his essays, *Almost Killed by a Train of Thought,* and ten novels, *Three's a Crowd, A Sunday Kind of Love, Summer of '68, Skulduggery in the Latin Quarter, Black Dragon, Jailbait, Bastard's Bluff, They Shot Kennedy, Fat Vinny's Forbidden Love, Woman Trouble* and *Witness to the Crucifixion.* As a journalist, Benjamin has edited newspapers, published and edited several magazines, and authored *SUMO: A Thinking Fan's Guide to Japan's National Sport.*

Since its launch in 2019, Benjamin's publishing imprint, Last Kid Books, has won thirteen independent press awards including, for *They Shot Kennedy,* the Midwest Book Awards' grand prize for literary/historical/contemporary fiction. His essays have appeared in publications that include the *Philadelphia Inquirer, San Francisco Examiner, Minneapolis Star-Tribune, Los Angeles Times, Chicago Tribune,* and *EE Times.*

Benjamin and his wife Junko Yoshida have been married for ages. They live sometimes in Madison, Wis., and the rest of the time in Paris.